The Girl's Got Bite

The Girl's Got Bite

An Unofficial Guide to Buffy's World

KATHLEEN TRACY

RENAISSANCE BOOKS

Los Angeles

Library of Congress Cataloging-in-Publication Data
Tracy, Kathleen.
    The girl's got bite : an unofficial guide to Buffy's world / Kathleen Tracy.
      p. cm.
    Includes bibliographical references and index.
    ISBN 1-58063-035-9 (alk. paper)
    1. Buffy, the vampire slayer (Television program)—Miscellanea.
    2. Buffy, the vampire slayer (Motion picture)—Miscellanea.
    I. Title.
    PN1992.77B84T73   1998
    791.45'72—dc21   98-33584
                                    CIP

Design by Joel Friedlander

10 9 8 7 6 5 4 3 2 1

Manufactured in the United States

Distributed by St. Martin's Press

To the Sweetness in my life

Contents

Introduction

As long as there have been demons, there has been the Slayer. One girl in all the world, a Chosen One, born with the strength and skill to hunt vampires and other deadly creatures . . . to stop the spread of their evil. When one Slayer dies, the next is called and trained by the Watcher . . .

Although loosely based on the 1992 feature film of the same name, the small screen version of *Buffy the Vampire Slayer* has an identity all its own—think *Xena: Warrior Princess* meets *The X-Files* in *Beverly Hills, 90210.* Ever since its debut on March 10, 1997, as a mid-season replacement show on the fledgling WB network, *Buffy* has been singled out for its uniqueness and high quality by enthusiastic critics, with *Entertainment Weekly* calling it that season's "most distinctive and sharply written new show."

Whereas the film version ended up more high camp than horror, creator Joss Whedon says the series represents his vision of what he originally intended *Buffy* to be.

"To me, high school *was* a horror movie," Whedon deadpans. "And that idea can sustain a TV show for years. For the series, we've broadened it out. This one community happens to be situated on a Hellmouth, which is a mystical porthole, and all different kinds of bad things like monsters, demons, and giant insects gravitate toward it. It's not a very good place to go to school."

The series follows the story of Buffy Summers, your average, slightly off-center, sixteen-year-old girl next door—who just happens to be the latest in a long line of female Slayers fated to protect their generation from the powers of evil. By day, Buffy is an average high school student constantly under fire for not living up to her potential. But by night, she's the Slayer, a martial arts expert with superhuman strength who spends her evenings battling vampires and other monsters—which leaves very little time for homework.

What Buffy really wants to be is normal, but her strange behavior keeps her out of the "in" crowd. Instead, she bonds with two fellow outsiders, Xander and Willow, who become her loyal allies in the fight against the terrors of the Hellmouth.

Responsible for looking after every Slayer is a Watcher. Buffy's is the school librarian, Rupert Giles, who himself comes from a long line of Watchers. It is Giles's job to help Buffy defeat whatever the local Hellmouth spits out at her by figuring out otherworldly signs and prophecies, and by guiding her through the realities of being both a Slayer and a teenager.

Adding both romance and danger is Buffy's object of desire, the seductive Angel, whose tortured past both repels and attracts the Slayer.

Bringing *Buffy* to life is a cast that includes newcomers Nicholas Brendon and Alyson Hannigan as Buffy's best friends Xander and Willow, and heartthrob-in-the-making David Boreanaz as Angel. Charisma Carpenter plays the image conscious, boutique-minded Cordelia, and Anthony Stewart Head is the occasionally flustered Watcher. Starring as Buffy is the Emmy-winning former *All My Children* star, Sarah Michelle Gellar.

What gives *Buffy* added depth and makes it more than just another spook show is Whedon's allegorical use of monsters and things that go bump in the night to represent the basic fears we all have about what we really don't know about the people around us.

"When it's somebody's parent or friend who turns into something horrible, it brings up issues that are real and therefore very scary," Whedon explains. "Then there's also your everyday terrors like death, maiming—and high school life in general."

Welcome to the Hellmouth . . .

Buffy

From Feature Film
to Television Series

efore there was Sarah Michelle Gellar and Sunnydale, there was Kristy Swanson and Los Angeles. But other than the title, the feature film incarnation of *Buffy the Vampire Slayer* is as different from the television series as Bela Lugosi's *Dracula* is to George Hamilton's *Love at First Bite.*

Buffy's evolution from a low budget, high camp feature film disappointment to one of the most distinctive and stylish television series in recent memory is reflective of both what's right and wrong with working in Hollywood and why it's important to retain creative control over a project.

It also shows that a good vampire story just won't stay dead and buried.

Buffy Goes to the Movies

When twenty-five-year-old Joss Whedon first got the idea to write his *Buffy the Vampire Slayer* screenplay, his intention was to create a supernatural heroine whose terrifying encounters were reflective of the anxieties all adolescents experience.

"The idea behind *Buffy* was to take someone who is living a normal life, put them in an abnormal situation and see if they rise to the occasion," Whedon explains. "My idea of the film was that no matter how ill-equipped someone may appear to handle their own life, there comes a time when they must take charge of their fate."

That's the *artiste* version. On a more superficial level, Joss just wanted this girl to have a little fun.

"Yeah, this movie was my response to all the horror movies I had ever seen where some girl walks into a dark room and gets killed. So I decided to make a movie where a blonde girl walks into a dark room and kicks butt instead."

Buffy the Vampire Slayer, which was Whedon's first screenplay, was optioned in 1988 by Sandollar Productions, the company that was founded by Dolly Parton and her longtime manager, Sandy Gallin. But it wasn't until two years later, in 1991, that the script finally passed from the seemingly eternal "development hell" stage to actual pre-production. That's when Sandollar executive Howard Rosenman approached the husband-wife team of Kaz and Fran Rubel Kuzui with the script.

Rosenman and his partner, Gail Berman, saw *Buffy* as a small budget, offbeat independent film. They hoped Japan-born producer Kaz Kuzui, who along with his wife Fran Rubel Kuzui, owned a distribution company that marketed American independent films in Japan, would produce *Buffy* and find Japanese investors to finance it.

The Kuzuis had been a producing/directing team since the couple married. Kaz came to America from Japan in 1977 to work as an assistant director on a Toshiro Mifune film, where he met Fran, who was the script supervisor. They married a year later. When Fran started spending half her time in Japan, she was hit with culture shock. "I didn't know anything about Japan when I met Kaz," she has said. "I hadn't even read *Shogun*."

Out of her experiences came the screenplay for the 1988 film *Tokyo Pop*. Although she had no previous directing experience— her background included a master's degree in film from New York University, working as an associate producer at WNET in New York and as a production manager for PBS—Fran was named the movie's director.

The film starred Carrie Hamilton, better known as Carol Burnett's daughter, as a struggling young singer who goes to Japan in search of fame, and once there finds out "what her place is in the world."

The first meeting between Howard Rosenman and Fran Kuzui didn't go well. "Fran was either an hour early or late and I had a manicure appointment," Rosenman recalled. "So I asked if she minded if I had my manicure while we talked and she said she didn't. But I later heard through her agent that she thought it was the most loathsome meeting she'd ever had. She hated me. To her, I must have seemed like the clichéd, high-handed movie producer. Which I may have been."

Despite the unfavorable first impression, *Buffy* would end up at Kuzui Enterprises. Then Fran surprised Rosenman by telling him she wanted to direct the film as well.

"The instant I saw the title, I knew this was a film I *had* to make," Fran enthused. "Five pages into the script and I was hooked. The more I read, the more I was attracted to the world that Joss Whedon had created. Here's a girl, a high school cheer-leader, who's suddenly being told she's part of something else.

"I think all of us, when we're kids, know we're part of *something*, and the process of being an adult is finding the something you're a part of. This is a story about a girl—and it's very impor-tant that it's a girl—finding out how powerful she really is."

Once the deal was set, Fran set about changing Joss's script. She made Buffy more lovable and asked Whedon to write in a female sidekick for the lead vampire. But the biggest change she made was one of tone, viewing *Buffy* through a pop cultural prism.

"I don't understand that approach," Joss admitted at the time, but as the screenwriter, he had no say in the matter. It was now the Kuzuis' picture to reshape as they saw fit.

The cast was a curious mixture, integrating pop culture of the moment with the respected tried and true. Although early in the film's development former *Who's the Boss?* star Alyssa Milano was briefly attached to the role, the part of Buffy eventually went to twenty-two-year-old Kristy Swanson, who was just coming off two films, *Hot Shots!* and *Mannequin Two: On the Move.*

"There are a lot of blondes and they're either funny or they're tough," Kuzui said. "When Kristy walked in wearing a black leather jacket and chewing gum, I knew I'd found my slayer. You just look at her and know she could kick some tush.

"The day I met Kristy, I understood that Buffy wasn't just pop and silly," she continued. "She could be really cool and tough. It was Kristy's idea that, while other girls wear sandals, Buffy wears Doc Martens as a way of saying somehow she always knew that she was born to be a Slayer." She predicted, "When people see her in this movie, they'll see: This is a star."

Despite her youth, Swanson had thirteen years acting experience behind her. A native Californian, Kristy was born in the well-heeled community of Mission Viejo near San Diego. By the time she was nine, Kristy had decided she wanted to be an actress. When a family friend suggested she get an agent, she sent some Kodak snapshots to the Mary Grady Agency, a well-known talent agency for children and young adults. Mary, whose daughter Lani O'Grady was a regular on *Eight Is Enough*, took a look at Kristy's pictures and liked what she saw. Within three days, Swanson had signed with Grady and had been cast in her first commercial, one of the more than thirty in which she would eventually appear.

When she was thirteen, Kristy was cast in her first series, *Dreamfinders*, on the Disney cable channel. With her family still living in Mission Viejo, it meant a three-hour round trip commute and being tutored while on the set. When the series ended, Swanson returned to school to discover that one of the teachers was going to fail her because she hadn't been in class. When her parents couldn't reason with the teacher, they took her out of the school.

Her parents, both teachers, decided to teach Kristy at home, following the local school district curriculum. Kristy thrived under the new arrangement, and graduated from high school when she was sixteen.

Although she didn't have to juggle work and school anymore, her age still posed a problem. She kept losing roles to older actresses who could legally work longer hours. So with her parents' blessing, Swanson filed for emancipation, and when it was granted, she moved to Hollywood on her own. Within a short time she landed parts in the horror films *Deadly Friend* (1986) and *Flowers in the Attic* (1987). Swanson's parents, whom she calls "my biggest supporters and understanders" both appeared as extras in *Buffy*.

When asked if she regretted missing the high school experience, Swanson was resolute. "I love every aspect of show business and that includes both the show part and the business part of it. I've always been this strong-willed person and I've always been in love with acting.

"I enjoy characters so I learned to study people—family, friends, everybody. That was more important than going to the prom. My sister-in-law, Jyl, was the model for Buffy. I observed her for weeks before shooting because she had that attitude. No professor can teach you that."

Unlike Gellar's Buffy, who is mostly fearless in pursuit of her Slayer duties but struggles with how the responsibilities affect her life and future, Swanson's Buffy was less angst-ridden and less thoughtful. She saw the character as someone going through personal growth.

"It's not about *I'm a woman and I can kick anyone's ass*. It's about change and challenging yourself, getting over your fears and taking it one step further. She may walk into the dark room, but she's still afraid. Her biggest fear is, *What are my friends going to think?* Because in the beginning Buffy knows the price of everything and the value of nothing—she's very shallow."

Interestingly, the movie Buffy was given some of the qualities that would later come to be associated with the Cordelia character on the series: she is consumed with shopping and fashion, is bent on running the school social scene, and is rather self-involved, with, as Swanson put it, "few concerns beyond what is hip and happening."

Cast as Buffy's boyfriend Pike was Luke Perry, then at the height of his *Beverly Hills, 90210* popularity, who was being touted as the next James Dean because of his brooding, bad boy portrayal of Dylan. His fans were exactly the people the producers wanted to attract. Ironically, Perry hoped that the comic elements of the movie would give him some distance from his TV alter ego.

"I can do more than stand and squint. I'd like to play character parts. Pike is very sweet, he just doesn't expect a lot from anybody or anything.

"There is a real role reversal in the movie," he noted. "Buffy's the one who's always having to save him, which is a nice change from the way these movies usually work. If Buffy can be seen as a hero, then I suppose Pike is the damsel in distress."

His fans didn't care what he was. Perry's heartthrob status carried over to the film production. In an attempt to keep his more aggressive fans from tracking his movements, Luke was listed on the call sheet as "Chet." When filming scenes at the Fashion Square Mall in Sherman Oaks, an upscale area in Los Angeles' San Fernando Valley, the producers were forced to hire six extra security guards just to keep the teen and pre-teen girls away from Perry.

Swanson revealed that Luke tried to downplay the intensity of his popularity by presenting himself as just an average Joe. "The word *simple* kind of fell into our vocabulary, because he'd always say, *I'm just a simple guy.* So I called him Mr. Simple. *Come here, Mr. Simple.*"

The reason Perry worked so hard to show he was unaffected by his white-hot popularity was his awareness that the idol label made people take him less seriously than they otherwise might have. "Elvis Presley said, *An image is a hell of a thing to live up to. I'm just a human being.* And me? I'm just a skinny kid from Ohio doing the best I can."

"A lot of people ask me if it's hard being so identifiable," Perry mused at the time. "It was a hell of a lot harder being completely anonymous and trying to get a job."

That said, he was still chagrined by the teen idol-ness of it all. "On the first day of shooting, about three hundred people showed up, most of them screaming girls. I was so glad Rutger Hauer and Donald Sutherland weren't working that day because I didn't want these two well-respected, well-established actors to walk on the set and think, *Oh no—we're making a movie with Frankie Avalon.*"

Donald Sutherland, whose credits range from *M*A*S*H* to *JFK*, played the mysterious Watcher, Merrick, whose job is to instruct Buffy in the ancient art of vampire slaying. Although he liked the script very much, the title left him befuddled. "When I first agreed to do this," he recalled, "I couldn't even say the title out loud. When somebody asked me what the name of the movie was I was going to be working on, I wrote it down on a piece of paper. They, in turn, fell on the floor laughing."

Rutger Hauer, the Dutch actor who had gained international fame and acclaim in films like *Soldier of Orange*, *Spetters*, and *Blade Runner*, was cast as the vampire Lothos. But only after, says Fran, "he overcame his resistance to a second-time female director."

"Lothos has been a vampire king for twelve centuries," Hauer said, explaining his character. "He's a parasite of history. While he is undoubtedly evil, I believe he is also a very romantic character; a sentimental guy who falls in love with the face of purity in the guise of Buffy."

As Buffy would say, *Huh?*

Kaz Kuzui later explained the cast mix as a financial necessity. "Luke Perry's name means nothing in Japanese markets or overseas, so we needed to make certain we had international names."

As it turned out, though, the need to find Japanese investors fell by the wayside. On the strength of Joss's script, and the cast, 20th Century Fox eventually agreed to pick up the $9 million budget in exchange for worldwide rights—on the condition that the movie be ready for release in the summer. That meant they could only spend five weeks in pre-production and six weeks filming.

"It's a kid's movie that Fox wanted made quickly so they could release it on the crest of interest in screen vampires," Kuzui explained. "However, it isn't a vampire movie, but a pop culture comedy about what people *think* about vampires."

Actually, as conceived by Whedon, it *was* supposed to be a vampire movie as well as a comedy, but by this time, the film being made had become completely different from the one Joss had written.

Among the other credited cast members were a curious collection of actors with pop culture credentials: future *Scream* star David Arquette, who at the time was best known for being Rosanna's brother, Natasha Gregson Wagner (Robert Wagner and Natalie Wood's daughter), syndicated columnist Liz Smith, Amanda Anka (Paul's daughter), Sarah Jones (whose father was the Monkees' Davy Jones), and *American Graffiti* star Candy Clark in a cameo appearance as Buffy's inattentive mother.

But the most interesting casting choice was for the part of Amilyn, Lothos' sadistic sidekick. Joan Chen had been set for the role, but left in a dispute over money. Reportedly, the producers had offered her $45,000 and she wanted more. When she didn't get it, she walked just before filming was scheduled to start. That was when Fran suggested the person she'd really wanted all along—Paul "Pee-wee Herman" Reubens. "I had never said anything because it was such a far-out idea."

At the time, casting Reubens was a risky choice because it would be his first job since being arrested in an "adult" movie theater and charged with indecent exposure, which had effectively ended his career as a children's show host. Reubens agreed to take the role—for $150,000—and for reasons never clearly explained, the producers attempted to keep his involvement in the film a secret. But on March 3, 1992, the industry trade paper *Variety* reported that "the film's producers and domestic distributor, 20th Century Fox, and Herman are all under a contractual press gag not to divulge Pee-wee's involvement until production is completed. Sorry guys."

Alyson Hannigan and Charisma Carpenter with creator Joss Whedon.

And except for the press leaks, it would have been fairly easy to keep Reubens' participation under wraps. Like Perry, Reubens had a code name—Beau Hunkus. But unlike the *90210* star, Paul was virtually unrecognizable in the film, with rat's nest hair and a goatee disguising his face. And Pee-wee's distinctive nasal preschool voice was replaced by a menacing, snarling one.

"We decided Paul would play the evil guy and Rutger would play the scary guy," Fran said in an interview. "And there's a distinction because usually what you're scared of is not the real evil.

"The thing that's great about directing a vampire movie is that it lets you create your own world. And talk about someone who creates their own world—Paul is somebody who created one of the most unique and, to me, seriously important pop characters ever. Pee-wee Herman is right up there with Mickey Mouse as far as

I'm concerned. So I was really interested in what he could do with a character like Amilyn."

In order to handle the movie's physical demands, prior to filming Swanson had ten days of intensive martial arts instruction from expert James Lew (*Big Trouble in Little China*) and Pat Johnson, who had worked on *Teenage Mutant Ninja Turtles*. During filming she was coached by the movie's leading stunt coordinator and second unit director, Terry Leonard, whose credits included *Romancing the Stone* and *Apocalypse Now*.

"They never asked me if I was a fighter but I did have a dance background," Swanson said. "At the end of the film, I had a lot of bruises and sore bones."

Rubel Kuzui takes credit for the martial arts aspect of the film. "I wanted to find some way for Buffy to slay vampires that had nothing to do with killing, since I was not interested in making a violent film. I am a great fan of Chinese martial arts films, which are, for the most part, pretty bloodless affairs. Since Buffy is a vampire slayer, not a killer, I had the idea that she would rely on the martial arts as much as possible to get the job done."

Filming began February 20, 1992—almost four years after Whedon had originally sold the script. The production filmed on location around Los Angeles, including Marshall High School, and on a soundstage built in a converted warehouse located in Santa Monica. What made the nine-week filming schedule particularly difficult was night shooting, which hit twenty-nine consecutive days at one stretch.

"The biggest challenge in making this movie was to make it through the night shooting," Swanson said.

"You *become* a vampire when you shoot a vampire movie," Perry joked.

"It's one of the unwritten rules of Hollywood—never take on a movie with the word *vampire* in the title," Fran noted. Although of anyone, Kuzui seemed to be the one enjoying herself the most, a boundless source of energy and optimism, even offering pearls of wisdom to veteran Swanson.

"Kristy's a self-sufficient young woman, so she had to learn to be taken care of a little bit," Kuzui explained. "I had to say, *You're the star. You have to act like the star.* We became very close. At the end of the shoot, I gave her a silver Celtic cross on a chain with the inscription *To My Favorite Slayer.*"

While Kuzui openly enjoyed her younger stars Perry and Swanson, who in turn got along so well together that they were rumored to be romantically involved, her relationship wasn't as warm with some of the other performers. According to Kaz Kuzui, Donald Sutherland and Rutger Hauer were not amused at the tone the film was taking.

"They were very difficult," he says directly. "They thought the movie was very serious and became insecure. They tried to make their roles more complex, more emotional."

In other words, the way Joss originally wrote the characters.

"Rutger tried to be the vampire Lestat from *Interview with the Vampire,*" Kaz continued. "He's very good but he depends on a lot of acting gimmicks."

Hauer acknowledged that it wasn't the easiest of work situations. "It *is* very difficult for me to come into something like this, because it's a supporting role—supporting a lot of young actors."

Swanson also admitted to having some problems with her film foe. "Our relationship was hot and cold. He was really trying to screw with me, to get some sort of rise out of me, I guess. He likes to mess with everyone. He'd stare at me with his Rutger Hauer look and it frustrated him because I'd just laugh and say, *You're not scaring me.*

"He'd ask me a million questions, like *Kristy, what does Lothos mean to you?* Finally I said, *Look, does it matter? You take care of your character, I'll take care of mine and we'll just leave it at that.*"

There was also an uncomfortable moment during a dream sequence in which Buffy and Lothos end up in bed together that Hauer wanted to play in the nude. After Kristy asked, though, he complied with her request that he wear pants.

But Sutherland, on the other hand, was a Swanson favorite. "Donald was unbelievable. I was blown away by how supportive and sweet he is."

After the production wrapped, Rubel Kuzui immediately set to work on post-production, having only four months to edit the film before its scheduled release date in late summer. Then the schedule became even tighter—the studio was so confident that the film would be a box office winner, they moved up *Buffy*'s release date to July.

"We really have our summer kind of scheduled around *Buffy*," said Fox's domestic marketing president, Andrea Jaffe. "This is a concept movie and we're going to sell the concept. It's what we have to do."

Jaffe wanted to follow the lead of what Disney had done earlier that season with one of their smaller budgeted films, *Encino Man*, starring Pauly Shore and newcomer Brendan Fraser. They had given the film extensive sneak previews, creating a strong word-of-mouth that translated into a healthy box office performance, making it one of the summer's surprise hits. But Jaffe claimed that by rescheduling *Buffy*'s release date, the film wasn't done in time to screen it as extensively as she would have liked.

For a small budget film, Fox gave *Buffy* a relatively huge promotional blitz, which included an extensive billboard marketing campaign. Actually, the film had more than one campaign. Initially, ads and billboards for the movie showed a cheerleader from the waist down, holding a pom-pom in one hand and a wooden stake in the other, with the tag line, *She knows a sucker when she sees one.*

Later newspaper ads showed Swanson holding a stake with Perry peering over her shoulder, with the banner: *Pert. Wholesome. Way Lethal.* Time would tell whether Jaffe's marketing plan would work.

Although the earlier release date meant going up against stronger competition, Kuzui seemed unconcerned about the switch. "There's probably not really a good time to open a movie. But by August, everybody is just interested in having a good time and I think that's what this movie will provide."

In press interviews promoting the film, Swanson was equally optimistic. "The guys are gonna go, *Damn*! They're going to think it's cool. I think the girls are going to think it's *really* cool—*I can kill vampires* and *get the guy in the end*."

However, in less spun moments, she was more ambivalent. "For all I know, it could be really hilarious, or it could really suck."

Perhaps the person with the most on the line was Luke Perry, at least as far as his film career was concerned. Although at the time he had a two-picture deal with Fox, Luke had been unable to get financing for his pet project, *The Lane Frost Story*, about the world champion rodeo star who died in a bull-riding related accident when he was in his early twenties. (The film was finally produced in 1994 as *8 Seconds*.)

"I learned I'm not bankable at the box office," he admitted. "I'm no one's first choice for a part. I'm behind fifteen other guys—if I'm thought of at all. I think Paul Reubens and I both came to this thing with something to prove. I think Paul wanted to prove that, whatever your preconceptions about him might be, he is someone who's truly funny and creative and talented.

"For me, I wanted to prove that I can do more than what I get to do on *90210*, where my role is basically a dramatic one. There's a real goofy side to me and I like to get that out once in a while. It was fun, after nine months of making Dylan as dangerous and problematic as I can, to come, fall on my ass, and make everybody laugh."

The depth of fan identification of Perry to the Dylan character was highlighted by the brouhaha that was ignited when it was revealed in pre-release stories that Luke shaved his trademark sideburns in *Buffy*. Perry explained to *People* magazine that Pike shaves off his sideburns "to show that his character is getting his act together at the end of the movie." A spokesperson for Perry assured distraught *90210* fans that the sideburns would grow back in time for the new season.

Buffy the Vampire Slayer opened on July 31, 1992 and floundered at the box office. Even the relatively unsuccessful Meryl Streep-Bruce Willis black comedy *Death Becomes Her* took in more money.

The executives at Fox had thought teens would be lining up in droves to buy tickets for *Buffy*, if just to see Luke Perry—but they were wrong. When trying to explain why, Joe Roth, then-chairman of 20th Century Fox Film Corporation, pointed the finger at the marketing. "We thought we had a campaign that really worked—and obviously we didn't."

Ironically, although teenagers stayed away, the adults who saw the film scored it very high.

"I took my son and his ten-year-old friend to see it," Roth recalled. "On our way out of the theater, the ten-year-old said to me, *This is a movie for adults, but there's no way they would know that.* I offered him a job."

The movie was generally skewered by the more important film critics.

Time magazine offered this assessment: "By now you are perhaps dreaming that the summer's most pressing need—for a funny sleeper—has been fulfilled. Wrong. Or as Buffy says, *Does the word* duh *mean anything to you?* It does to director Fran Rubel Kuzui, whose frenzied mistrust of her material is almost total."

Newsweek's Charles Leerhsen noted, "The film's basic problem is that it fails to create what might be called the vanilla fudge effect—the delicious swirling of the scary and the funny that marked, say, *Abbott and Costello Meet Frankenstein.*"

Many critics, such as the *Washington Post's*, were disappointed that such a promising premise hadn't lived up to its potential. "Its comic creativity is patchy; that final match with Hauer is a distinct letdown. *Buffy* is amusing for a time but its destiny is to die in a disappointingly, long-winded conclusion."

Michael Price of the *Fort Worth Star Telegram* was more pointed. "If it were not for the saving grace of Paul Reubens' show-stopping vampire act, a script too witty for director Kuzui's dreary handling and Kristy Swanson's energetic title portrayal, *Buffy the Vampire Slayer* would be unwatchable."

That pretty much summed up Joss Whedon's sentiments as well. He now says bluntly of the film, "The director ruined it."

Although *Buffy's* disappointing reception did not adversely affect Whedon's career, it was a setback for both Swanson and Perry. Kristy has continued her film career, with roles in *The Program* (1993), *The Phantom* (1996), and *8 Heads in a Duffel Bag* (1997), among others.

Luke Perry would eventually leave *Beverly Hills, 90210* to pursue, among other things, a film career that never came to pass. When last seen, he had been taken over by an extra-terrestrial life form in the 1997 NBC miniseries *Invasion.*

Fran Rubel Kuzui has yet to direct another film, although Kuzui Enterprises has produced two other films—the 1997 release *Telling Lies in America*, a coming-of-age story starring Kevin Bacon and Brad Renfro, and a 1995 gem called *Orgazmo*, in which a young Mormon actor/preacher becomes the star of a porno film, and discovers his costar has invented a ray-gun, called Orgasmorator, which emits a light beam that causes the most intense orgasm in whoever it hits. Two of the actors in the film,

Trey Parker and Matt Stone, would later go on to find fame and fortune as the creators of Comedy Central's animated series *South Park*. In Hollywood, it really is six degrees of separation—if that much.

When the final figures were tallied, *Buffy the Vampire Slayer* grossed a little over $16 million in domestic box office, but because the budget had been ultra-modest to begin with, the studio managed to turn a small profit. However, nothing could compensate Whedon for his profound disappointment over how his vision of the script had been so thoroughly compromised.

"When you wink at the audience and say nothing matters, then you can't have peril."

Three years later, Whedon would unexpectedly get a second chance to do *Buffy* the way he originally intended.

Turning Buffy into a Television Series

Although they carry the same name, the television version of *Buffy the Vampire Slayer* is dramatically different from the feature film incarnation. Whereas the movie substituted tongue-in-cheekiness for any sense of menace, on TV, *Buffy*'s creatures do a lot more than merely go bump in the night. More so than on any other series in memory, a character who is here in this episode may very well come to a gruesome end in the next.

Despite its seemingly quiet, small town appearance, Sunnydale is actually a hotbed of mystical happenings and a magnet for evil creatures of all types, not just vampires. Why? No, not because of its proximity to Los Angeles, which is some two hours away, but because it sits on what is vividly called a Hellmouth—think of it as a Club Med for the demon set.

During the day, Sunnydale is bright and antiseptic, lacquered in promise and possibility. But at night, its dark and deserted streets insinuate the unseen danger lurking beneath the dank surface, and when Buffy hears the footsteps of someone following her, the sense of danger and jeopardy is surprisingly intense.

"In the movie, the director took an action/horror/comedy script and went only with the comedy," explains Joss Whedon, who is executive producer of the series. "In the television show, we're keeping to the original formula. We take our horror genre seriously. We are not doing a spoof. It's larger than life but we are very much involved with these characters. This is not *Clueless* or *Party Girl*. The description I like best is *My So-Called Life* meets *The X-Files*."

Welcome to the world of *Buffy the Vampire Slayer*, television style.

The idea for resurrecting *Buffy* began in 1995 when Gail Berman, an executive at Sandollar, the production company that originally optioned Joss's screenplay back in 1988, approached Whedon with the suggestion of making the 1992 film into a television series.

"What's ironic is that when I first read Joss's screenplay for the movie years ago, I thought then it would make a great television show," says Berman. "But when the movie came out and didn't do that well, the idea of a series sort of went away."

But like the vampires she fights, *Buffy* wouldn't die. It became a surprising video hit, prompting Berman to exhume her series idea from the development graveyard in her head.

"I called Fran Kuzui, who had produced the movie and we discussed doing a series for syndication. Neither of us thought Joss would have the time to do a series because of his screenwriting. But when we called his agent and asked Joss, he surprised us by coming back and saying, *Yeah, this is what I really want to do*."

"I thought about it for a while then decided that I *was* interested because it would be very different from the movie," explains Joss, who would have creative control—something he did not have

The Chosen One: Sarah Michelle Gellar won the role of Buffy

with the film. "I thought there was an idea in the 'high school hor-ror show' that would sustain a television show and keep it going for years.

"I think high school has become a popular setting for new shows because there's never a time when life is more like a TV show, whether that's a horror show or a drama or anything else. Everything is so turgid when you're in high school, everything is so powerful and so dramatic. I don't think there's any other time in life when you feel that way except high school. So when people see high school characters, it's very believable and very relatable.

"If you look at movies like *I Was a Teenage Werewolf,* you'll see this combination of teen angst and horror has been going on for a long time. So it was a very appealing idea to me for a show, but one I honestly hadn't thought of until they brought it to me."

Not everyone was thrilled with Whedon's decision to go forward with the idea for a series, however. "My agent *begged* me not to do it," Whedon laughs.

But Joss ignored the advice because he was being given a chance to do something few screenwriters get to do—get it right the second time. This time, although the Kuzuis and Sandollar share screen credit as producers, Joss would be the man in charge.

"I really hated what they had done to my original script," Whedon says bluntly. "To me, making a movie is like buying a lotto ticket—the writer is just not that important. Being a screenwriter in Hollywood is not all it's cracked up to be. People blow their noses on you. When I went on the set of *Alien*, people are nice enough but I'm standing in a corner. On *Buffy,* I'm telling these stories. Not only am I telling them, I'm telling them every eight days," he says, referring to how long it takes to film each episode.

"The movies I write, if they even get made, take several thousand years. But television is a writer's medium so there's a better chance things will come out the way you originally envisioned them. With television, it's like getting to make an independent movie every week.

"Besides," he says smiling, "it was a way to get back at everyone I went to school with."

Once the decision was made to go forward with the project, Whedon and Sandollar set out to find the series a home.

"The first place we took *Buffy* was Fox because it seemed like a good fit, but they passed," Whedon recalls. "But the WB liked it right off. I like to think Fox is bummed they passed but I also like to think chicks dig me, so it's possible I'm wrong."

Jamie Kellner, CEO of the WB, says he knew immediately that *Buffy* was a perfect fit for his network. "More and more we can get the sense now when we look at something whether that's for us. I saw *Buffy* and said, *That's for us.* When you put a program on, you have to have confidence in your judgment. I certainly do. There wasn't even a tinge of a question mark in my mind about *Buffy.*"

Whedon says they worked on the show for about a year before filming actually began. During that time he ironed out the show's concept and solidified the characters. In the film, Buffy's original Watcher, Merrick, dies. Donald Sutherland's Watcher was almost as old and musty as some of the vampires.

"Merrick was so caught up in the Gothic horror movie world he lived in that he was constantly confounded by the superficiality of Buffy's life," Whedon says of the character.

For the series, Whedon wanted a Watcher slightly less strange, although no less confounded by his charge. He also wanted this Watcher to be ever so slightly less sure footed, more human.

The Buffy character would also be adjusted. To begin with, in the film, Buffy was a senior, but Whedon wanted her to be younger, so he made the TV Buffy a sophomore. Gone is her preoccupation with clothes and her insider status with a vacuous circle of friends—those traits were incorporated into Cordelia, who serves as a visual example of the kind of person Buffy might have grown into had she not been the Slayer—and in their place are a deep sense of angst and friends who are anything but in. Also, although she might not be a straight-A student, the TV Buffy exhibits far more intelligence.

For the series, Buffy's mother became much more than the fleeting joke presence she was in the film. Whedon sought to make Joyce Summers a parent more grounded in the reality of having to deal with a daughter who seems compelled to do unexplainable things, like burn down the gym and constantly get into fights. In the film, Buffy barely dealt with complex emotional conflicts, but in the series, she deals with them on a daily basis.

It was also vitally important to set the right tone from the very first scene. "Where the movie was camp, the television series is grittier," Joss says. "I wanted to give the series a wider range; by making it a little more serious, I felt that would help open it up. So it's not just vampires she has to fight, it's all kinds of different things—monsters, robots, witches, giant insects, demons—anything we can come up with. And there's plenty out there.

"Action and horror are actually more antithetical than comedy and horror, I think, because horror is so much about not being in control of your environment. And in a way, comedy can be the same thing. So it's really going from the comedy and horror to the action, where Buffy is in control, that's a difficult balance to maintain."

Despite the horror premise, Whedon believed that playing it straight would lessen the suspension of disbelief necessary by viewers.

"We set up the premise that the town is located on a Hellmouth so it would be understood that our characters who know what is going on, who know that Buffy is a vampire slayer, would understand that mystical and strange things will happen in Sunnydale.

"The rest of the school just sort of takes it for granted that the school is a strange place to be, but they've never gone anywhere else. It's like people living in the world with Superman—they take it for granted, and if they see a werewolf next week, they'd be okay with that."

In March 1996, the WB put the series into development for the 1996–97 season and began casting, which became a long, drawn out process. Sarah Michelle Gellar recounts how she first learned of the series.

"My manager spoke to the WB and they mentioned they had this *Buffy* show and he thought it would be a great opportunity for me to use my Tae Kwan Do, which I had studied for four years."

However, the producers had already approached Charisma Carpenter, who was just coming off Aaron Spelling's short-lived prime-time serial *Malibu Shores*, for the part of Buffy. Gellar, who had been set to audition for the role of Cordelia, was determined to play Buffy and badgered the producers into letting her read for the lead.

"I probably had eleven auditions and four screen tests," Gellar says of the nerve-wracking process. "It was the most awful experience of my life but I was so driven to get this part.

"I had read the script and had heard about how wonderful Joss Whedon was and I went to audition the week he had been nominated for an Oscar for his *Toy Story* screenplay. I thought, *I'm going to have this role.* Later, Joss told me I nailed it—but I still went through eleven auditions."

"There was no second place," says Whedon. "We read tons of people and several were staggeringly untalented. Buffy is a tough part; it is a character actress in the body of a leading lady. She's an eccentric. This girl has to look the part of a blonde bimbo who dies in reel two but turns out to be anything but that. You don't find those qualities very often in young actresses who also happen to be beautiful, but Sarah gave us a perfect reading.

"And then she says, *By the way, I'm also a brown belt in Tae Kwan Do. Is that good?*"

After seeing Sarah, Whedon offered Charisma Carpenter the role of Cordelia instead. The cast, which also included Anthony Stewart Head as Giles, Alyson Hannigan as Willow, and Nicholas Brendon as Xander, was coming together.

Then the series hit a snag. Instead of putting the show on in September, the network decided to hold it for the mid-season. Although the delay was disappointing at the time, Gellar says it actually worked out for the best. "The show wasn't ready so it was a blessing to wait. The extra time really gave us a chance to fully develop and flesh out the show and we're stronger because of it." When they were finally ready to film, a last minute decision was made to recast the role of Angel. David Boreanaz was cast the night before he was scheduled to show up for filming.

Once his cast was set, Whedon was satisfied he had the right group. "I like all the characters because they are either parts of me or parts I wish I had. You know, I took a bunch of pieces and put them on a page and when these guys came in, they not only got them exactly, but since we've been doing the show together, have shaped them. So right now, the characters are a real hybrid with everybody bringing something to their character that wasn't there before. Although the characters started off with me, now they belong to the actors and I just write to them.

"What Sarah brings to the part is her intelligence. At the same time, she's got that hormonal goofiness that makes Buffy not just the Terminator. I think Nicholas Brendon is the closest to his character and Charisma and Tony Head are the least. Unlike their characters, she's very nice and he's not stuffy at all.

"I'm very fond of everyone in this cast and I've worked with *plenty* of people I can't say that about," he laughs. "It's not easy to find the right balance—people who are mature enough to do the hard work, but who still have that youthful energy that's genuine. It's not easy, but we got 'em. Everyone in our cast is very professional but they don't read old on screen and I don't think they ever will. I actually think we have the youngest median age for actors of any high school show out there. There's not a gray hair among them.

"And you know, you definitely have people come in who are too old to read high school but who are still reading high school and it's awkward. But these people are *sooo* immature," Whedon laughs teasingly.

Executives at the WB were more than pleased with the work Whedon and his cast were doing. Susanne Daniels, executive vice president of programming for the network, is one of the series' biggest boosters. "Every once in a while you meet a writer whose passion and vision just blows you away and that's what happened when we met with Joss Whedon for the first time," she says.

"As soon as we saw his pilot script, we knew we had something unique, but it wasn't until the casting process, when we met Sarah, that we knew we had our first potential breakthrough show. *Buffy* is really scary, it's really sexy, and it's really funny. We think it's a show that has it all."

The WB, which is going after the same audience Fox went for in its early days, felt *Buffy* would appeal to their target demographic, the 18–34 age group.

"In internal meetings we described this show to other executives as *Beverly Hills, 90210* meets *The X-Files*," Daniels says. "We

---

Spells

Spells are a means of communicating with a deity to request a specific event to occur. They are mystical recipes that usually require ingredients such as herbs, certain animal body parts, or a personal possession or lock of hair from the person the spell is intended to effect. The spell-casting ritual also incorporates incantations, incense, lit candles, and other accessories.

The typical stereotype of a witch's spell, especially in Sunnydale, is a malevolent curse or hex arising out of black magic. Modern witches who practice "white witchcraft" take the attitude that spells are not inherently "good" or "evil"— spells are what you make them.

thought it was a show that would appeal to both the *Goosebumps* audience as well as the viewers who like *X-Files*. I personally think Buffy will do for the WB what *21 Jump Street* did for Fox—it attracted new teenage viewers and got critical acclaim as well and helped put the network on the map."

Co-producer David Greenwalt says, "What I love about what Joss has done with the show is to take something that is very real in high school, like sexual tension, and then fulfill that by having a guy trapped with a giant bug in a basement who's going to eat him."

"Or Joss can take the psychological truth behind the true story of the mother who had her daughter's rival killed because she didn't make the cheerleading squad, and turn it into a story of a mother who takes her daughter's body so she can relive her glory days as a cheerleader.

"I like that he takes very real issues and then magnifies them. It's fun doing that."

Buffy the Vampire Slayer debuted to some of the highest critical praise of any show in the 1996–97 season.

People's Tom Gliatto graded it a B+ and added these words of praise: "Sarah Michelle Gellar plays the part with the right degree of put-upon resentment, and the cast—including Anthony Stewart Head as the school librarian—is as smooth an ensemble as you could wish in an hour-long series. All in all, this looks like one of the brightest new shows of the season."

The *San Francisco Chronicle*'s TV critic, John Carman, also lauded the show. "*Buffy the Vampire Slayer* is as surprisingly engaging as the film that spawned it. The Buffy role seems to have been altered a bit for Gellar. This Buffy is primed for martial arts action, but she's also notably nimbler in the cranium. It's a decent role, and Gellar handles it with wit, confidence, impressive athleticism and a fetching off-center smile. *Buffy* takes itself just seriously enough to ladle moderate suspense between chuckles."

Still, not everyone was enchanted with the series. *TV Guide*'s Jeff Jarvis was one of the few who faulted the show's production values. "I can't decide whether to praise *Buffy* for being different or to make fun of it for being so B-movie cheesy."

But overall, the response was more in line with Kristen Baldwin's brief critique in *Entertainment Weekly*. "Infinitely more entertaining than the cute but forgettable 1992 movie it's based on, *Buffy the Vampire Slayer* is this mid-season's most distinctive and sharply written new show."

"The word of mouth has been excellent and there is a buzz about *Buffy*," Kellner said in an interview in July 1997. Although the show did indeed attract the expected young audience, it also attracted its fair share of older viewers.

"The producers and I were out scouting locations one day when this old man who must have been eighty walked by and asked if we were the *Buffy* people," Gellar recalls. "We thought he was going to complain about us filming in the neighborhood but instead he smiled and said, *That's the best show. I never miss it.*"

Gellar feels that the series is so different in execution and tone from the film that the people won't equate the two. "I look at the series as being loosely based on the movie. In my mind, all we did was take the idea of *Buffy*, not the story or the character. Not to mention the fact that the movie came out so long ago, I think few people are going to be comparing one against the other.

"Joss's vision for *Buffy* was something a little darker, a little more on edge, a little less camp. It's really a brilliant idea, that the scariest things in life are things that are based in reality. What scares you the most are things that could possibly actually happen.

"And what's scarier than high school? Nothing. I think high school scares everyone. I think that no matter how popular you are, or how unpopular you are, high school is a scary place and the show touches on that a lot. When I was in junior high, I didn't know where I fit in. I tried to be a jock, then I tried to be cool but I couldn't find my place. I think that is what Willow, Xander, and Buffy are all going through and that is what makes it interesting and believable. Buffy is a person who is lost and who doesn't know where she belongs and you feel for her.

"The situations in our story lines are ones kids can relate to— loving a friend, being at an age when you're having problems with Mom, wanting to be an adult and a child at the same time. These are situations teenagers understand because it's happening to them right now."

That said, Whedon is adamant to keep the series from becoming an issue-of-the-week soapbox.

"We are not going to get terribly or overtly issue-oriented. We will deal with teen subjects, because that is where all of the interesting stories come from. The horror isn't just, monsters attack and we fight them. The horror and the stories have to come from the characters, from their relationships and fears—otherwise, it won't really be interesting. So when we deal with teen stuff, it is really the more emotional stuff, not the 'issue' oriented.

"The way a lot of teen shows deal with issues are like, they learn that racism is bad. But I don't think that's the way teens operate. As I've said before, there will never be a Very Special Episode of *Buffy*."

But as for what exactly Joss has planned, the cast claims they are the last to know. "Joss won't tell us," Gellar says, in mock outrage.

Head says, "When I found out that Giles's dark past was going to be revealed I asked Joss what it was. And he refused to tell me because he knew that subconsciously I would immediately start to play that; there would be some little undertone in there somewhere. As actors, we just can't leave things alone—and he knows that."

But the one thing that anybody who knows Whedon can be sure of, is that the story lines reflect his personal outlook and fears, which he admits have been present for as long as he can remember.

"Yes, I was the odd child," Joss laughs. "I wish it were different. I wish I had been Mr. Popular, but then *Buffy* would be a very different show.

"In the series, we have taken real-life situations that reflect a grotesque parody. Most people remember high school very clearly, so they understand how horrific it all can be. When I get together with my writing team, I ask them, *What is your favorite horror movie? What's the most embarrassing thing that ever happened to you? Now, how can we combine the two?*

"What's fun about the show is that we never know from scene to scene which way it's going to go. A scene that starts out very dramatically could end up quite funny, or something truly horrible could happen in it. We don't do, *Okay, now here's the funny part and now here's the scary part.* We never really know what's going to be highlighted until it's over."

To Gellar, it doesn't matter what direction the scenes take. "I love all genres—comedy, horror, action, drama—and what I think is so wonderful about our show is that we have all of those different aspects," observes Gellar. "It's interesting when you go from being a child actor to an adult actor. *All My Children* was really that transition for me and *Buffy* is really a wonderful opportunity for me to play someone a little closer to myself and situations I've been in—minus the vampires."

Nicholas Brendon, who plays Xander, likes a more macabre aspect of the series. "One thing that I like about the show is that in every episode, somebody dies—and you never know who it's going to be. I mean, you could have a bond with, say, me—and then I'm dead. So if someone is in danger, they might actually die and not come back, which I think is nice."

"Yeah, it makes for real job security on our show," Charisma chimes in.

Whedon says it was always his intention to introduce characters that wouldn't make it through the end of the season. "Not that we feel we have to kill someone every week, but we like to let people wonder. We like to show people that the peril here is real, that the horror is real and there's something at stake."

"But it's not what you might expect," Gellar points out. " It's not the person you think will die who does."

"Basically," Joss sums up, "the only ground rules we have is that Buffy won't be killing puppies."

Anthony Stewart Head believes one reason for the show's success is that Whedon goes straight for the gut. "Joss's vibe has always been that what he writes is an extension of the pain and torture that we've all been through in our teens and adolescence—there's definitely a dark side to all of us.

"Joss is at his best when he directs his own words. He knows exactly what he wants and knows to the finest detail every nuance. It's a joy. But we've had some other really good directors and the show is developing a serious edge."

While some have wondered whether part of *Buffy*'s success might be the result of television's sudden love affair with all things fantasy-horror, from *The X-Files* to *Sabrina, the Teenage Witch*, Whedon is convinced that his show, and others like it, are well received because they fill a need.

"I have no doubt *Buffy* would have gotten on the air whenever it was pitched. When we started production, *Sabrina* wasn't on the air yet, and anyway, it's a very different show. *Sabrina* is a very young comedy. *Buffy*, I think, is a little older. And because it's a horror show I think it owes more to *X-Files* than to *Sabrina*.

"But actually, if I wanted to be compared to anything, it would be *My So-Called Life* and *Party of Five*," Whedon said. "Those shows were as much a template for *Buffy* as *Twilight Zone* or *Dark*

Shadows. Whenever we do a tender, poignant scene, we say, *There's a 'Party of Five' moment coming up.* They're both genuine dramas about genuine teen concerns that are not soap operas starring young people the way *Beverly Hills, 90210* is."

But the core of the show is and will always be its central theme of horror. And although some people might view the horror genre as currently being "in," Whedon doesn't think it ever really went away or that it can ever be replaced.

"In the same way I don't think horror stories have replaced cowboys and Indians because I think Colombian drug dealers and cops have replaced cowboys and Indians, but seriously, I do think horror shows have an important place. The reason horror stories are popping up again is because people *need* horror stories. They need the Big Bad Wolf and they need something to latch on to, something to project their fears on to. But horror had disappeared somewhat in movies which is why it is showing up on television. And it hadn't been on television for a long time, either. It was *The X-Files* that sort of brought it back again."

But *Buffy's* action quotient is reminiscent of another genre altogether—Hong Kong action cinema. In order to perform the extensive fighting sequences, Gellar's training schedule rivals that of any professional athlete—or Jackie Chan.

"I'm taking kickboxing, boxing, and street fighting and gymnastics," she says nonchalantly.

"She's very tough in story meetings," quips producer David Greenwalt.

Maybe now, but early in the production, Gellar was a little squeamish about the realistic fighting sequences. "I had never done street fighting before. Tae Kwon Do is really an art form so I never actually used it in combat," she explains. "So the very first time I had to break a broom over some guy's head, I didn't want to do it. I had never hit anybody before so I was shaking and crying. Now it's like, *Give me the broom—let me hit somebody.*"

Buffy the Vampire Slayer is filmed primarily in a warehouse in Santa Monica, California. Each episode typically has one major fight scene, which can take as long as two eighteen-hour days of rehearsed choreography to film. There are also two or three minor sequences which require much less time.

"We shoot the fight scenes very, very carefully and usually just tag the other actor, which is sort of a light kick," Gellar explains. "And we use stunt doubles when necessary if it's really dangerous."

The second season of the series picked up where the first ended, with lots of critical raves and ever-improving ratings. Of course, ratings are relative, and what is positive for the WB would be disastrous for one of the Big Four networks. But *Buffy* had become the weblet's highest-rated show and more importantly, it's most recognizable and talked about series. If there was any concern, it was over the show's title.

"I think, from a title standpoint, we would have been better served by not having *the Vampire Slayer* in the title," says WB CEO Jamie Kellner. "Because I think that the movie conjured up, in some people's minds, negatives that we would have been better off not having to sell against."

Actually, the WB wasn't even so keen about having *Buffy* in the title, either, initially thinking the name was way too '80s. But Whedon prevailed on that argument and prevented the network from renaming her Samantha or some other '90s name. However, for the second season promotional campaign, the network began referring to the series simply as *Buffy*, with *the Vampire Slayer* tag pushed far into the background, although the words still appear on the show's title card.

"It's sort of a slang name for the show, marketing slang," says Lou Goldstein, co-head of marketing for the WB. "It's what happens to any show that becomes a hit that has taken on a whole other mystique. Like the way *Beverly Hills, 90210* became known as just *90210*."

The reason the network didn't adjust the name in the beginning was that the marketing department felt it would be worse to debut a new show just named *Buffy*. But with one season under its belt, the show was well enough known to make the switch.

There was also some tinkering going on with the show itself. The producers had decided to increase the romance quotient, in order to broaden the appeal and attract even more women to the show.

So far, *Buffy* has exceeded all the expectations the WB had for it. Sarah Michelle Gellar has become a sudden movie star and is appearing on magazine covers everywhere, David Boreanaz is getting noticed as one of television's newest hunks, and the quality of the show keeps getting better with every episode. And in perhaps the most telling indicator of popular culture interest, new Web sites devoted to the series and its stars are popping up weekly.

As a result, WB executives decided to have *Buffy* anchor Tuesday nights, as the network expanded to four nights of programming. Beginning on Tuesday, January 20, 1998, *Buffy*'s new time slot was 8:00 P.M., followed by *Dawson's Creek*, the critically acclaimed new series from Kevin Williamson, who wrote *I Know What You Did Last Summer* and the *Scream* films. Although 8:00 shows are traditionally more family-oriented, Whedon did not make any changes to his series, either tonally or plot-wise due to the new time slot.

Joss Whedon

There's no question that Joss Whedon has a fertile imagination. He has conjured up some of the most inventive screenplays in recent movie history, from the genre-bending *Buffy the Vampire Slayer* to his Oscar-nominated work on *Toy Story* to breathing vital new life into *Alien Resurrection*. His talent is unquestioned.

The question is, just what happened to this guy in childhood that so skewed his way of looking at the world?

"Yes, I was a strange, unlovable child," laughs Joss, whose name means "luck" in Chinese. "I was afraid of the dark and had a very vivid imagination. I think the thing I was most afraid of was my big brother. So if you see big brothers being eviscerated in some show of mine, you'll know where that came from.

"The truth is, I like monsters. The thing I like best is when the monsters jump out of the closet or when there are demons with horns. If it's a cheesy horror film, I've probably seen it."

Admittedly a painfully shy adolescent, who says he was inspired by Buzz Aldrin because "Dammit, he's number two but he was still on the moon," Joss spent much of his youth escaping into reading—comic books like Spiderman, Dracula, and the Fantastic Four, and authors Frank Herbert and Larry Niven.

"A lot of kids get into comic books, but with me it was deeper, more consuming than with other children. While they were outside playing, I'd be tucked away inside the house with a stack of comic books to read.

"I think one of the reasons I got so into reading is that as a kid we had a farm and there was absolutely nothing to do. I think all children should have nothing to do for long periods of time."

Not that Whedon literally grew up on a farm. He was raised in Manhattan and attended high school at the exclusive Riverdale School in New York. Posh or not, Joss hated it and many of the recurrent themes found in his writing can be traced back to his teen years. "For me, high school *was* a horror movie," he says. "Girls wouldn't so much as poke me with a stick."

During his senior year, Joss transferred to Winchester College, an all-boys school in England that was built over six hundred years ago and is renowned for its academic qualifications.

Whedon, with Nicholas Brendon and Alyson Hannigan, discusses *Buffy* at the L.A. Comic Book and Sci-fi Convention. © Sue Schneider/Flower Children Ltd.

"I started quoting Monty Python routines and they accepted me," he jokes. "Actually, I studied the classics and saw a lot of movies," says Joss of his time there.

Whedon returned to America to attend college in Connecticut at Wesleyan—the original Wesleyan. The distinction is important because there are twenty-two schools that have Wesleyan as part of their names, referring to John Wesley, the founder of Methodism. Originally a Methodist college, Wesleyan is now a small, exclusive university on the Connecticut River with a student body of less than three thousand students.

"College rocked," Joss says. "I mean, I was still miserable most of the time, but in a party way."

Whedon majored in film and when he graduated, he had a degree and a diploma but not much else. "I was broke and without a single job prospect," he recalls.

Not that he was without options. Although it's true he was unemployed, Joss knew what he wanted to do. "Writing is the thing I understand best," he says unequivocally.

As it turns out, he was simply joining the family business. His grandfather John wrote for *Leave It to Beaver, The Donna Reed Show,* and *The Dick Van Dyke Show.* And his dad Tom wrote for series such as *Alice, Benson,* and *The Dick Cavett Show,* and produced *The Golden Girls.*

"Actually, my father didn't want me to be a writer but after college he suggested I write a TV script so I could earn enough money to move out of the house," jokes Joss.

So Joss got busy and started churning out spec scripts on his typewriter.

"I wrote a sickening number of scripts, most of which were returned to me. The rejection notes usually said something like, *Very charming. I do not wish to have it.* But the thing is, the only way to get a career is to do a lot of it. You have to do the hard work and create the spec scripts. You have to write as many as you can and send them around, even if it takes a large number."

Joss's dream was to get a job writing for *The Simpsons* or *Twin Peaks.* Instead he had to settle for one of the highest-rated sitcoms on television. When he was twenty-five, he was hired as a story editor on ABC's *Roseanne.*

"I literally went from working at a video store on a Friday to working on *Roseanne* on Monday," says Joss, who vividly describes his experience with the mercurial performer.

"It was baptism by radioactive waste. She was like two different people. One was perfectly intelligent and good to be around. The other was very cranky and not so good to be around. You never knew which would show up.

"I was on staff for a year and then I quit."

Instead of looking for another television series to work for, Joss turned his attention to feature films and hit a home run on his first at bat when his *Buffy the Vampire Slayer* screenplay, which he had written while working on *Roseanne*, sold in 1988.

"The first screenplay I ever wrote was in high school but I never finished that one, so my first real one was *Buffy*," he says. "I got the idea from watching too many movies where the bimbo gets killed by the monster. I remember thinking, *I'd love to see a movie where she kills the monster*."

One of the biggest drawbacks to working in features, though, is the time it takes to go from *We love your script; we gotta have it* to actually seeing the movie on film. So while waiting—and waiting—for the *Buffy* movie to be made, Joss worked for a brief stint in 1990 as a co-producer and writer on the NBC series *Parenthood*.

When *Buffy the Vampire Slayer* was finally released in 1992, Joss hated what he saw. "I wrote the movie as a comedy-horror-action movie and all three elements were equally important," Whedon says. "Unfortunately the director decided to take out the horror and to make it camp instead and ruined my film."

Despite the mixed reaction to the *Buffy* film, Joss's screenwriting career suffered no setback. Over the next two years, he sold two more spec scripts—meaning he wrote the screenplay first then sent it around hoping someone would buy it, as opposed to being commissioned to write it for a specific producer or production company.

In June 1993, Largo Entertainment bought Whedon's script *Suspension* for $750,000 against a $1 million total price. It was an action-suspense film that took place on the George Washington Bridge, which connects northern New Jersey with Manhattan. Industry insiders described it as *Die Hard* on a bridge. Largo announced it wanted to begin filming before the end of the year—but it didn't. Perhaps the failure of Largo's *Judgment Night* (starring Emilio Estevez and Denis Leary) earlier that year doomed *Suspension*, but for whatever reason, the movie was never made.

The first time Joss was hired to "doctor" a script—add scenes or dialogue to punch it up—was for the 1994 Keanu Reeves-Sandra Bullock blockbuster *Speed*. Then in the summer of 1994, Whedon became part of the adventure known as *Waterworld* when he was hired by Kevin Costner to work on the script. Joss should have known that any $100 million-plus movie that begins production without a finished script is not going to be a dream job.

The film was also marred by a bitter falling out between Costner and director Kevin Reynolds, and although the two men blamed each other, an anecdote from Joss gives an indication of what the problem was. "I was on location in Hawaii for seven weeks and nearly every single idea I wrote down was thrown into the garbage by Kevin Costner. I became the world's highest-paid stenographer," says Whedon, who was not given any screenwriter credit.

In September 1994, Columbia Pictures paid a reported $1.5 million against $2 million for another spec script from Whedon, called *Afterlife*. The movie was a love story in which a scientist's mind is implanted into the body of a younger man so the scientist can continue his research project and get back with his loving wife. The catch is, the body belonged to a well-known serial killer.

Once again, the studio announced it would immediately give the project a green light. And this time, they even had a star attached to it—Jean-Claude Van Damme. But a few months later, the muscles from Brussels backed out of the project and the film was never made.

Despite such disappointments, Joss was still one of the more sought after screenwriters in Hollywood and soon it seemed as if everyone was clamoring for his services.

Then came *Toy Story*, the animated movie that almost didn't get made after Disney executives viewed the first story reels. Disney was wary about the kind of computer animation being used, which was quite different from classic Disney. But the biggest problem was that the two lead toy characters were sarcastic, antagonistic, and generally unappealing—particular the cowboy doll, Woody (voiced by Tom Hanks).

As Joss puts it: "Let's face it, Woody was a thundering asshole. So it was my job to make him somewhat likable." For his efforts, Whedon and the six other credited writers were nominated for an Oscar for best original screenplay. The *Toy Story* group lost out to Christopher McQuarrie, who penned *The Usual Suspects*.

But the nomination cemented Joss's reputation and put him in the upper echelon of script doctors, who can command $100,000 a week for their services, which is what Whedon reportedly received for punching up the script for *Twister*, the 1996 film that starred Helen Hunt, Bill Paxton, and a lot of windblown animals, cars, and houses.

When executives at 20th Century Fox decided to revive one of their most successful film franchises, Joss got the call. The result was *Alien Resurrection*, which took the original concept and turned it on its ear by combining the Ripley character (played by Sigourney Weaver) with the alien. Literally. In the process of resurrecting Ripley from some tissue and blood samples, her DNA mixes with the DNZ of the alien creature she had been carrying inside her. The result is an incredibly strong Ripley who can spit acid.

"I made Ripley very strange and morally ambiguous and Sigourney Weaver went for it," Whedon says with classic understatement.

Ironically, despite his reputation as a horror/suspense writer, Whedon claims he is not necessarily a one genre kind of guy. "Although it has some horrific aspects, *Toy Story* isn't a horror

Fangs

Vampires haven't always had fangs and in fact, European vampire lore does not list fangs among a vampire's definite traits. Historical accounts of vampires include blood in the coffin and blood on the mouth, but no fangs. Nor do any of the early works of fiction dealing with vampires, such as Dr. John Polidori's *The Vampyre* (1819), speak of fangs.

The advancement of fangs corresponds to our increasing scientific knowledge of animal physiology and biology. Therefore, it wasn't until the 1800s that vampires in literature started being described as creatures with elongated canine teeth. Obviously, this made it easier for the vampire to puncture the skin of the neck and the jugular vein while feeding.

It isn't until the first chapter of *Varney the Vampyre* (1840) that the idea of fangs appears. "With a plunge he seizes her neck in his fang-like teeth."

The movies jumped on this visual aid. However, in the 1931 film version of Bram Stoker's *Dracula*, Bela Lugosi refused to wear any dental prosthetic and is noticeably missing anything resembling fangs (even though in the book, the Count has sharpened incisors). In the classic *Nosferatu* (1922), the vampire wore his fangs proudly.

Then as special effects improved, vampires with retractable fangs began showing up. In *Buffy*, the vampires' teeth are normal until the demon face appears. And in the series *Forever Knight*, Nick's fangs only protrude when his vampire nature is released through anger or extreme emotion.

film," he points out. "I love all genres. I'm not *just* a scary person—there's a nice part of me. They're just all a little different, that's all."

But for all the success he has had in the film world, Whedon remains surprisingly ambivalent about movies. "I have always felt my movie career was an abysmal failure," he says.

While it brought him wealth and the respect of his peers, his film career failed to satisfy the part of him that wanted to see *his* work on the screen. That is why the television version of *Buffy the Vampire Slayer* is so important to him. "It's the first time I've gotten to write something then see it the way I intended on film."

After an executive from Sandollar came to Joss with the idea of turning the film into a series, Whedon realized it was his chance to finally get his words right—he would finally get the chance to see his vision on film, which is the reason he started writing in the first place as a teenager. Perhaps that's why he named his production company Mutant Enemy.

"Mutant Enemy was the name I gave to my very first typewriter," he explains. "I named it after a song by the group Yes, and that's why the company is called that."

Although Joss, who is now married to interior designer Kai Cole, says the workload of *Buffy* is more than he ever imagined it would be, he swears he has never been more satisfied in his professional life.

"As far as I'm concerned, the first episode of *Buffy* was the beginning of my career because it was the first time I told a story from start to finish the way I wanted it told."

The Characters

Main Characters

Buffy Summers (Sarah Michelle Gellar)

All Buffy really wanted was to be a normal teenager, but fate had other plans for her. Much to her dismay, she is the Chosen One, the one girl in all the world with the power to slay vampires and other creatures of evil. This not only puts her in constant danger, but also puts a severe crimp in her social life.

Buffy's biggest dilemma is in the realm of romance. She is in love with Angel and this is no ordinary Romeo and Juliet problem. He's a vampire, and her duty as the Slayer calls for her to kill him—but she can't because she senses he's not your average, evil, murderous member of the undead. At least, not any longer.

So Buffy must figure out a way to balance her responsibilities as the Slayer with her academic obligations while trying to maintain a relationship with someone she can never see in the daylight—and keeping her mother in the dark about all of it.

WHAT OTHERS SAY:

JOSS WHEDON:

Buffy may grouse about it, but she has heroic instincts; she's somebody who really takes control of her environment.

DAVID BOREANAZ:

Buffy kicks ass. Even when she's down and out, whatever power she has makes her come back with a flair.

KRISTINE SUTHERLAND:

All teenagers have a part of their lives that by necessity they keep a complete secret from their parents. In Buffy's case, it just happens to involve vampires and monsters.

SARAH MICHELLE GELLAR:

Buffy is really dealing with whether she's an adult or a child. She has a life I can really understand—you want to go to the prom but you can't because you have work obligations. Do you have a date or go sit in the cemetery all night?

I think Buffy is an amazing role model because the one thing I was able to do at my high school was be an individual. The problem with most schools is that they don't stress individuality. Buffy is a total individual and shows girls it's okay to be different, which is wonderful because she proves you don't have to fit in. You can be different and still find happiness.

She always finds something good even in the midst of all the evil that surrounds her. Buffy has an amazing spirit and I hope that is never broken.

Alexander "Xander" Harris (Nicholas Brendon)

Xander is the kind of guy who gets along better with the girls in school than he does with the guys. He's too sensitive and sardonic to hang out with the jocks, and too cool to be a nerd. Although bright and street-smart, Xander struggles with certain subjects like math, unsure what the point of learning it is, but he is kept on the academic straight and narrow by his best friend, Willow.

Xander comes from a family of blue collar workers, like his uncle, who was a janitor at a local computer company that went belly-up. Like Willow and Buffy, he is an only child, and in many ways, Buffy, Willow, and Giles have become his surrogate family.

From the moment he first set eyes on her, Xander has loved Buffy. Even though he now knows there will never be a romance between them because her heart belongs to Angel, having Buffy in his life in any capacity is better than no Buffy at all, so he has become her most doggedly loyal friend and protector, willingly—and often recklessly—putting himself at risk to help her battle the forces of evil.

WHAT OTHERS SAY:

NICHOLAS BRENDON:

I'm Joss in high school, which is very intelligent, meaning I have to look up a lot of the words that are in the script. In the series, he's the comic relief guy and I relate to his sense of humor. We both see the funny side of things.

Xander is the person who laughs at all the horrific stuff that's happening and then says, Whatever . . . life goes on. So in that way,

Xander helps people better understand what's going on and accept it.

I can also relate to his feelings and emotions, and especially his insecurity. He's got a crush on Buffy and doesn't hide it. Xander may not be as attractive as Angel, but he has a good heart and he has gotten stronger as the series has progressed and I like that.

Willow Rosenberg (Alyson Hannigan)

A computer whiz kid, Willow is a gentle soul who tends to give people the benefit of the doubt. Although she can be wonderfully ironic in her observations of others, she's not mean-spirited and never goes out of her way to insult or offend anyone. While she is shy and unassuming in front of strangers, Willow is quite capable of taking charge, speaking her mind, and calling people on the carpet if the situation demands it—and there's no other alternative. In some ways, she almost serves as Giles's second, helping him rummage through volumes of lore in search of an answer to the latest challenge the Hellmouth has thrown Buffy's way.

Although Willow is confident in her intellectual abilities, she is stunted in the self-image area, which hasn't been helped along by her ongoing pining for Xander. Though they have been friends since childhood, Willow dreams of Xander being her boyfriend. But whereas the Buffy-Angel pairing tends to carry a jolt of sexual heat, Willow's fantasies are filled more with visions of *amour* than erotic encounters, which is another reason other guys scare her off. In more ways than one, Xander is very safe.

The reality is, Willow knows she and Xander will never be more than friends, despite almost kissing one night in a moment of affectionate sentiment. The real problem for Willow is finding someone sensitive and nice enough—and being aware enough to know it when he comes along.

WHAT OTHERS SAY:

ALYSON HANNIGAN:

She's shy and much more computer literate than I am. I like that she's so smart. We're kind of alike in that she's not the most popular girl in school, she has crushes on guys who don't have crushes back on her and she can retreat to her own little world.

Rupert Giles (Anthony Stewart Head)

Responsible for looking after every Slayer is a Watcher, and Buffy's mentor is the school librarian, who himself comes from a long line of Watchers—his father and his father's mother were Watchers.

Before coming to Sunnydale, Giles worked at the British Museum. Although he is educated and can speak five languages, rather than being some didactic know-it-all, Giles admits that he is often just as unsure and without answers as Buffy is. While most Watchers would have refused to allow others into the Slayer inner circle, Giles accepted Willow, Xander, and Cordelia without much fuss—and even brought Ms. Calendar in of his own accord—realizing that there might very well be strength in numbers. Although it is his duty to make sure the Slayer follows the rules, his number one responsibility is to keep Buffy alive. So if that means bending—or completely ignoring—the Slayer code of absolute secrecy, then he's willing to do that.

Part of the reason Giles is more flexible than Watchers of the past is that he understands the conflicts Buffy is going through—if given the option, Giles would have been a pilot or a grocer or anything other than a Watcher. In fact, he was so resistant to his fate that during his college days he rebelled by falling in with a group who practiced black magic—a decision that would one day come back to haunt him.

Because he spends so much time with books and teenagers, Giles's social life is nearly nonexistent. And when he did take a liking to the school's computer teacher and resident techno-pagan, Jenny Calendar, a run-in with a demon put a frost on the budding relationship.

Although he sometimes flusters easily and loses his patience with the often laid-back attitudes of the teenagers he's become a father figure to, Giles is still the steadying force for Buffy. And he's open enough to take advice, and occasional words of comfort, from her.

WHAT OTHERS SAY:

ANTHONY STEWART HEAD:

It's Giles's duty to teach Buffy how to deal with vampires because she is the One. She is the one who possesses all the talents and he is the Watcher. In the beginning the fact that she resists getting on board was infinitely annoying to Giles, but now he's come to understand her better.

Giles gives the series roots. He anchors it because he knows what needs to be done, even though he's not up to it. That's Buffy's job. At his strongest, he's like Alan Rickman; at his weakest, he's like Hugh Grant.

Angel (David Boreanaz)

Angel is a 242-year-old vampire. Born in 1755 in Ireland, he was "made" by Darla when he was a young man. As Angelus, the vampire with the angelic face, he spent the next hundred or so years terrorizing people all across Europe—until he killed a gypsy girl and her clan put a curse on him, restoring his soul and with it, his conscience.

Overcome with guilt over the horror and carnage he had caused, Angel came to America and swore never to feed on a human again. Rejecting his former family, which included Darla and the Master, the oldest known vampire on record, Angel chose to live above ground with humans and do whatever he could to atone for his evil deeds of the past—including helping the Slayer kill as many vampires as possible.

What Angel didn't plan on was falling in love with Buffy, which forced him to openly renounce his undead brethren, making him just as much of a marked man as Buffy is a marked woman.

WHAT OTHERS SAY:

JOSS WHEDON:

> *I loved Interview with the Vampire as a kid and Angel probably owes something to that.*

DAVID BOREANAZ:

> *Angel is a good guy in a bad situation—he's torn between two worlds and is in love with the girl who should kill him. Angel has a lot of passion he hasn't bitten into yet.*
>
> *The best thing about being a vampire is that Angel has a sixth sense that lets him anticipate danger at all times. The biggest drawback is that he can't drive to Las Vegas during the day in an open convertible.*
>
> *But what Angel would love to do more than anything is watch the sunrise with Buffy. He would love to possess some kind of special powers that let him go back into the sun, at least for a little bit.*

Cordelia Chase (Charisma Carpenter)

On the surface, Cordelia Chase is that girl every high school has—the one who is completely self-absorbed and self-obsessed. Cordelia is the prettiest and most popular girl in school. She has her choice of boyfriends, despite their noticeably high mortality rate. And while Cordelia does have a tendency to act as if she is the center of the known universe, there is more to her than meets the eye. She's very well aware that much of her social life is superficial and that many of her so-called friends are only there to glow in her reflected light of popularity. But she's honest enough to admit it's better than being alone.

When Buffy first came to Sunnydale, Cordelia was one of the first students to extend a tentative hand of friendship. But when Buffy rejected Cordy's "in" group for the company of outsiders Willow and Xander, Cordelia bid her good riddance. Her opinion of Buffy plummeted even further due to Buffy's tendency to always be around weird happenings, like students being killed and monsters taking over the local hangout.

But Cordelia is a pragmatist and when her own life was in danger, she turned to Buffy for help, thereby opening the door to an edgy alliance. As time has passed, Cordelia has reluctantly but steadily been drawn into the fold and learned the truth about Buffy being the Slayer. Although she'd really rather be out shopping for the newest designer fashions, Cordy has proven she can be counted on to show up when needed because it's the right thing to do—even though she will complain endlessly about it afterward because she finds it all so . . . distasteful.

WHAT OTHERS SAY:

CHARISMA CARPENTER:

Joss and I had a conversation one day on the lot. He said, 'You know how Ashley [the character Carpenter played on the series *Malibu Shores*] *was kind of Joan Collins bitchy? Well, we don't want to go there.' We want Cordelia to be a little more witty. It's more intimidating when she's smart, when you bring that aspect into it, rather than just being mean or evil.*

My perspective is that Cordelia is a little misunderstood. She can come off as a snobby witch but I see her as a survivor. Her mother had Epstein-Barr and there was a lot of neglect. So she's learned by survival skills to use her sexuality and to use aspects of her personality that maybe she wouldn't have to use had she had an attentive mother.

If I look at Cordelia that way, then I can more easily relate to her. And as far as inspiration, I based Cordelia's character on everyone I've met in L.A.

JOSS WHEDON:

> *There's a story behind the character's name. My wife went to school with this really mean girl named Cordelia, so it was kind of a way of getting back all these years later.*

Recurring Characters

Jenny Calendar (Robia La Morte)

A self-professed techno-pagan, Jenny combines old-fashioned mystical beliefs with Information Age technology in keeping an eye on the forces of evil. In her spare time she reads rune stones and attends pagan festivals.

As Sunnydale High School's computer teacher, Jenny is often at odds with Giles over the value of cyberspace and Internet information; she sees it as the dawn of a new era, he sees it as temporal and elusive. To him, a book represents knowledge forever; to her, writing can be elitist and difficult for the common person to access.

Add to that her easy sensual aggression and his shy eagerness and it's a match made in the Hellmouth. Although attached to him, Jenny must come to grips with the reality of Giles's life as the Watcher and the daily dangers anyone involved with him must necessarily face.

WHAT OTHERS SAY:

ANTHONY STEWART HEAD:

> *She's gorgeous, like a David Bailey picture.*

Joyce Summers (Kristine Sutherland)

After Buffy was kicked out of school for burning down the gym, her mom decided to leave Los Angeles and start a new life in Sunnydale. As a divorced single mom, Joyce is often too preoccupied with trying to get her new business, an art gallery, off the ground to have the time to pay close attention to exactly what her daughter is doing.

Used to big city cynicism, she believes that Giles is simply a concerned teacher trying to help her often academically troubled daughter. She takes Buffy's sometimes moody behavior as typical teenage angst, unaware that her child faces life-threatening danger on a nightly basis.

But for all her worries, Joyce also ultimately has faith in Buffy and sees her daughter as a self-reliant young woman who is not afraid to intervene on the behalf of others. Now if only she would do her homework.

WHAT OTHERS SAY:

KRISTINE SUTHERLAND:

Buffy and Joyce have a really good relationship and ultimately, a trusting one. Both are trying to make new lives for themselves in a place very different than what they are used to. Whatever disagreements they might have, the bottom line is there is a strong love there. Joyce just wants the best for her daughter, and for herself, too.

Hank Summers (Dean Butler)

Now divorced from Joyce, Buffy's father lives in Los Angeles and is the ultimate weekend dad—he sees his daughter only a few weekends every year. Because of the distance that separates them, both in miles and due to Buffy's tendency to withdraw into herself, Hank worries that he's lost the ability to communicate with his daughter. Unaware of her conflict about being the Slayer, he naturally thinks the divorce is the reason for her reserve.

WHAT OTHERS SAY:

DEAN BUTLER:

He'll never be more than peripheral in Buffy's life. He shows up on occasion to see her but their paths seldom cross.

Principal Flutie (Ken Lerner)

A kinder, gentler kind of administrator, Mr. Flutie believed that even the most incorrigible students would come around given enough support and understanding. He ultimately learned just how woefully wrong his philosophy was.

Principal Snyder (Armin Shimerman)

Children, shmildren. This administrator sees his students for what they really are: horrible little troublemakers who would just as soon eat you than pick up a book and study. Sneaky with a mysterious aura, Principal Snyder is a man who knows more than he lets on.

He also has made it his mission to make Buffy's school life miserable. He considers her one of the school's most troublesome students and goes out of his way to see she stays on the straight and narrow by forcing her to participate in school activities she would otherwise spurn.

WHAT OTHERS SAY:

JOSS WHEDON:

> *There are some people for whom teens are simply vicious little statistics. Snyder is one of those guys.*

The Vampires

The Master (Mark Metcalf)

The oldest and most powerful vampire on record, the Master is a megalomaniac bent on destroying humankind and reclaiming the earth for the "old ones." After being trapped in a mystical portal beneath Sunnydale when his plan of opening the Hellmouth was interrupted by an earthquake, the Master spends his time plotting evil schemes and using ancient prophecies in hopes of being set free so he can begin his long-anticipated extermination of man.

WHAT OTHERS SAY:

MARK METCALF:
> The reason the Master was in such an evil mood was it was really hot and dusty where he was imprisoned.

Darla (Julie Benz)

The vampire who sired Angel prefers dressing up in Catholic school uniforms when she leads young men expecting a good time to their unexpected deaths. When Angel was at his worst, they roamed the streets of Europe leaving death and horror in their wake. When Angel went over to the other side, Darla was determined to win him back, or failing that, kill him. It never occurred to her that the tables could be turned.

WHAT OTHERS SAY:

JOSS WHEDON:
> Darla's a popular girl. Time just won't seem to let go of Darla; she stays with you.

The Anointed One (Andrew J. Ferchland)

The Anointed One was one of five people killed by vampires in order to fulfill an ancient prophecy. The twist was that the One chosen was a child, who was destined to sit at the right hand of the Master when Armageddon came. Although he still had the body of a child, the Anointed One's ruthlessness was second only to the Master's.

WHAT OTHERS SAY:

JOSS WHEDON:
> He's really annoying.

Drusilla (Juliet Landau)

Not only is Drusilla a vampire, she's certifiable—as in nuts. She was driven to madness by Angel, who killed off her family one by one just for fun, before turning Dru into a vampire.

But an attack by an angry mob in Prague nearly killed poor demented Drusilla, so she and her constant companion, Spike, headed for the Hellmouth in order to find a cure. The thought of a physically hale Drusilla is a terrifying one because while most vampires are simply evil, Dru is evil *and* insane, a decidedly unpleasant and unpredictable combination.

WHAT OTHERS SAY:

JULIET LANDAU:

> *Drusilla was a lady with servants and wonderful friends, and she ate them all.*

JAMES MARSTERS:

> *The moment Spike saw Drusilla, he knew he would love her until the moment he died—which was about three minutes later.*

Vampire Mask

When Angel gets angry, his face abruptly changes, revealing the demon inside his body, a transformation that takes mere seconds. However, it takes David Boreanaz considerably more time than that to turn into his vampire alter ego.

"It takes on average about an hour and twenty minutes to put on my vampire face," says Boreanaz. "And then about forty minutes to take it off."

The vampire mask, designed by John Vulich, is a prosthetic piece of latex that fits around the actor's nose and is applied by Todd McIntosh.

"Then they paint the face on by using make-up to blend it in and *that's* what takes all the time. Once they're done with that, you just put in the contact lenses and the teeth and you're ready to go."

Spike (James Marsters)

Also known as William the Bloody, Spike got his nickname from his penchant for torturing people with railroad spikes. But his one soft spot is for Drusilla, for whom he would go to the ends of the world, which he has by coming to Sunnydale in order to help Dru regain her health. Not one to follow tradition, Spike has no time for most ancient prophecies and he certainly can't be bothered with taking orders from a pip-squeak Anointed One.

But if there's one thing Spike in particular can't stand it's a Slayer. He's already killed two within the last hundred years and plans on making Buffy the next notch on his fangs.

WHAT OTHERS SAY:

JAMES MARSTERS:

[Spike's] very good at gouging. Eyes mostly. It's pretty well a lost art.

A Brief History of the Vampire

The creature we know today as the vampire—a reanimated corpse that rises from the grave to feed on the living by drinking their blood—has been around certainly since the time of the ancient Greeks and possibly even since the beginning of recorded time. There have always been vampire-like creatures in the mythologies of many cultures.

The Romans and the Serbians of Eastern Europe had specific names for these blood sucking monsters—*sanguisuga* and *vukodlak* respectively. Many scholars believe that the Slavic countries of Eastern Europe were the hot zone of early vampire belief from the Middle Ages on, and that our current perception of the vampire can be traced back to there.

Between 1600 and 1800, the number of suspected vampire cases reported reached epidemic proportions. Although it started in the Balkans region, vampirism eventually spread west into Germany, France, Italy, Spain, and England. There were so many purported occurrences of vampire activity that writers of the time began to use the myth as the basis for literature.

The word "vampire" became part of the English language in 1732, when investigators for two British periodicals, *Gentleman's Magazine* and the *London Journal* reported on the chilling case of Arnold Paole, who was accused of killing people in the town of Meduegna between 1727 and 1732.

At first, nobody believed the ramblings of Paole, who, while lying on his deathbed, claimed that he had been bitten by a vampire and that was the reason he was dying. But after his death, villagers started disappearing, and people began to believe Paole had risen from the grave and was feeding on the locals.

So a group of townsfolk dug up Paole's body and drove a stake through its heart. According to eyewitnesses, the body appeared unnaturally fresh for having been in the ground so long, and seemingly fresh blood squirted from the wound. On the heels of the Paole incident, more vampire attacks were reported in Serbia, and subsequently, eight more "preserved" corpses were dug up and burned.

Another famous case of vampirism involved a seventeenth-century countess named Elizabeth Bathory, who belonged to one of the wealthiest and oldest families in Transylvania, an ancient area located in what is now Romania. Among her many powerful relatives were clergymen and political leaders, including a monarch—King Steven of Poland (1575–86).

Elizabeth married Count Ferencz Nasdasdy when she was just fifteen years old. As was typical in those days, he was away most of the time fighting one battle or another, so while Elizabeth sat home at Castle Csejthe, she was introduced to the occult by one of her servants.

In 1600, her husband died, and Elizabeth's behavior took a decided turn for the dark. According to the story, one day a servant girl accidentally pulled the countess' hair. Furious, Elizabeth hit her so hard she drew blood, a drop of which landed on her skin. Elizabeth was so taken by the effect of the girl's blood on her skin that she ordered the servant's blood drained into a huge vat, which she then used as a beautifying bath treatment.

It took ten years for authorities to learn of the horrible atrocities occurring at Castle Csejthe. It eventually came out during the trial that nearly forty girls had been tortured and killed. The countess herself would often stab them with scissors, letting the blood drain out slowly. However, Elizabeth Bathory was never convicted. Even then, if you had enough wealth and power, you could get away with murder. Instead, she was literally walled up inside her bedroom and was found dead in 1614.

Interestingly, Elizabeth's family was connected to another family whose name would become synonymous with terror—and vampires. Back in 1476, Prince Steven Bathory helped a Romanian prince named Dracula regain his throne.

Although it's been the subject of great debate, the general consensus seems to be that Bram Stoker did indeed base his Count Dracula character on the real-life historical figure of Vlad III Dracula—also known as Vlad Tepes or Vlad the Impaler (the surname Tepes means "The Impaler" in the Romanian language).

Ironically though, the historical Dracula—although it is acknowledged that he committed atrocities against his own people—is remembered in Romania as a national hero who resisted the Turkish invaders from the east and maintained the national monarchy in the face of the powerful Hungarian empire.

Dracula was born in 1431, the son of Vlad II Dracul, who was the ruler of Wallachia, a Romanian province south of Transylvania, north of Bulgaria, and west of the Black Sea. At that time, the area was in a constant state of political turmoil, with the Turks trying to invade on one side and Hungary trying to swallow up the other. After Vlad II was assassinated, Dracula (which means son of Dracul) seized the Wallachian throne in 1448, with a little help from the Turks. He was forced off the throne two months later and fled the area.

He retook the throne in 1456 and ruled until 1462 and it was during this time that he became known as the Impaler because of his unimaginable, torturous cruelty. Death by impalement, where a stake is gradually forced through the body—often until it emerged from the mouth—was an unspeakably gruesome way to die. The victim would sometimes linger for days, often hung upside down.

To amuse himself, Dracula would often arrange the impaled bodies in geometric designs or set up rings of impaled victims outside of the next town he intended to attack. The most shocking aspect of his pastime is that he also used impalement against his own people as a way to maintain authority. The elderly, the ailing, women and children, pregnant women—nobody was safe. He was known to impale thousands at a time, and then eat dinner sitting amidst the carnage.

So when Stoker needed a model for his vampire, Dracula no doubt seemed a perfect choice. Outside of Eastern Europe, Vlad the Impaler was an obscure historical figure, and those who did recognize the name would associate it with horror and unspeakable cruelty. One change he did make concerned locale—he moved Count Dracula's castle from Wallachia to Transylvania, which, during Stoker's time, was an area that remained medieval in appearance and outlook.

Up until the seventeenth century, vampires were mostly an oral tradition, frightening tales passed down through generations through verbal retellings. But as vampires became a staple of literature, the very mythology of the creature began to change, until it became a reverse reflection of the society from which the authors sprang. In ancient times, vampires were evil creatures to be feared, avoided, and killed. But as they were analyzed through literature, they also became creatures to be understood, because at their core, they represented mankind's deepest, darkest fears about death.

Vampire Mythology

Although Bram Stoker did not invent the vampire, his Count Dracula character certainly helped form the modern mythology of the vampire, which has changed drastically over the centuries. For example, early mythological vampires did not sleep in coffins, for very good reason. Up until the nineteenth century, only the very rich could afford coffins. So all a vampire needed to "rest" was a mound of native soil. Which is why, in Stoker's book, Dracula brings several crates of Transylvanian dirt with him. The only reason it became common to depict a vampire resting in a coffin is simply because in modern times, we bury the dead in coffins.

Although Christians have long associated vampirism with Satanic evil, it was not until Stoker's *Dracula* (published in 1897) that the crucifix—a cross with the figure of Christ—was seen to wield supernatural power against the vampire. The cross, symbolic of goodness and holiness, became a mystical weapon to be used against the abject evil of the demon vampire. In *Dracula*, the crucifix could both weaken the vampire physically as well as burn its flesh.

Over the years, the powers attributed to the crucifix were carried over to any cross. However, in recent years, some writers, including Anne Rice, have broken with that tradition by depicting vampires that are immune to the effects of the cross and other religious symbols. That's because these vampires are not associated specifically with Satan—consider them secular blood suckers—therefore, religious artifacts have no effect. However, in the *Buffy* vampire mythology, crosses and holy water are still used to repel and ward off Sunnydale's brand of vampire.

But where the cross is falling out of favor in certain literary circles, garlic is making a leap in popularity. Since ancient times, garlic has been used as both a food and a healing agent, and in modern times it is valued for its ability to help strengthen the human immune system. In medieval times, garlic was either worn or hung outside a house to ward off vampires. Some cultures stuffed cloves of garlic in the mouth of a suspected vampire—after its head had been cut off the body.

It was also believed that you could use garlic as a kind of vampire detector—if a guest in your house refused to eat garlic, they could be a vampire. Again, the first literary reference to garlic was in *Dracula*. Van Helsing, the vampire hunter, puts it around Lucy's neck to keep Dracula away from her. Since then, garlic has become a major tool for vampire hunters everywhere, and even Buffy carries garlic cloves around in her Slayer satchel.

However, being the rebel she is, in *The Vampire Chronicles*, author Anne Rice tends to disregard garlic's effectiveness.

Rice does ascribe, however, to the long-standing belief that fire is a sure way to kill the undead. Culturally, it makes perfect sense, because the flames of fire have been used since caveman days as a symbol of cleansing and purity. Ironically, *Dracula* is one of the few references—oral, literary, or cinematic—that doesn't make mention of fire. In Rice's *Vampire Chronicles*, fire was the *only* way to destroy a vampire—not even staking would do the trick.

Killing a vampire by stabbing it through the heart with a wooden stake has been the method of choice in vampire mythology for centuries. Initially, the stakes were used to literally spike a corpse to the earth, which would prevent the body from rising.

But after coffins became a regular feature of burial, the stake became a way to actually kill the creature. However, there have been questions whether it was the actual puncturing of the heart that did the trick, or the wood itself that was necessary. In *Buffy*, as with most other depictions, it is necessary for wood to go through the heart. Anything else leaves a wound but the vampire keeps going. As a result, certain woods were favored over others by vampire hunters, the most highly recommended being ash and juniper.

One of the aspects of vampire mythology that has changed drastically over the centuries is the effect of sunlight. Although most modern stories, including *Buffy*, hold that sunlight is absolutely lethal to vampires, that wasn't always the case. In medieval times, people believed that vampires walked around just as easily as humans during daylight. But as the literary vampire developed, so did its aversion to the sun.

In *Dracula*, Stoker's vampires were able to be out during the day, however exposure to sunlight made them considerably weaker. But since then, vampires have been portrayed as being lethally vulnerable to the sun's direct rays. In the 1990s supernatural television series *Forever Knight*, the cop/vampire can go out during the day, but must avoid letting the light come in direct contact with his skin. However, like Dracula, just being in reflected light saps his strength.

In *The Vampire Chronicles*, Anne Rice—ever the one to turn the mythology upside down—devised vampires that become immune to the sun's rays if they live long enough.

The idea that vampires are able to alter their appearance or shape-shift, has been part of the mythology for hundreds of years, but it was cemented by Stoker's description of how the count was able to turn into a bat or disappear in a spray of mist. However, that ability has frequently been discarded in other literary and film depictions, including *Buffy*, where the closest thing to a disappearing act is the way Angel can leave a room without anyone hearing him—all they see is the swinging library door.

The single aspect of vampire mythology that hasn't changed regardless of the culture or era is the creature's need to drink blood in order to survive. Deprive a vampire of its blood supply and it will grow weak and eventually wither away. But when it comes to why exactly the vampire needs blood, there are varying interpretations. Like *Buffy*'s vampires, Anne Rice's undead in *The Vampire Chronicles* are inhabited by a demon that makes them lust for blood. In early literary works, it was inferred that vampires suffered from a sort of anemia, so they needed fresh blood to stay healthy and strong.

One trait of vampirism that seems to hold true across the board is that once a person becomes a vampire, they stop aging. Hence, the young girl in *Interview with a Vampire* remains a young girl throughout. It is also the reason why *Buffy* creator Joss Whedon found it necessary to kill off the Anointed One—the actor was visibly aging before viewers' eyes.

As far as physical attributes go, it is generally agreed that vampires have good eyesight and excellent hearing, most likely because those are traits associated with other nocturnal creatures. A vampire's skin is usually pale, which makes sense if sunlight never touches their skin. However, some literature indicates that a vampire will get a glow to his skin after feeding.

In *Buffy the Vampire Slayer* and many other depictions, the vampire possesses superhuman strength, but this wasn't always the case. Centuries ago, vampires tended to only attack vulnerable victims, such as old people or children. But in more recent literature and film portrayals, vampires are powerful creatures with few weaknesses. That's what made *Buffy*'s Drusilla character so unique—she was powerless and completely dependent on Spike, until revived through the ritual with Angel.

Now we come to the question many *Buffy* fans have debated—can vampires have sex, either with each other or with humans? The answer is yes, on both counts.

In some literature, vampires are simply not interested in sex, considering such carnal desires as beneath them. But by and large, vampires have come to be seen as highly erotic, sensual creatures, although there are some definite drawbacks to becoming intimately involved with one.

The first problem is their skin temperature. Vampires are technically dead and therefore cold to the touch. All over. In some portrayals, vampires are shown as bloodless, with no circulation. But the *Buffy* vampires bleed when hurt, so Angel would have blood circulation, which, for all males—including vampires—is important for a romantic interlude.

The biggest hurdle to overcome during physical intimacy with a vampire is the danger that the vampire will lose control and go into a feeding frenzy. If the point of the seduction is to feed and kill, then that's no problem. However in the case of a long-term relationship, such a loss of control would be disastrous. Recall the first time Angel kissed Buffy; the first thing that happened was his vampire face appeared. Some literature details how a vampire may feed just a little bit on a human lover, enabling the undead one to have normal sexual function. It's believed that true love tends to keep a vampire from going into a feeding frenzy during sex. Which also means that one night stands usually don't stand a chance.

And yes, vampires can have children. The offspring of a vampire and a human is called a *dhampir*. Traditionally, the father is a vampire and the mother human. And usually, the baby is male. Because of his unique parentage, dhampirs are said to have the ability to ferret out vampires and many, in fact, became vampire hunters. The dhampir's special sensory abilities could be passed down to his children and were believed to last many generations.

Vampires in Film and TV

Although the modern view of vampires has its roots in Bram Stoker's *Dracula*, the creature has been refined, and redefined, by more recent works of literature—most notably Anne Rice's *The Vampire Chronicles*. But the art form most responsible for shaping the current view of the vampire is film.

The granddaddy of vampire movies has to be the 1931 Tod Browning film *Dracula*, which starred Bela Lugosi. Although by today's standards the film is pure camp, at the time, women were passing out in theatre aisles from fright. It was also the genesis for the horror film genre that Universal made into a cottage industry.

Lugosi's Dracula was a gothic figure, a man of the shadows. Because of his accent and foreign appearance, the film promoted the image of the alien vampire, the stranger who walks among us.

In a little known bit of vampire movie trivia, studio executives believed that *Dracula* would do very well in the overseas markets, so a second film was shot in Spanish using the same sets just days after *Dracula* wrapped. This version starred Carlos Villarias as Count Dracula and was directed by George Melford. Some film historians consider the Spanish version to be superior to the Browning version.

Although film vampires have tended to stay in the tall, dark, handsome, and mysterious vein, two distinct types of Hollywood vampires have emerged—the old-fashioned, courtly vampire who possesses an Old World air and tends to shy away from interacting much with humans; and the modern vampire, who

He vants to suck your blood: Bela Lugosi in *Dracula* (1931). Photo courtesy Photofest.

often conceals his identity by hiding in plain sight, living among humans and interacting with them aside from feeding on them.

Initially, all vampires were ultimately evil and better off dead. But as vampires have become ingrained in popular culture, that menace has become optional. On occasion, vampires have become lovable comic foils, as in the 1960s television series *The Munsters* and the films *Love at First Bite* (1979) and *Dracula, Dead and Loving It* (1995).

Buffy the Vampire Slayer straddles both approaches. Most of the vampires the Slayer encounters are soulless monsters out to hunt and feed on humans. But Angel is a vampire of a different sort because he's been cursed with a conscience, so he keeps the demon inside him in check, and refrains from feeding on humans. He's got all the eroticism and power without the killer mentality.

No doubt much of the change in attitude towards vampires has to do with the times in which we live. During Victorian times, the qualities embodied by the vampire—the lusty, erotic, dangerous creature not bound by social conventions—reflected the very aspects of man that the era sought to repress. The sensibility of those times was incorporated in both 1992's *Dracula*, directed by Francis Ford Coppola, and the 1994 film adaptation of Anne Rice's *Interview with a Vampire* starring Tom Cruise.

While the majority of vampire portrayals maintain the convention that the undead are monsters who must be stopped, some opt for a more complex identity that in many ways reflects our own dual natures as creatures that can embody the greatest good and the worst evil. Now with our "I'm okay, you're okay" openness, vampires don't have to represent all that is evil.

Although vampires have populated close to a hundred films and have been the topic of literature for the past several centuries, television has been slower to jump on the vampire bandwagon. Part of that is the nature of a series—how does one incorporate a vampire over an extended period of time?

The easiest way is through comedy. In *The Munsters*, Lily and Grandpa were vampires but without any bite. And in the 1988 animated series *Count Duckula*, a vegetarian duck battles against everyone's attempt to turn him into a blood sucker.

Developing a dramatic series starring a vampire as a lead character had proven to be a trickier matter, but in the right setting,

Max Schreck starred in the classic *Nosferatu* (1922). Photo courtesy Photofest.

vampires have shown they can be TV stars, too. In 1967, ABC introduced the gothic soap opera, *Dark Shadows*, about a 200-year-old vampire named Barnabas Collins. Using soap conventions, *Dark Shadows* managed to milk the vampire myth for five seasons. Part of its success was due to the willingness of daytime viewers to accept the Gothic setting. Plus, daytime serials tend to move at a slower pace than prime-time shows, so it fit traditional vampire storytelling conventions.

The Night Stalker, one of the better scary television movies ever made, starred Darrin McGavin as reporter Carl Kolchak, who investigates a series of gruesome murders in Las Vegas. But when ABC made the 1971 telefilm into a series in 1974, it proved impossible to sustain the story lines—which branched out beyond vampires into monsters of all kinds. But the genuine fear factor that had made the original telefilm so effective mutated into toothless camp and the show was canceled after a year.

The 1990s series *Forever Knight* and *Kindred: The Embraced* both took the "vampires are people too" approach. In *Forever Knight*, an 800-year-old vampire works as a Toronto homicide detective, in an attempt to atone for his past sins and somehow regain his mortality.

In *Kindred: The Embraced*, a vampire named Luna is the prince of several clans of vampires, or kindred, living in San Francisco. It's his job to maintain peace between the clans and enforce the Kindred rules against taking a human life or turning humans into vampires against their wishes.

The lead characters of both series are reminiscent of *Buffy*'s Angel—vampires who have maintained some remnant of their humanity or are attempting to repent for atrocities they've committed earlier during their lives as vampires. This trend of humanizing some vampires while acknowledging the overall evil of the species seems to be the most successful way to portray vampires in a series, because in television it's important for people to want to invite the show back into their homes week after week.

Buffy offers viewers the best of both worlds. The lead character is a Slayer, the vampires she hunts are unequivocally evil, but her love interest is the only vampire who, through a gypsy curse, has a conscience and is able to control the demon within—for the most part. Angel takes the appeal of the tortured soul to a new level. By combining the traditional Gothic elements of vampire lore with the modern twist of redemption, *Buffy* has further developed the ongoing mythology of vampires.

While the classic elements of vampire mythology will undoubtedly endure in future films and series, as evidenced by *Buffy*, individual vampire characters will continue to diversify and grow in complexity because at their core, they are simply a mirror into the dark side of our own hearts.

Cast Biographies

Sarah Michelle Gellar

There's a stigma attached to being a kid actor. In order for pre-school aged children to succeed in such a highly competitive business they must be precocious, willing to please, possess a premature ambition, *and* be cute as a button to boot. Child actors must have at least one parent who steers them toward the spotlight, who at some point agrees to expose their son or daughter to the often ego-punishing world of show business. No matter how much a child maintains their desire to act, the fact is, unless the parent becomes part of the process, it simply wouldn't happen. Many kids aspire to be in show biz, however, the majority are gently told they can do whatever they want—once they are old enough to get to auditions on their own.

The biggest criticism of child actors is what happens to them when they become adults. The film and television industries are littered with reminders—Dana Plato, River Phoenix, Todd Bridges, Macaulay Culkin, Danny Bonaduce, Corey Haim, to name just a few—of what can happen to young people who are subjected to the pressure of being the family's primary bread-winner; of juggling the angst of growing up with the responsibilities of an adult job; of not only achieving success, but maintaining it.

Some of the most vocal critics are former child stars themselves, such as *The Donna Reed Show*'s Paul Petersen (founder of A Minor Consideration, a group which advocates the rights of child performers), who says that the entertainment industry's tendency to view people as disposable goods sets young people up for a devastating fall once they literally grow out of their careers.

Of course, not all former child actors end up robbing dry cleaners or overdosing on city sidewalks or marrying eight times and becoming the poster girl for the Betty Ford Clinic. Nor do all fail to make the transition to an adult career. Jodie Foster, Henry Thomas, Jerry O'Connell, and dozens of others are living proof that you can be a child actor, grow up to become a relatively well-balanced adult, and continue in your chosen profession.

Sarah Michelle Gellar can be added to that list of adjusted overachievers.

Gellar (pronounced Gell-are, not Gell-er) has been a professional actor for fifteen of her twenty-one years, and she is a bit weary of people making assumptions about former child actors.

"I'm tired of people who say, *Acting corrupts these young people*," Gellar has said. "You know what? There are a lot of actors who have been working since a young age and they're just fine. I was not meant to be in Little League or the local ballet school.

"My mom is not living vicariously through me. It has always been my choice to act—and if my grades ever fell below an A, I had to stop working for a while. When I was old enough, it was my decision to go to college or pursue my career. If at any time I wanted to give it up, she would be behind me 100 percent."

That said, it was actually an agent who first got the idea that Sarah had a face a camera could love. Born April 14, 1977 in Manhattan and raised on the Upper East side, Sarah was discovered in a Lana Turner moment while eating lunch with her mother in a restaurant.

"This woman walked up to me and asked if I'd like to be on television," Gellar says. "And I was like, *Yeah, okay!*"

Sarah was four years old and a would-be star was born.

A short time later, Sarah got her first national exposure when she was hired to play Valerie Harper's daughter in a CBS movie-of-the-week, *An Invasion of Privacy*, which also starred Jeff Daniels.

"The day I went in, I was supposed to read with Valerie but she'd already gone home. But that was no problem; first I read my lines and then I read hers—in Valerie's voice. I was hired on the spot."

Sarah played Burt Young's daughter in the 1983 feature *Over the Brooklyn Bridge*, and she filmed a guest spot on the Tony Randall series *Love, Sidney*, but she worked mostly in commercials during those early years. She did over one hundred television spots, thirty of them for a long-running Burger King campaign.

"I was the little Burger King girl who couldn't say the word 'burger.' Actually, they sent me for speech lessons and eventually I could say the word, but unfortunately I couldn't say anything else," she laughs.

Child star no more: the beautiful Sarah Michelle Gellar. © Albert Ortega/Flower Children Ltd.

However, what happened later was no laughing matter. At the tender age of five, Sarah learned just what a cutthroat business entertainment was when she was named in a civil lawsuit filed by McDonald's against Burger King. Although a common practice now, the suit stemmed from Burger King daring to openly disparage rival McDonald's in a television commercial.

"The commercial I did was one of the first to ever directly challenge another company. In it, I said the lines, *Do I look 20 percent smaller to you? I must to McDonald's because their hamburger is 20 percent smaller.* And they're not flame-broiled, either, as we all know.

"Well, McDonald's was very upset by this commercial so they turned around and sued Burger King, J. Walter Thompson—the advertising company that came up with the idea for the spot—and me. I couldn't even say the word *lawyer* and a few months later I was having to tell my friends, *I can't play. I've got to give a deposition.*"

The case, dubbed by the New York papers as the Battle of the Burgers was eventually settled out of court in 1982, and Sarah and her career sailed along untainted by the legal maneuvering.

Sarah says the lawsuit was the least of her concerns at that age. Worse was her truth-in-advertising contractual obligation to only publicly endorse Burger King. "When you're five, where do all of your friends have their birthday parties? Answer—McDonald's. So there I was going to birthday parties wearing a big straw hat and sunglasses."

By 1986, Sarah's career was gaining momentum. She played a little girl in the hospital on an episode of *Spenser: For Hire* with Robert Urich, and made her Broadway debut in the drama *The Widow Claire*, which was staged at Circle in the Square. Sarah played the role of Molly opposite a still up-and-coming Matthew Broderick.

"But then *Ferris Bueller* came out and Matthew left the show," Sarah recalled. "But he was replaced by Eric Stoltz. Then Eric's film, *Some Kind of Wonderful* came out and suddenly *he* was really big. And I became the most popular girl in school because I got to work with both of them."

As positive and bright as her career was, Sarah's home life was decidedly darker. Her mother, Rosellen, then a nursery school teacher, and her father Arthur, a salesman, were in the throes of a crumbling marriage. As an only child, Sarah had no sibling to turn to for comfort.

Although Sarah has steadfastly refused to discuss her parents' split, an interview Arthur gave to a tabloid in 1994 strongly indicates that Rosellen's support and encouragement of her daughter's acting career was at least one cause of friction.

Arthur, then an unemployed textile salesman, told *Star* magazine that he never wanted Sarah to go into show business because he worried about the effect it could have on her, having seen firsthand via some of his relatives what troubles life in the fast lane can bring.

"I just wanted Sarah to have a normal life. Kids in the business grow up too fast," he said.

Arthur and Rosellen divorced in 1987, after thirteen years of marriage. For a while, Arthur and Sarah maintained contact, but by 1990, when she was just eleven, all communication had been broken off. Even though they lived in the same city, Sarah wouldn't lay eyes on her father for many years.

As late as 1994, Sarah would respond coldly whenever asked about her father. "My parents divorced when I was very young and I don't see my real dad. We never got along, so when he left it was a much better environment. And he's out of the picture. My mom's fiancé is the one who sat in the front row at school recitals with the camera."

Despite his daughter's apparent anger and resentment, Arthur maintained he held no grudges. "I love Sarah very much. And even though I haven't seen her in years, there isn't a night that goes by that I don't think of her—but it's too painful to even watch her on TV."

Sarah's resentment against anyone, her father included, who questioned or criticized her or her mother over her acting career would be a recurring theme for many years. But whatever emotional toll it took, it did nothing to slow Sarah down. If anything, she sped up.

Not only was she pursuing acting with a passion, but Sarah was also a jock. "A lot of kids took ballet and jazz but I was a bit of a tomboy, so I started training in Tae Kwon Do when I was nine. It just seemed like something interesting to do at the time," she smiles. "I thought it would be fun—kick around a few people, get a couple of aggressions out."

She was also a competitive figure skater for three years, ranking third in the New York State regional competition.

"What was happening was, I was going to school, acting, skating, and taking Tae Kwon Do all at the same time. I would get up in the morning and head straight to the ice rink to practice. Then I'd go to school, then when school let out I'd go on auditions, then take Tae Kwon Do classes in the evening."

Can you say, Type A personality?

Despite her amazing determination, stamina, ambition, and drive, Sarah eventually discovered she wasn't superhuman.

"No human being can keep up that kind of schedule, and I was cracking," she admits. "So finally my mom stepped in. One day she sat me down and told me I could only do two things. One was school, so that left me the choice of picking the one thing that was my big love. And I chose acting."

Although Sarah had weathered the storm of her parents' divorce, she was about to embark on a new emotional tidal wave.

The good old days of being one of the gang invited to birthday parties at McDonald's gave way to a miserable junior high existence.

"I went to a normal private school. Although it may seem odd to people in the Midwest, everyone goes to private school in Manhattan," Gellar says.

Well, everyone who can afford to, anyway.

At New York's exclusive Columbia and Preparatory School, Sarah was a fish out of water. "I didn't have anything in common with the kids because so many students there were used to having everything handed to them on a silver platter," she says. "Everything I got I worked hard for and got on my own."

Despite her talent, intelligence, and desire to fit in, Sarah was the class outcast during her junior high years, surrounded by schoolmates unimpressed by her achievements as an actress, which by that time included parts in the features *Funny Farm* with Chevy Chase, and *High Stakes* with Sally Kirkland.

"No one cared what I did. I was very into studying and I was not the most popular. I was a nerd. I was an outcast. Kids were so hard on me. I never liked to talk about my acting because if I did, I was branded a snob. And if I didn't, I was still a snob.

"I do feel I was sort of punished for what I did. I was always excluded from everything because I was different. That's difficult when you're a child. I used to cry because I didn't understand why people didn't like me."

Sarah believed the other kids resented her professional achievements, which made her start being secretive about her extracurricular activities.

"In 1990, I had more absences in the first month than you're supposed to have in an entire year. I was telling them I had back problems and had to go to doctors all the time. I guess they believed me—until *A Woman Named Jackie* aired."

In that 1991 miniseries, Sarah played the young Jacqueline Bouvier. Besides being delirious at the opportunity to spend time away from the nightmare that was school, Gellar was excited to be involved in a project about the former First Lady. "I had always been fascinated by Jackie Kennedy so to play her as a teenager was really a thrill," Sarah says.

The older Jackie was played by future *Touched by an Angel* star Roma Downey, to whom Sarah became instantly devoted. "I wanted to be just like Roma. Not just in the movie but in real life, too. If she sat down, so did I. If she walked, I walked. I tried to do *everything* she did. And fortunately, Roma was great about it. She didn't mind me becoming her little shadow at all."

If not for the joy Sarah experienced at work, her painful existence during those difficult school years might have left lasting emotional scars. As it is, her junior high school experience may be the genesis of her self-admitted penchant for sarcasm. She's honest enough to admit that whatever the cause, her sarcastic nature certainly started as a defense mechanism against the hurts she suffered at the hands of peers. "Sarcasm *is* a defense mechanism. Absolutely. It's that, *screw it, what the hell* attitude. But at the same time, it's funny. There's no ill will meant in my sarcasm. But now it is part of me, it's who I am. So take it or leave it."

Peer problems aside, Sarah's professional life was only getting better. She was a co-host on the series *Girl Talk* and traveled to Europe to film the internationally syndicated series *The Legend of William Tell*, which in some areas was known as *Crossbow*. The 1991 series starred Will Lyman as William Tell, who was searching for his wife and son. Lyman was fresh off the short-lived 1990 series *Hull High*, NBC's failed attempt at a musical series.

The Legend of William Tell was canceled after thirteen episodes but Sarah wasn't out of work for long. In 1992, she appeared in Neil Simon's play *Jake's Women* at the Old Globe Theater. Next she was cast in *Swan's Crossing*, a much-hyped syndicated teen soap opera that was produced by WOR in New York. It was Sarah's first chance at ongoing national exposure and she went into the project with high hopes that it would be her break-out role.

Swan's Crossing debuted on June 29, 1992. According to the promotional material, the serial focused on the lives, loves, and intrigues of a dozen privileged New England teenagers and pre-teens living in the fictitious coastal town of Swan's Crossing, who "stir up scandal and excitement in their small town."

In an ironic foreshadowing of her future *All My Children* role, Sarah played Sydney Rutledge, the mayor's scheming daughter. Among the other characters were the requisite ladies' man, an evil ex-boyfriend, a former television star, and a young scientist working on formulating world's first self-perpetuating rocket fuel.

Sarah's big chance didn't last long. After just three months on the air, *Swan's Crossing* ceased production on September 25, 1992.

TV Guide's soap columnist, Michael Logan, said bluntly. "Basically, it starred too many young people—Sarah excepted—who couldn't act."

The original episodes were rerun over the next three months and despite a fervent outcry from the few but hardcore fans, the show faded way. But it didn't exactly disappear. In large part because of Gellar's current stardom, *Swan's Crossing* has been rediscovered by a new group of would-be fans and resurrected as an Internet entity. Web sites about the show are popping up in surprising numbers and "new" stories involving the characters are being written by devoted fans who refuse to let the show die.

After *Swan's Crossing* went off the air, Sarah shook off the disappointment and looked forward to her next chance at television notoriety, which came within a matter of months.

For a few years, the producers of *All My Children* had been contemplating introducing a new character as a foil for Erica

Kane, and were just waiting for the right moment. The time finally came in 1993, just as Erica (played by daytime diva Susan Lucci) was settling into engaged bliss with new love Dimitri (played by Michael Nader). So the casting call went out for a young actress to play the part of Kendall Hart, Erica's long-lost daughter.

The soap's producers were determined to keep the shocking story line a secret, so during the casting process the actresses were told that Kendall would be Erica's new assistant.

"I didn't know when I auditioned for Kendall that she would turn out to be who she is," Sarah said. "I had heard rumors, but everybody was denying it. Besides, I was scared enough at the thought of working with Susan."

Practically every teenage girl in New York auditioned for the plum role, which eventually went to Sarah, then fifteen. Besides bearing a resemblance to Lucci, Sarah had the acting chops and the forceful personality needed to go up against Susan Lucci. After all, this daughter was supposed to be a chip off the Kane block.

"When they told me I would be playing her daughter, I was like, *What!? Daughter? Me?*

"I remember on my first day when I walked into the rehearsal hall, Susan and Michael were rehearsing a scene. I was very nervous. I kept thinking, *What if I'm really bad and they fire me?* I just snuck in the back and tried to blend in with the coffee machine, when all of a sudden, Susan said, *Hold it, we need to stop for a minute.*

"Then she walked over to me and said, *Congratulations! I'm very glad you're here.* She put her arm around me and said, *Don't worry, nobody bites.* And then she introduced me to everyone who was there. She really did help me and always made sure I was okay during my first couple of weeks when I was still unsettled. Both Susan and Michael made me feel comfortable."

But it wasn't a complete set of strangers. Also there to hold her hand was actress Lindsey Price (who played An Li Chen), who happened to be an old school friend of Sarah's.

The February 24, 1993 broadcast introduced Kendall to the unsuspecting audience as Erica's new twenty-two-year-old assistant. Eventually, the truth was revealed—Kendall was Erica's long-lost daughter. She was also mad as hell for being abandoned at birth—even if the pregnancy had resulted from a rape—and determined to exact revenge against Erica.

Although Gellar admits Kendall was the most terrible daughter on daytime during her reign—during her first week on the show she locked her little half-sister in a crypt, tried to seduce her stepfather Dimitri, and when he turned her down, slept with the stable boy, after which she cried rape and he went to jail—she refuses to admit she was evil.

"I chose to see Kendall as misunderstood, which was how as an actress I justified her actions. It was amazing, though, playing a psycholooney."

As Kendall became more central to the story line, Gellar's workload increased, making her school obligations that much more difficult to meet. This time, however, there was no talk of Sarah having to sacrifice work for grades.

"In the beginning of high school, I had the typical high school experience," she says. "But it became incredibly difficult because of my work schedule. Then after I started working on *All My Children*, where we were shooting five episodes a week, it became impossible.

"Soap operas are so demanding; you can shoot over fifty pages a day, and let's be honest, on *All My Children*, I was doing soliloquies out there. The amount of work is so demanding that eventually, I had to transfer to a school specifically for children with different schedules. It was called Professional Children's School and it is for musicians, ballerinas, writers—just the most talented group of young people. Kids from all over the country, as well as from all over the world, go there."

Finally, Sarah had found an environment in which she could flourish without feeling guilty about her career or having to compromise her ambitions.

"I thank God for that place. It's an amazing place because all of the kids who go there are very talented. And it's a place where your talent is special, but it doesn't affect your schoolwork. Everyone there had a talent and everyone there was respected for that talent. If someone didn't like you, they simply didn't talk to you. They didn't make fun of what you did or punish you for it.

"When I enrolled, I felt amazingly untalented. But they gave me a chance to find myself. That school was my lifeline."

And *All My Children* would prove to be a gold mine for Sarah. Longtime fans of the soap saw Sarah as the second coming of Erica. The more she showed she could handle the work, the more the writers showcased her. Gellar's social life became a whirl of soap-related activity and for the first time in her career, she became a household name, at least to the legion of faithful daytime viewers. Fans wrote to tell her she reminded them of Natalie Wood, people stopped her in the street, and even New York cabbies took notice.

Sarah recalls the time she got in a taxi and was greeted by name. "I had no idea who this guy was. It turns out his son was the doorman at my apartment building."

In addition to the adoration of fans, Sarah was also initiated to the perks of celebrity. And she quickly realized it was a lifestyle she could easily get used to.

While buying a ticket to see the movie *Guilty As Sin*, Sarah was recognized by the theater manager who was so excited to have her there, that he treated Sarah to a free movie and complimentary concessions. It was a memorable day because, as Sarah said later, "It was the first time anyone had gone out of their way like that for me."

But not the last. During an affiliates event in West Virginia, Gellar and costar Eva LaRue were given the royal treatment at the resort where they stayed. After mentioning they were hungry, the chef came out and personally took their order, and when the actresses asked if they could go swimming, the resort opened the closed pool area just for them.

Although Sarah was still in school, *All My Children* had become the center of her life. She became friends with several costars, including Kelly Ripa and Eva LaRue. LaRue, who had joined the soap around the same time Sarah had, and who was ten years her senior, became Sarah's best friend, especially after Lindsey Price left the soap. (Price later landed on *The Bold and the Beautiful* and *Beverly Hills, 90210*.) Both shrugged off the age difference and became inseparable during Gellar's tenure on the show.

Their friendship began when they were assigned the same dressing room and they found they had a lot in common, including work, a love of shopping, and a tendency to leave clothes laying around. Sarah also found someone who understood the pressure and dedication daytime work requires; who understood what she was going through in a way that someone who hadn't experienced it could not.

"I think what I love most about her, is that Eva's one of those people who I know will always be there for me," Sarah once said in an interview.

In 1994, Sarah proved that she wasn't only a fan favorite but a respected member of the acting community when she was nominated for a Daytime Emmy Award in the Outstanding Younger Actress category for the 1993–94 season. Gellar landed an extra coup when she was asked by *Entertainment Tonight* to be a guest correspondent and provide a behind-the-scenes look at the Emmys. On the *E.T.* broadcast, she exuded an easy charm and affability that once again belied her years.

Although she lost the Emmy, Gellar wasn't disappointed. She had come a long way in a short time and knew she was only going to get better. But life can be a lot like a soap opera at times. While Gellar's working relationship with Susan Lucci began cordially enough, over time it began to subtly, then blatantly, deteriorate.

The year of Sarah's discontent had begun.

****

It wasn't long before the rumors started. Some reports insinuated that Lucci, who has made a cottage industry out of not winning an Emmy, was miffed that Sarah was nominated her first year out, the same year Lucci failed to earn a nomination of her own.

"The truth is," says a show associate, "Susan was against the idea of the Kendall story line to begin with because she didn't really want Erica to be seen as the mother of a daughter in her twenties. Ironically, one of the ways the producers convinced Susan to accept the plot was to convince her that this was the story line that would finally win her the Emmy."

Soon, Sarah began spending a lot of time denying the rumors of tension. But according to a source on the show who requested anonymity, their personality clash actually began shortly after Sarah's arrival.

"Susan actually made Sarah's life hell from the beginning by doing things to undermine her. For example, she would play a scene one way during rehearsal then abruptly change it when the cameras were rolling. Then when Sarah would stop short, confused, Susan would chastise her, telling her she should really be more professional and learn her lines before shooting a scene.

"Susan would also make cutting little remarks about Sarah's acting and a few times, Sarah was reduced to tears. The rest of the cast thought Susan's behavior was appalling."

But another person familiar with the conflict says that contrary to the perception at the time, it wasn't just Susan contributing to the tension.

"In many ways, Sarah was just as guilty, although it wasn't as obvious as Susan's snits. Sarah was, and is, intelligent and aware and she knew how to push Susan's buttons. She just did it subtly and with a smile.

"Lucci is an old pro and has long had a reputation for being a generous performer. But then along came Sarah, who makes sly jokes about Susan's age and pushes other hot emotional buttons and before you know it, the set becomes thick with tension. They were just a bad mix.

"Plus, Sarah loved being the center of attention and she wasn't shy about how her career was heating up," says a former soap employee, who claims the situation between Gellar and Lucci deteriorated to the point where they simply stopped talking.

"They would be professional and perform their scenes together then leave and not say a word once the cameras stopped rolling."

It didn't help that Sarah, who was frequently referred to as the Baby Erica, was being groomed to be the next major leading lady in daytime—and made it clear she was up to the challenge.

In fact, by the end of 1994, Sarah had developed a different attitude toward her acting. Instead of just being something she did for fun, it became a more serious pursuit. "If you train when you're young, I think it ruins your spontaneity," Gellar explains. "Kids have a natural honesty that no adult really can and at some point, you lose it. It wasn't until I got *All My Children* that I started to study and see it as a craft."

In a 1994 interview, Gellar responded sharply when asked if she didn't sometimes wish she could have enjoyed a traditional high school experience.

"I don't feel like I'm missing out on anything," she said. "Your childhood is what you make it. I do all the normal things that most teenage girls do, like go to the movies, hang out with friends and go on dates.

"At the Professional School, I get to have it all. I go to proms and I go to formal dances and you know what? I yawn."

Now, though, Sarah is more thoughtful when asked the same question. "I don't feel I missed much, especially because high school is a scary, scary place. I managed to avoid some of the problems that I think everyone faces because most of the children that I went to school with were so into a specific activity.

"I had the same kind of decision Buffy has—do I go to a school dance or slumber party or do I go to an audition? But I don't have any regrets. I've done a tremendous amount of traveling and it's given me the opportunity to see all the different things that are out there in the world."

But in 1995, Sarah was too busy to spend much time on philosophical reflection. She was preparing to graduate from high school and for the second year in a row she had been nominated for a Daytime Emmy. As luck would have it, the award ceremony fell on the same night her prom was scheduled, but there was never a question which event would win out, especially since Sarah was considered the odds-on favorite to win the Outstanding Younger Actress Emmy.

But what only a handful of people knew as the Emmys approached was that win or lose, this would be Sarah's soap swan song. She had asked to be released early from her contract, which wasn't officially up until February 1996.

"I had decided not to renew my contract some time before and told the show very far in advance, because I felt that was fair. Then, when my story line slowed to one day a week, I asked to be released even earlier. I'm the type who needs to be acting eight days a week, twenty-five hours a day."

Besides the inactivity, her contract—and the show's unwillingness to accommodate her—was preventing Sarah from pursuing other opportunities. "I was offered two other projects, which I was not released to do," she says pointedly. "And to be honest, I was a little bitter about that."

The producers reluctantly agreed to release her but the network insisted she keep the departure a secret until after they made the official announcement—after the Emmys. Sarah agreed, although the decision would later come back to haunt her when it put her in a bad light with fans of the show.

"The timing was terrible because it made me look incredibly bad," she says.

As expected, Gellar won the Emmy. As was also expected, Lucci didn't win in her category. So when news broke the following week that Gellar was leaving the show, one of two assumptions was made. The first was that Lucci was so beside herself over Sarah's Emmy win that Gellar was practically forced out of the soap. The other was that Sarah was so full of herself, she abruptly decided to quit and go to Hollywood.

The charges stung and Gellar felt compelled to confront the rumors. "Contrary to what one newspaper reported, I was *not* fired because I won the Emmy and Susan Lucci didn't," Sarah laughs. "Nor, as another one claimed, did I win the award on a Friday night and quit the following Monday morning because I got *too big for my britches.*"

Gellar's last day on *All My Children* was July 3, 1995. Although she continued to downplay the acrimony between her and Susan

Lucci for a while, these days Sarah can speak about the situation with the dispassion of distance.

"It wasn't an easy time in my life. Susan and I didn't have the most amazing relationship; we were not best friends and we're never going to be. I denied it for a long time because that's what you're supposed to do, but it also wasn't as bad as people made it out to be. The thing I said to her, that I was not competing against her, was the truth. She was in the leading actress category and I was in the younger actress category. And let's be honest; leading actress is a much more difficult category. And you don't work alone—I won for scenes submitted with her; for work we did together.

"We worked very well together, but it wasn't the easiest working relationship. Basically, the best I can say is that we worked together, *on top* of each other, for so long that problems were inevitable.

"But would I do it all over again? Absolutely. Being on a soap is the best training in the world because technically, it's a very difficult medium to work in. I feel that if you can do daytime, you can do anything. There's nothing like it; you can't compare the small time for preparation and the actual work to anything else. To do theater is one thing, but with daytime, it's a new script every day. I had two and a half years of that. And contrary to popular belief, we did not have cue cards. Now, I walk on a set and don't worry about hitting a mark or being in someone's light or shadowing myself. It's second nature now and I don't even think about it."

Now having the perspective of time, it's easier for Sarah to explain her soap experience in a larger context.

"Winning the Emmy was one of those things that I think everybody dreams about," she muses. "You know, you do your work and it's wonderful that people respected it and that's what the Emmy was to me—that people respected and enjoyed my work.

"But the overall work experience was very difficult. I think at the time I was probably the only contract player on a soap under eighteen. And after I started, they started bringing other people on but because of the hectic schedule, very few soap operas like to hire younger people.

"So I was in an environment surrounded by adults with an immense amount of work to do. And not only was I learning forty pages a day, I was also trying to graduate from high school. So it was really difficult. But I still loved it."

After leaving the soap, Sarah prepared to make her next big move—relocating to California. In an interview given shortly before her move to Hollywood, Gellar expressed her determination to be picky about what work she took. "The most important thing for me is to do work I enjoy, that I'm proud of and respect. If it takes me time to find work, then it will, but I'm not going to jump on the first things that have been offered because they're not what I'm interested in. And if I wanted to do another soap, there'd be no reason for me to leave *All My Children*.

"It's been an amazing two years, but I want to spread my wings and do other things, something totally different."

Gellar technically moved to Los Angeles in August, but resisted putting down roots—a common syndrome that afflicts many New Yorkers when they first relocate to the West Coast. Despite coming fresh off of an Emmy win, the door of Hollywood didn't exactly spring open for Sarah. She auditioned for, and lost, several high profile parts, including *Romeo and Juliet* to Claire Danes.

"I had a lot of offers for movies-of-the-week, disease-of-the-week, this girl in peril, that girl in jeopardy and I turned them down. I was really waiting for the role that was going to be special; the role that could establish me more seriously. I had to wait about a year and a half before I started working again."

Apparently temporarily putting aside her desire to be taken seriously, Sarah appeared in the ABC telefilm *Beverly Hills Family*

Robinson, opposite Martin Mull and Dyan Cannon, which filmed in 1996.

Then she was sent a script and immediately sensed this was the role she'd been waiting for. The script was for a WB network series called *Buffy the Vampire Slayer*.

****

Buffy the Vampire Slayer was going to be the small screen version of the 1992 feature film that had starred Kristy Swanson as a vampire killing high school student. Gellar knew she was perfect for the part of Buffy. Unfortunately, though, she had been asked to read for the part of Cordelia, the school's most popular, and most annoying, girl.

When Sarah requested to read for Buffy, she was politely but firmly turned down. Repeatedly. But she hadn't moved cross-country to let a golden opportunity slip by so she fought to change the producers' minds.

"I really wanted Buffy, but when they were auditioning, I had long dark hair and very light skin. I kept trying to convince people to let me read for Buffy. They kept saying, *You're not Buffy.* And I kept saying, *I can be Buffy.*"

Her persistence, and her offer to dye her hair blonde so that Buffy would remain a quintessential-looking California girl, eventually wore creator Joss Whedon down. After two readings, Whedon was convinced he had found his Buffy, except for one last detail.

"For both auditions, I wore this ankle-length dress with sneakers and they were afraid I was trying to hide a really ugly pair of legs," Gellar laughs.

Sarah and her costars shot a two-hour pilot then went back to New York for six months. After WB gave the series a go-ahead as a mid-season replacement and scheduled it for a January 1997 debut, the cast reassembled and filmed ten additional episodes.

Buffy debuted on March 10, 1997. It received rave critical response and quickly generated a host of Web pages devoted to the series and its stars, especially Sarah. However, she wasn't around to witness the *Buffy* buzz because she had just landed her most important film role to date in *I Know What You Did Last Summer*, which costarred Ryan Phillippe, Freddie Prinze Jr., and *Party of Five*'s Jennifer Love Hewitt.

"It was about two weeks before *Buffy* was scheduled to go on the air. I was on a press junket for the show when I heard about the movie and I went and auditioned. I found out I got the part on March 9, the day before *Buffy*'s first airing.

"Screaming was my entire screen test for the movie. I just stood there and screamed for about five minutes. Gut wrenching. Love has this really pretty, high melodic scream while mine sounds like a cat in heat.

"I got *I Know What You Did Last Summer* the week *Buffy* first aired," Gellar explains, "so I was off to North Carolina. We were filming in this very small town in Sonoma County that only got *Buffy* on a little cable station. And believe me, most people there didn't have cable. So for two and a half months I was spared from it. I never heard about the Web sites and didn't see any of the billboards that WB put up all over the place.

"So I had two months to prepare for it."

In *I Know What You Did Last Summer*, Gellar played the upscale local beauty queen, Helen Rivers, who plans to use her good looks as her ticket out of town. On a fourth of July weekend, after an evening of partying, the car she's a passenger in accidentally hits and kills a man. After the driver freaks out, he convinces the others that unless they cover up the accident, their lives will be ruined. So Helen helps dump the body in a local lake. A year later, the four friends are stalked by a crazy guy wearing a rain slicker and wielding a very sharp hook.

Sarah says, "The good thing about working on a movie in a small town is that it was an amazing bonding experience, because the four of us didn't have anybody else but each other down there. We had one local movie theater and I think it was playing *Tootsie* as a first run. There was no Starbucks and everything closed at nine."

The last of the four main characters cast, Gellar admits she was still carrying around Buffy's attitude when she first started filming. "In the beginning, the director would have to tell me that I wasn't running a triathlon—you can't kick the guy. It was also hard just because of my training and what I had gotten used to on a day-to-day basis. I'm so used to being the aggressor in a fight."

She's not kidding. Once while visiting Knott's Berry Farm, a Los Angeles-area amusement park that hosts annual Halloween fright nights, Sarah punched a park employee/vampire who jumped out of the shadows to scare her.

"Yeah, the guy grabbed me and I hit him," Sarah says, chagrined. "It was just an instinctive reaction."

So it took a while for Sarah to tone down her survival instincts and get into the head of a beauty queen noticeably lacking in self-reliance. "It was important to me that Helen wasn't just a big-breasted babe-running-through-the-woods joke. I wouldn't have wanted to be in the film if that were the case. In the movie, Helen *is* a little vacuous, because she's never been asked to be anything but pretty. For the first time she's in a situation where she's asked to handle things—and she doesn't know how."

The day production wrapped on *I Know What You Did Last Summer* in June, Sarah flew to Atlanta to begin work on *Scream 2*, in which she played one of star Neve Campbell's sorority sisters.

She got the movie by pure coincidence. Although she had already been cast in *I Know What You Did Last Summer*, writer Kevin Williamson had never met her. After running into her on a plane, Williamson was professionally smitten and recommended

Sarah to director Wes Craven for the part of Cici, a character who doesn't make it to the end of the film.

"I didn't have to push very hard because Wes fell in love with her, too," Williamson says. "It's a juicy little part and she's rocking. I want her in every one of my movies because you know when you hire her to do a job she's not going to be in the trailer complaining about everything. She's going to be right out there giving you the tenth take in the freezing cold."

For all of Williamson's high praise, Gellar was a basket case when she got to the location. "I got down there and was so intimidated and in awe that the day before we finished the read-through I literally called my manager and said, *I'm going to pack my bags. I'm going to be fired. I'm coming home.* Actually, I do that at every job after a read-through. I did that at the first read-through for the first season of Buffy—and after the second season I *still* thought I was going to be fired."

It's an actor's version of buyer's remorse.

"This is what I've waited for my whole life and now it's happening. But I'm worried that something's going to go wrong. Lately, I have been feeling a little intimidated by everything—it makes me nervous that things are going so well. I keep thinking I'm going to mess it up somehow."

Scream 2 was still in production when it was time to report back to *Buffy*. Unlike the *All My Children* producers who prevented Sarah from doing outside projects, Whedon and the other executives worked around Sarah's movie schedule.

"Basically, I'd work on *Buffy* Monday through Thursday, then I'd start *Scream* on Friday, wouldn't finish until Sunday and just basically go straight to *Buffy*, shower, and start work there."

And as Sarah can attest, filming *Buffy* is exhausting enough by itself. "It's a real difficult show to shoot, and I never have a day off. Sometimes they don't finish shooting until 2:00 A.M. and sometimes I have to be there at five some mornings. So there were

Sarah with costar Alyson Hannigan. © Albert Ortega/Flower Children Ltd.

times when I did feel as if I was in over my head. One day I was driving to work. I had the top down and I noticed people were looking at me. I look down and realize I'm only wearing a slip because I had forgotten to put my dress on.

"But I've learned I can juggle things."

Even so, Gellar admits it took some time to get acclimated to working on the series again. "It was an adjustment going back to

Buffy after working on two films back to back. Suddenly, the schedule seemed really hard and it seemed as if we were always rushed, never had enough time for takes, didn't get the scripts far enough in advance . . . . I had to stop and remind myself that on *All My Children* I used to learn a new script *every day*. It's amazing how quickly you get used to the slower pace of movie making."

Right now, her pessimism aside, Gellar's future is so bright, she ought to be wearing shades. If nothing else, to cover the dark circles.

"I've definitely been tired. I go to work. I scream. I yell. I come home. I go to sleep. I don't really have much of a life beyond work and I wouldn't mind just relaxing for a little bit but I'm really not complaining. This is something I want to do and twenty years is kind of the time to do it. I can sleep when I'm dead. Besides, how many people get to release their inner demons for a living?

"On the other hand, when I do get a day off, I don't know what to do with myself. Usually, I spend the day doing things like paying phone bills and trying to run errands. People think I'm so together—if they only knew."

The hardest part of her new-found notoriety is the effort it takes to keep her public life separate from her personal one.

"It has been a little difficult because privacy is hard. I keep a really separate private life that is my own, and that keeps me grounded. I like to think that if I walk into a roomful of people in the business I have something interesting to say to them, but I also want to be interesting to a group of people who know nothing about what I do.

"Going to premieres, doing the Hollywood thing, it's just not me. It's not my life, that's the thing. It's my job. I am a really private person and don't talk about my personal life or family. And I work very hard to maintain a separate life outside of what I do."

Part of that life these days apparently includes her once-estranged father, Arthur. A friend of Gellar's let slip that Sarah has reestablished communication with Arthur and now sees him. And although she has gone to great pains to avoid mentioning it, the same friend revealed that Sarah's mother is currently living with her in Los Angeles.

When asked why such basic daily family realities that most people share without a second thought are kept so guarded, a longtime acquaintance of Sarah shakes their head. "Who knows? The mere fact your mom is living at your house is such a non-issue that it actually draws more attention to it when you go out of your way to deny it. Yeah, true, on one level it's nobody's business. But really, it's such an innocuous topic that it might make people begin to wonder why Sarah is so reluctant to talk about her family at all—even in good terms.

"Privacy is one thing, denial and stonewalling is quite another. And it can lead to the conclusion, rightly or wrongly, that Sarah's familial relationships are troubled."

For her part, Sarah steadfastly maintains that her silence is simply a way to protect her own personal space in a business where loss of anonymity is the accepted price for fabulous wealth and fame.

Her desire to be in control is not only reflected in her jealously guarded personal life—which of course means no details of any romantic life will be forthcoming—but even in her reluctance to relinquish even household chores to others.

"I now have a maid that comes once every two weeks—and this was a big step for me. But I still do my own laundry and wash my own dishes and I still don't have an assistant."

Interestingly, the part of fame that is most bothersome to many celebrities is the part that Sarah accepts with little trauma.

"I had my first scary situation when I went to Freddie Prinze Jr.'s premiere of the *House of Yes* and my car got followed. I got followed. People were grabbing at me. It was incredibly scary, but it is something that comes with the job and if you are not prepared to deal with that, then you are in the wrong business."

What is known about Sarah's current life is that she recently bought a new house and a brand new sport utility vehicle in her favorite color, red. And according to the actress, she doesn't have a boyfriend—not that she'd admit it if she did—because she simply doesn't have the time.

She has commented that she's so busy, she doesn't even have time to call back her *I Know What You Did Last Summer* costar, Freddie Prinze Jr., who seems to come up a lot in conversation. In addition to her story about attending the *House of Yes* movie premiere, one writer commented in print how Prinze tried to climb through the window of the hotel room in which Gellar was being interviewed. He has also taken it upon himself to make sure that Sarah doesn't waste away.

"During the time I was promoting *Scream 2*, I was really stressed out and exhausted and just not eating. One night I got home to find Freddie and several of his friends in my kitchen cooking up a feast. Then they wrapped up the leftovers to make sure I would have plenty of food in the refrigerator.

"Freddie's my baby."

Although Sarah won't comment on specific romances she has had in the past, she will talk about her philosophy on relationships in general.

"I'm very outgoing until it comes to actually seeing a guy and meeting him for the first time. Then I'm very quiet and I can't think of a word to say and I just go, *Uh, hmmmm.* Once I get in a relationship, though, I can initiate things, but when it comes to that first move, I can't do it.

"I do think you have to have some compromise to make a relationship work but I would never change drastically. You have to be true to yourself and I think if you're not happy with what you're doing, you've crossed the line.

"You shouldn't be going out with someone just to say you're going out with them. You're going out with them, hopefully, because you enjoy who they are and they enjoy who you are."

When Sarah was still on *All My Children,* there was a curious incident involving costar Windsor Harmon, who was one of the "pretty boy" actors on the soap. Once during an interview, Harmon announced that he and Sarah were a romantic item.

"Sarah was outraged," says an acquaintance. "But whether she was outraged because it was not true, or because he had let the cat out of the bag, nobody was completely sure. In the end, most people figured that Windsor was just trying to up his profile by attaching himself to Sarah.

"As it happened, he left the show shortly after that, moved to California, joined *The Bold and the Beautiful* and is now married with a family."

Sarah admits that her current schedule limits her ability to meet potential dating material not involved in the industry. "Right now, because all I do is work, the only people you meet are actors, and I'd rather not date actors."

That's quite a change from her sentiments of just a few years ago when she extolled the virtues of dating an actor because he'd be able to understand "what it means to have a bad hair day."

But the actor/non-actor issue aside, Sarah maintains the point is mute. "Right now, I really don't have time for a relationship."

As for her future, Sarah says she's not worried about being typecast as the horror maven for the new millennium. "I took these roles because they are the ones that were the three most interesting, diverse roles offered me. Most teenagers are written very one-dimensionally.

"What Joss and Kevin have created is like a new genre—it's action, it's horror, it's drama, and it's comedy. And you know, if I get stuck doing work like this, I should be so lucky."

Sarah spent part of her second season hiatus from *Buffy* filming *Cruel Inventions* with Ryan Phillippe and Reese Witherspoon. Also forthcoming is a costarring role in a 20th Century Fox release, *Vanilla Fog*, opposite Sean Patrick Flannery and Amanda Peet.

Despite her surprising film success—*I Know What You Did Last Summer* was the number one film at the box office for three consecutive weeks—Gellar says she's committed to *Buffy* for the long haul. "As long as Joss Whedon is there, we'll all be there. He has no plans to go anywhere so I have no plans to leave. I have done two really good feature films, but it doesn't mean if I leave tomorrow there will be more. You know, for every Claire Danes there is a David Caruso.

"I have had other offers but I wouldn't have gotten anywhere without *Buffy* so my loyalty has to be to that show."

David Boreanaz

Although David Boreanaz wasn't exactly born in a trunk, you could say that show business is in his blood.

"I was brought up in an entertainment family," the twenty-seven-year-old actor explains. "My dad, who goes by the name Dave Roberts, started out as an entertainer and is now the weather forecaster for WPVI in Philadelphia. So I was around a performer all my life.

"However, the thing that really inspired me to be an actor was a production of *The King and I* they took me to see when I was seven. I was really taken in by Yul Brynner's performance and it was a real inspiration."

Although by that time, David had already shown definite signs that show business was to be his life.

"When I was four years old, I used to perform for my family—the Rumplestiltskin Theater, live at home. I had extremely long, curly blonde hair back then, although it got darker as I got older. Actually, my hair is still curly but I straighten it for the show—if I didn't, I would get this funny wave in it that I don't think would look good."

Boreanaz graduated from Malvern Prep in Philadelphia, then went to Ithaca College, an expensive private school located in central New York. David enjoyed his college education and eventually earned a degree in film.

"My intention at that time was to get a job on the production side of the business," David says. "I love the whole process, the preparation. Television has much more of a turnaround time—you see the results faster, but film is much more of a process. It's like two different kinds of paints on a canvas—oil and water. They are different kinds of art but both are beautiful."

Had David succeeded in forging a career in production work, he would have been following in his sisters' footsteps. His sister Beth is a production coordinator for *The Rosie O'Donnell Show* and Bo is a costumer who has worked on a number of films, including *Escape from L.A.* and *Barton Fink*.

After graduating, David packed his bags and set off for California, driving cross-country with his dad for a week. He made the rounds, trying to get hired on a production crew. He found work as a prop master, but his job hunt ended up bagging him a different career.

"I had gone to apply for crew work on a couple of commercials and got hired to be *in* them instead. My first job was in a spot for Foster's Beer—but it was never aired because they said it was 'too dark,'" David laughs.

Once David decided to pursue acting fully, he supported himself by working an assortment of struggling actor type jobs, such as house painting, working at a gym, and parking cars at the Beverly Wilshire Hotel.

"That wasn't one of my favorite jobs," David admits. "But I've had a lot of jobs I dreaded doing at times, although I always tried to find ways to have fun with them. I figured if I was going to be stuck working there, then I'd better have a good time. I wasn't going to be miserable in a miserable situation.

"My philosophy was, I know these jobs are only temporary, so why hurt myself even more? I mean, sure, there were times when a job was terrible and I'd get depressed but then I'd remind myself it was only temporary then go on and make the best of it."

Boreanaz admits that getting his acting career going required a lot of determination—and a lot of patience. His first film jobs were little more than extra work, which is why his name doesn't even appear in the credits of two 1993 films, *Aspen Extreme* and *Best of the Best II*.

Aspen Extreme starred two future television series stars—Paul Gross, who would later star in *Due South*, and Peter Berg of *Chicago Hope* fame. *Best of the Best II* starred Eric Roberts and Chris Penn as martial artists. David also appeared in a film he remembers being called *Eyes of the World*, which never saw the light of day.

His first credited role came in 1993 when he was cast in the "Movie Show" episode of *Married . . . with Children*, which aired April 11. David played Frank, the new biker boyfriend of Christina Applegate's character, Kelly. The plot has Kelly breaking a date with Frank because her parents want to take her to a movie for her birthday. But when they get to the theater, Kelly finds Frank with another girl.

"*Married . . . with Children* was a laugh," David says. "If you can get beat up by Al Bundy, that's just a great experience in itself. It was a lot like theater because it was shot in front of a live audience."

Soulful and sexy: David Boreanaz. © Albert Ortega/Flower Children Ltd.

While waiting for his breakthrough role, David sought out theater work to sharpen his skills. He appeared in productions of *A Hatful of Rain, Fool for Love, Italian-American Reconciliation*, and a 1996 Equity Waiver production of Sam Shepherd's *Cowboy Mouth* at the Hudson Theater in Hollywood.

"I believe you've got to do lots of theater," David says. "You've got to stand up in front of live audiences because it helps you become confident and you learn to work off your mistakes. In order to succeed and become a stronger person, you really need to fail and fall down."

If that sounds suspiciously like advice you might find in a new age self-help book, it just might be, since one of David's favorite authors is self-help guru Og Mandino.

"My father turned me on to Og Mandino when I was in grade school and gave me his books for inspiration, which they were," says David, who is extremely well-read.

"I love reading and I have a library of tons of different authors so I can pick up a book that matches whatever I'm feeling. Even if I've read it before, I'll read it again. And I'll often have three or four books going at the same time."

In 1996, David auditioned for the producers of a new WB series who were desperate to cast the part of a character named Angel.

"It turns out they needed someone to be on the set the next day," David recalls. "I think what might have gotten me the role, actually, was the sense of humor I brought to the character. At the beginning of the audition, I was trying to turn the rocking chair into a motorcycle and got everybody laughing. And just like that, at the eleventh hour, I got the part.

"Because it happened so quickly, I hardly knew anything about the show. I didn't even have a full script, just the eight pages that Angel was on and I was shooting the day after I was cast. I didn't get to read the script until after work."

What started out as an occasionally recurring character has become a full-time costar of the series and has made David one of television's newest sex symbols. But unlike many other young actors who have no frame of reference when it comes to dealing with sudden notoriety, Boreanaz is familiar with being around "celebrity."

"A lot of times while growing up, I'd be out with my dad and people would come up and say, *You're Dave Roberts!* And he's such a kind man, he *always* took time to stop and talk to these people—I saw that my whole life.

"And now it's slowly starting to happen to me, little places, on and off. And I'm trying to handle it the same way my dad always has. If I get a letter that I can really feel and get in touch with, I would write the person back personally. I wouldn't use e-mail or call, I'd write a real letter.

"I have called some people on the phone, out of the blue, just to surprise them. Sometimes, they don't believe it's me but all I have to do is refer to the letter they wrote and then they trip out. I think that's kind of neat."

Though his fans include throngs of ardent female admirers, David only has eyes for one special woman in his life. He recently married his longtime girlfriend, Ingrid, who hails from Dublin, Ireland.

David refuses to let his new-found star status change his perceptions. "Fundamentally, nothing has changed because I'm the same person. It's a big misconception that everything changes. I've never looked at myself as being a famous person and probably never will. That's a really strange concept to me. I'm fortunate enough to work on a show and enjoy what I do.

"Famous is kind of a strange word and one I want to stay away from, only because I consider myself one of the people. I always want to be just a regular person. And I know that's a lot easier to say than it is to do, because the public perceives you as this other person, or people see you as this other character you play. And I love that, I think it's great—but I kind of want to keep check with that. You know, remember my roots and where I come from.

"It's a weird medium we're in. The camera gets turned on you and you become famous—the same thing happens when you put cameras on lawyers, as we've seen."

Although when pressed, David admits there are material differences that happen when you're suddenly starring in a popular television show. "You do get little perks—free stuff in the mail, or a nice pair of Nike shoes, which was nice. Those things come with the territory. Sometimes now I'm able to get a table more quickly at a restaurant—and I can buy my dogs more food."

David's dogs are a big topic of conversation with him. "I hang out with my dog, Bertha Blue. She's a pound dog, a Lab with a little Greyhound mixed in, that I rescued when she was a puppy. She's a real sweetheart."

David also has a Chinese Crested, which looks like a bald Chihuahua with tufts of hair sprouting from its head and around each paw. "It's a real trip—it could be a circus dog," he laughs.

When he's not playing Angel, the vampire cursed with a conscience, David can be found hitting the links. "Yeah, I have become a big golf fan," David admits. "I always played a little bit here and there, and in college, I played with my friends but then I stopped. But once I got to California, I started playing again and got hooked. It's a great game for focusing and relaxing.

"I used to play a lot of basketball but my knee slips out all the time. That's why I can't play hockey anymore. What I'd like to do is take the time to go have my knee fixed by having the ligament replaced so I can do all my sports again."

Other than regaining joint mobility, David's hopes for the future include a chance to do some feature film work and a long run for *Buffy*. "The best thing about this show is working with the people on it. It really is just a big happy family. I just want to do good work and whatever comes my way, I'll feel blessed with."

Nicholas Brendon

Like a surprising number of actors, including Jack Wagner and Dean Cain, Nicholas Brendon started out wanting to be a professional athlete. Brendon—called Nicky by friends and family—grew up dreaming of being a baseball player. His goal was to play ball in college and, hopefully, get signed with a big league team.

But first, he had to get through high school. Nicholas and his identical twin brother, Kelly, were born April 12, 1971, in Los Angeles. They have two younger brothers, Christian and Kyle. Unlike costar Sarah Michelle Gellar, Nicholas did not attend private school. Instead he was educated at very public schools.

"I went to L.A. Unified, which was a very scary experience," Brendon says, referring to the notoriously troubled Los Angeles school district. "I learned a lot of lessons but it was a horrible experience. High school isn't really great to many people. It's like a mandatory prison sentence. In Israel they make you join the army, in America we go to high school."

The normally traumatic high school experience was not made any easier by Nicholas's introverted tendencies and a terrible stutter that plagued him throughout his youth.

"I wouldn't even talk to people," Nicholas says. "I was very shy in high school. Actually, I *still* keep to myself a lot but now it's out of choice. And I never dated—one of the scariest things about going to high school was dealing with girls.

"My first kiss happened in eighth grade but it was awful because our friends were spying on us. I was so embarrassed at being caught that I had to break up with the girl and that started a long dry spell. I didn't date that much in high school, although there was one girl I longed after. She was beautiful but we were good friends and I just couldn't tell her."

Once he was through with high school, Nicholas went on to college, but his dreams of a baseball career ended abruptly after he broke his elbow while playing. But it wasn't the tragedy it could have been because by that time, Nicholas had already decided he wanted to try acting.

"The thing is, even though I was shy in school, with my family, I was the entertainer and I loved making everyone laugh," Brendon says. "One day, when I was eighteen, I just said, *I have to try this.* After that, I sort of fell into it.

Once shy, Nicholas Brendon enjoys interacting with fans. © Sue Schneider/Flower Children Ltd.

In a way, acting was a family business, of sorts—his mom is an agent.

"My mom, who had just gotten a divorce, sent me out on stuff, so that was a help. But I overcame the stutter on my own. My first job was in a Clearasil commercial."

He appeared in the play *Out of Gas on Lovers' Leap* at the Pasadena Playhouse in 1991. An odd job here and there, especially in small theater productions, is not enough to pay the bills. Nicholas still needed to scramble to support himself. So while he waited to get back in front of the cameras, he worked behind the scenes, which ultimately led to his first break in prime-time.

"What happened was, I was a production assistant on the sit-com *Dave's World* and they allowed me to audition for a guest spot—and I got it. After I taped the episode, they fired me as a

P.A. but told me they really liked my acting and that I should pursue it full time. That was pretty much where it started."

Other small parts in television and movies followed. He was cast as "Basketball Player One" in the 1994 feature film gore-fest *Children of the Corn III*, and appeared on *The Young and the Restless* and *Married . . . with Children*. Nicholas was also active in theater and starred in Los Angeles productions of *The Further Adventures of Tom Sawyer* and *My Own Private Hollywood*, both Equity Waiver productions, in which the theater is required to have ninety-nine seats or less and paying the actors is optional.

At this point, Brendon really was just acting for the love of it. His first big chance to break out came when he was cast in the television pilot *Secret Lives*, but the show—which presented dramatizations of real-life marriages—was not chosen to go forward as a series.

"I also turned down a part because of nudity once," he says. "It was one of the *Friday the 13th* movies, something like part 8 or 9. That was a line I wouldn't cross."

Although acting had become Brendon's passion, he also realized that he couldn't stay an unemployed actor forever. "There was a time in my life when I almost gave up acting completely," Nicholas reveals. "I gave myself one year and told my family that if my career still hadn't gone anywhere, I would quit and go back to college and study medicine."

The year had almost gone by and Nicholas was still praying for his big break while waiting tables at Kate Mantilini restaurant, a longtime celebrity hangout located on the edge of Beverly Hills. Then his agent set up an audition for a series being cast at the new WB "weblet" called *Buffy the Vampire Slayer.*

"I was surprised they were making the movie into a show," Brendon admits. "And then pleasantly surprised when I read the script. The writing was so intelligent. I really have to thank Joss for hiring me because I don't know where I'd be if he hadn't."

Within six months of *Buffy*'s premiere, Nicholas had joined the ranks of TV heartthrobs. At fan events, girls and women line up to flirt and express their approval of both him and his character, Xander. It's a mantle Brendon wears a little uneasily. "It's weird to hear myself referred to as being hot or cute because I don't see myself that way. It makes me feel really shy."

Maybe so, but you couldn't tell by watching him. Brendon seems to genuinely enjoy interacting with fans and, along with Alyson Hannigan, regularly attends fan events. At one gathering in November 1997, Nicholas even treated the cheering crowd to an impromptu exhibition of Xander's gyrating dance moves.

Although he's not necessarily stopped wherever he goes, Nicholas is aware that others are becoming aware of who he is. "I do get a lot of glances now, although I don't think I have *that* many fans yet. I can still go into a grocery store and not get harassed, so I have the best of both worlds right now. However, once I got groped by a fan—that was the worst experience I ever had. But doing things like signing autographs is new so I like it.

"It's funny because since I have an identical twin, when I get recognized, he does too. He'll say to me, *Hey Nick, we got recognized again.*"

Nicholas now shares his Hollywood Hills home with his twin. When not working, he passes his time reading, going to auditions, and playing guitar. "I like to sit on my balcony in my rocking chair and look at the Hollywood Hills, watching old movies. I like old movies more than new movies. They were made differently back then. My favorite is *Some Like It Hot*—although I did like *Sling Blade.*"

After years of struggling, Brendon is both gratified and relieved to be in a successful series. He's far too grateful to have any complaints. However, if pushed, he does admit that the demands of filming an hour adventure show are difficult.

Nicholas demonstrates Xander's gyrating dance moves. © Sue Schneider/Flower Children Ltd.

"The hardest thing about filming *Buffy* are the hours; the endless, ungodly hours. A typical day on the set is a lot of waiting and a lot of bagels. And because I'm so much more busy now, I don't get to see my family and friends as much as I would like to. But that's the only real drawback and one I can live with."

What makes the time demands easier to handle is his sheer enjoyment at being able to work. "If you allow acting to be fun, it can be very fun and easy—except for the stunts," he says. "I do all my own stunts so when it looks like I'm getting hurt, that's because I really am."

Looking back now at all the earlier missed chances or jobs he didn't get, Brendon is philosophical. "I think everything is fated to happen—you just don't realize it until three years later."

He is the first to admit that had he gone back to college to pursue a different career, his heart would have been elsewhere. "If I wasn't acting, I'd be wishing I was acting. What I've learned is that if you want to do something, do it. The last thing you want is to be forty and be saying, *I wish I had done that.*

"To me, acting is a blessing and I hope to be able to entertain people for as long as I possibly can."

Alyson Hannigan

Like costar Sarah Michelle Gellar, Alyson Hannigan has been acting almost as long as she has been talking. Born in Washington, D.C., in 1974, her family moved south to Georgia a few years later and, just like Gellar, Alyson started working when she was four years old.

"I started out by doing commercials in Atlanta," says Alyson. "I had always wanted to act and I loved it. But at the same time, I don't really consider myself *an actor* because it's not necessarily who I am, it's just what I do."

Although she was the only one with acting aspirations in her family, Alyson's family moved to Los Angeles in 1985 so she could try to break into films and television. Her first break came when she was cast in the 1988 sci-fi spoof, *My Stepmother Is an Alien*, which starred Dan Aykroyd and a just-starting-out Kim Basinger. In 1990, she appeared on an episode of *Roseanne* as a friend of the eldest daughter, Becky, then played by Lecy Goranson. In the show, Roseanne gets a job waiting tables at the mall restaurant where her two daughters hang out.

Alyson Hannigan plays whiz kid Willow. © Paul Fenton/Flower Children Ltd.

From there Alyson was hired on her first series, the short-lived *Free Spirit*, which ran on ABC from September 1989 to January 1990. The show was an updated take-off on *Nanny and the Professor*, in which a widower with three children hires a housekeeper named Winnie (played by Corinne Bohrer), who is actually a witch. Alyson played thirteen-year-old Jessie Harper, the lone daughter.

Alyson's next project was the television movie *Switched at Birth*, based on the real-life story of Kimberly Mays, who was switched at birth with another child, Arlena Twigg, who later died. Alyson played Arlena's sister Gina, from ages thirteen to sixteen. Bonnie Bedelia played her mother.

In 1992, Hannigan graduated from North Hollywood High, glad to be leaving high school behind. "My theory on high school was, get in, get out and hopefully I won't get hurt," Alyson says. "Basically, it's a miserable experience, because you're a walking hormone in a place that is just so cruel. There were times that were okay, but it's not the little myth that high school is the best years of your life. No way."

According to Alyson, not only were other kids mean, some were just plain strange.

"There was this one guy who went to a dentist and had his teeth sharpened into fangs. It was so insane. I mean, how would you even find a dentist who would do that?"

In 1993, Hannigan made two guest appearances on NBC's *Almost Home*, which was a reworked version of *The Torkelsons*, about a single mom raising her five children. In the episodes, originally aired April 17, 1993 and June 5, 1993, Alyson played a tomboy named Sam, who is friends with the son of Mom Torkelson's boss.

She also appeared in episodes of *Picket Fences* and *Touched by an Angel*. Alyson's last pre-*Buffy* job was the ABC television move, *The Stranger Beside Me*. In this woman-in-peril thriller, Tiffani-Amber Thiessen, who had just made a splash as the new girl on *Beverly Hills, 90210*, played a recovering rape victim who is swept away by a seemingly perfect guy, played by Eric Close, who is actually a Peeping Tom.

Then came *Buffy*. In addition to the prospect of getting another series, Alyson had another reason to be thrilled about the audition.

"Even before I met Joss, *Toy Story* was my favorite movie. I'm actually slightly obsessed with that film because when I was a kid, I would spend countless hours trying to sneak up on my toys

Before *Buffy,* Alyson Hannigan starred on another otherworldly series, *Free Spirit.* Photo courtesy Photofest.

because I *knew* they had secret lives. I was determined to catch them in the act but I, uh, never did."

The casting process was a long, drawn out affair that tested Hannigan's nerves. "I auditioned way too many times and finally they couldn't find anyone else who looked as young and acted as immature, so I got the job," jokes the baby-faced actress, who says she still gets asked for I.D. when going to see an R-rated film.

Although she's worked steadily since moving to Los Angeles, *Buffy* is the first time Alyson has starred in a project that has had such high visibility. The resident cyber nut, Alyson often communicates with fans over the Internet via posting boards and is the subject of many adoring Web sites.

The intense media interest in the show took her off guard in the beginning. The first time the cast en masse met with assembled television critics from all over the country in January 1997, Hannigan was so intimidated that she literally only uttered a sentence or two—and that was under duress.

But away from the press, Hannigan is much more relaxed and comfortable. In front of fans at sci-fi conventions and other *Buffy*-related events, she's positively outgoing and gregarious, displaying a quick wit and charming personality—even when discussing things that go bump in the night.

"I think the idea of vampires and the occult is very interesting," she said at one conference. " I've always been intrigued by vampires, and anything else that's different from everyday, normal, blasé people. My attitude about vampires is that I'm not going to say they don't exist, because then if they do, they'll feel the need to prove me wrong. So I say, you never know, they just could exist."

Hannigan admits it is somewhat ironic that she should be costarring in a horror series because when she's in the audience, scary movies have her under the seat. "When I saw *Scream* I nearly broke my nose from trying to cover my eyes," she laughs. "I was terrified—but laughing at the same time. I am the biggest wimp when it comes to watching horror films but I love them. I also like *The X-Files*."

And she'll even watch herself on *Buffy*, normally a true exercise in horror for her. "That's how I know *Buffy* is the favorite project I've worked on—because I usually don't like watching myself. But I love this show so much that I actually don't mind."

Hannigan says that although she has always loved the environment of television and movie sets, there is something special about working on *Buffy*. "I love everything about this show. Even doing the stunts, although after some of the action scenes you definitely get bruised up. And the people on *Buffy* are wonderful. I love them very much and everyone has become like family. And the show itself is a lot of fun to work on."

When asked to share some of the raucous good times she's had while working on *Buffy*, Hannigan is aware that some of the hilarity might be lost in the translation. "Most of the stories are of the *you had to be there* variety. Like the time I 'pantsed' Nick. Sarah is the one who told me to do it because she wouldn't—she chickened out. So I did and accidentally pulled his pants all the way down.

"Another time, I had these really stale animal crackers that I had given to Joss's assistant, George. He tried to be polite and eat them but they were just so stale. Then Nick comes along and starts eating them and didn't notice they were stale. I was crying I was laughing so hard."

Away from the set, Alyson, who is single and not presently dating anyone, uses her precious free time during the season to play with her animals. "And I do a lot of stuff that's exercise but you don't know it's exercise, like bike riding."

Although she's not looking past *Buffy*, Alyson says she hopes that one day she'll be established enough to be able to pick and choose the scripts she'd like to work on, rather than audition out of necessity. Other than that, her needs and wants are simple.

"You have to go for the good things, like world peace, a cure for everything—and a really cool house."

Charisma Carpenter

Had things gone the way Charisma originally intended, right now she'd be standing in front of a classroom somewhere trying to get a roomful of students to pay attention to her. While working at a Los Angeles restaurant in order to save money for college, Carpenter caught the eye of a commercial agent who took her on as a client, and before you can say *homeroom*, teaching became a faint memory.

Born in Las Vegas, Nevada, Charisma spent most of her youth being trained in classical dance, starting ballet lessons when she was just five. Her family picked up stakes when she was fifteen and moved to Mexico, settling just across the border from San Diego, California.

She continued to study dance throughout her high school years, commuting to, and eventually graduating from, the School of Creative and Performing Arts in Chula Vista, a community near San Diego.

Instead of enrolling in college right away, Charisma took off for Europe. When she returned to the States, she moved to San Diego and worked at a variety of odd jobs, including working as a clerk in a video store, teaching aerobics, and waitressing.

In 1991, Charisma, who had been a cheerleader in high school, landed a job as one of the cheerleaders for the San Diego Charger football team. "Yes, I took cheerleading to the nth degree and was a professional, but only for a year," Carpenter says, who adds that unlike high school, where the cheerleaders tend to pair off with the class jocks, fraternization with the professional players was strictly prohibited.

"It was in our contracts that we didn't mingle with the players," Charisma explains. "I guess some player's wife found out about a cheerleader-football player romance and nixed any mingling."

After leaving her Charger Girl pom-poms behind, Carpenter headed two hours north to Los Angeles. She got a job working as a waitress at Mirabelle restaurant, located in the heart of the Sunset Strip—three blocks west is Johnny Depp's club, the Viper Room, and across the street is Wolfgang Puck's famous restaurant, Spago.

Her plan was to save enough money to continue her education. "I was going to be a teacher but acting kind of came to me.

The sweet smell of success: Charisma Carpenter was named after a bottle of perfume. © Robert Leslie Dean/Flower Children Ltd.

And it became my passion."

After signing with the keen-eyed commercial agent, Charisma appeared in over twenty commercials. One, a spot for Secret Ultra Dry that was filmed on top of a Manhattan building, ran for almost two years. Although commercial work wasn't terribly fulfilling, it paid very well and allowed Carpenter to concentrate full time on acting.

And by the way, Charisma isn't a *nom de plume*. "I got my name from a very smelly, tacky bottle of Avon perfume," she laughs. "That scent was very big in the '70s. My grandmother brought it to my mother, who thought it was putrid—but she liked the name."

Despite her inexperience in front of a camera, Carpenter was able to make the transition into acting by relying on things she already knew.

"I think dancing helped prepare me because it taught me to deal with stage fright and have the experience to be able to perform on the spot. And I'm pretty determined. My mom taught me not to take things personally, such as rejection, because it's only the opinion of a select few.

"But acting *is* challenging. Dancing always came easily but acting does not. I'll take acting lessons on scripts that I feel most challenged by then I stay up writing my lines over and over again to memorize them so they come across naturally."

Carpenter's hard work finally paid off when she landed her first theatrical job—a small role on *Baywatch*. The part attracted the attention of talent agent Wendy Green, who tracked Charisma down and signed her as a client. Not long after that, Charisma was cast in Aaron Spelling's new teen-driven prime-time soap, *Malibu Shores*, playing bitchy rich girl Ashley Green, who holds the Valley dwellers in nothing but contempt.

Often compared to *Beverly Hills, 90210*—and not just because it starred Spelling's other child, Randy—the series featured a cast of attractive young actors and featured a wrong-side-of-the-tracks romance as its central story. In this case the upscale girl was from the exclusive oceanfront burg of Malibu and the underclass boy was from the San Fernando Valley. Another gimmick was that after a fictional earthquake severely damages their school, the Valley kids are bussed to Malibu, where the two factions square off. Forget the fact that Malibu is its own city and not part of L.A. anymore—the writers did.

The series lasted just ten episodes before getting yanked. Two episodes never aired.

Often, after an actor finishes shooting the initial number of episodes ordered by the network and is waiting to see whether or not the show will be picked up, they will keep auditioning for other projects. While NBC pondered the fate of *Malibu Shores*, Carpenter was facing a dilemma of her own because she had just been offered the lead in a new WB series called *Buffy the Vampire Slayer*.

"It's true—I was ready to go as Buffy, but then they thought I'd be better suited as Cordelia," explains Charisma. "Actually, though, I wasn't going to do the show at all. I was already on *Malibu Shores* when *Buffy* came up and after they asked me to do Cordelia, I was leery about it because it was the same kind of character. But I guess it was fate because *Malibu Shores* got canceled and I was able to follow through with the commitment on *Buffy* and I'm glad that I did."

Carpenter admits that after coming off a big budget NBC show, she didn't know what to expect from *Buffy* as far as the production values of the show go.

"The first time I saw the show I was surprised by its quality," she says. "Everyone else had been watching the dailies, but I had decided to wait because I wanted to reserve my judgment until we had gotten a few in the can. Then one day I watched some of the show with the producers and I was just so impressed."

Although her character has evolved, with some of the rougher edges slightly smoothed down, Charisma sees Cordelia Chase as someone who simply speaks her mind, without fear of how self-centered it may sound. Her only concern is that she worries that people might mistake her for the character.

Before being "totally over it" on *Buffy*, Charisma (far right) costarred on *Malibu Shores*. Photo courtesy Photofest.

"It does bother me in a way because people *do* tend to confuse reality with fiction," she points out. "And they might think that I'm really this awful person—but I'm not. I just hope they remember I'm really a normal human being like everyone else and give me support."

Unlike some of her costars, who recall their high school years with a shudder, Carpenter had no such traumas. "I went to three high schools: Gorman Catholic High School in Las Vegas, Bonita High School in Bonita, California, and I graduated from Chula Vista High School, which was a performing arts school—and I had a great time at all of them. I had wonderful friends.

"I was actually a cheerleader, too—but there were always people more popular than I was. One thing, though—I did have to deal with a lot of preconceived ideas of what I was like. My personality was kind of intense and that was misconstrued occasionally as being snobby. I can be very pensive and it comes across the wrong way sometimes."

Like everyone else on the show, Carpenter says it's a great working experience because everyone gets along. "I had a great time on *Malibu Shores*, too," she says. "I got to be really good friends with Terry Russell, Susan Ward, and Tony Lucca, and some others. And I've definitely maintained those relationships and will continue to maintain them. But I'd have to say *Buffy* is a little more fun because it is bizarre to sit across from a vampire at lunch time.

"But while I'm pretty close to a lot of people I work with and have worked with, I only have two or three friends I would do anything for."

When she's not working on *Buffy*, Carpenter says she spends her time outdoors. Whether it's hiking or rock climbing or running a 5-k race for a breast cancer benefit, she loves being outside. When she is indoors and sitting still, she relaxes by writing, something she's done since she was a child.

Although she's quite content with the work she's doing on *Buffy*, Charisma is anxious to work in independent features. "I had a couple of offers before I was going back for the second season but we couldn't work out the schedule—they were shooting too near the start date of *Buffy*. So unfortunately, I had to turn down a couple of things, which really broke my heart. But I want it to work so I'm getting it together for the next hiatus."

As far as long range personal goals, Carpenter fantasizes herself successful and living in wide open spaces. "Some day I would like to live on a ranch somewhere with my dogs and have a horse. I would like to be married, with children, and have a successful enough career that allows me to live comfortably—and out of L.A. I don't care for L.A. that much but I have to be here for work.

"I like Andie McDowell's lifestyle—she's got a beautiful husband and kids, cooks, and comes in and out of town as required. Now that's a great lifestyle."

Anthony Stewart Head

It's ironic that when *Buffy* first began airing, people would have immediately recognized Anthony Stewart Head but have no idea what his name was because to most Americans, he's simply been known as the Taster's Choice guy for the past eight years.

"It is always nice being recognized for whatever reason, but *Buffy* is very different from anything I've done before so it's been really cool."

Unlike his stammering, somewhat stodgy television alter ego, in person Tony Head is an earring-wearing, confident charmer who has been acting his entire adult life, his career spanning more than twenty years. Born in the Camdentown area of North London, Head grew up in nearby Hampton and trained for the theater at the London Academy of Dramatic Arts.

His first role after leaving school was Jesus in the national tour of *Godspell*. Over the years Tony has maintained his ties to the theater, appearing in *Yonadab*, *Chess*, *Lady Windermere's Fan*, and *The Heiress*. He also donned fishnets and a dress to play Dr. Frank N. Furter in a West End revival of *The Rocky Horror Picture Show*, and most recently, he starred in *Rope*.

In addition to his theater work, Head has worked steadily in British television, amassing a résumé full of credits, from the 1978 war drama *Enemy at the Door* to *The Detectives* (1989), *Ghostbusters of East Finchley* (1995), and the current mystery *Jonathan Creek*.

Tony has also been able to move easily from television to features, working in films such as *A Prayer for the Dying*, the 1987 drama that starred Mickey Rourke as an IRA bomber and 1991's

Coffee peddler to vampire expert: Anthony Stewart Head takes his success in stride. © Paul Fenton/Flower Children Ltd.

Lady Chatterley's Lover, opposite Sylvia Kristal, who is best known for her soft-porn *Emmanuelle* movies.

Even though Head has appeared in his fair share of American series, including guest spots on *NYPD Blue* and *Highlander*, and a regular role on Fox's 1995 sci-fi series *VR.5*, it was his commercial work for Taster's Choice, as a man who becomes smitten with his neighbor after she borrows some coffee from him, that made Tony a household face.

The budding romance that began in 1990 evolved in thirteen different spots that eventually included the woman's son and ex-husband. And the end may not yet be in sight.

"It's a yearly contract, which they've been renewing every year," Tony says. "But there has been some problem about availability. When I've been free to shoot, Sharon hasn't and now

Sharon's husband Trevor is involved, so there are three of us to move around."

Because of the ads' popularity, there was actually talk of turning the commercial romance into a television series. "Yes, it's been talked about turning the commercials into a series and people have actually approached us with scripts, but the bottom line is, it's all kind of said in a fifty second commercial, you know? We've been doing it for eight years now so unless the scripts that came to us were radically different or somehow managed to expand the characters, there was never really any point in doing it.

"I have said to the producers, *Enough is enough.* The story lines are going nowhere. I wonder how they can be made more intriguing, how they can be given more spice. I don't know where else we can go, but we are talking.

"Personally," Tony smiles, "I'd like to do them as a musical."

While Head isn't convinced the commercials have much life left in them, he'll keep going as long as the coffee maker wants him to.

"While Taster's Choice hasn't made me wealthy for life, the commercials did give me the money to have a very nice house, a very nice lifestyle," he acknowledges. "The money has also put me in the position that actors dream about, which is the luxury of picking and choosing jobs. I don't have to take a job just to make the rent or feed the kids. And that's quite nice."

In fact, Head and his longtime partner Sarah and their two children, Emily and Daisy, have homes in both Bath, England, and Los Angeles. They split their time between the two residences.

Unlike many American actors who act as if it's mandatory to denigrate L.A., Head is unabashedly delighted with the city.

"I love Los Angeles because you can almost feel the creativity in the air."

Prior to *Buffy*, the last time Tony spent extended time in California was when he was cast as Oliver in *VR.5*. When asked if it's just coincidence that he seems to frequently get cast in science fiction and fantasy roles, Head admits it's a genre he particularly likes.

"Yes, I do seem to gravitate toward science fiction and fantasy and I do love it. I used to be a serious fan of Ray Bradbury when I was young. It's wonderful stuff and I've always been attracted to it. But more than that, as an actor, I'm attracted to good roles. *Highlander* was a wonderful opportunity and *VR.5* was a great series; it was sad that it didn't go a second season. I think it might have been just a little ahead of its time."

It was also not the easiest plot to follow. The series starred Lori Singer as a telephone technician who accidentally discovers a way into the fifth level of virtual reality, in which all five senses are involved. She could bring other people into VR.5 and create the setting—but had no control over the outcome. When she tried to use the technology to uncover the truth about her father's suspicious death, she was thwarted at every turn by the mysterious Committee.

VR.5 was canceled in May 1995, after only two months on the air. Tony headed back to England, where he worked in theater and did a couple of television productions. Then he was sent two scripts for a new television series.

"Joss sent me the first two episodes of *Buffy* and they were seriously special," Tony says. "The timing was wonderful because I had been asked if I wanted to do the series *Poltergeist: The Legacy* and to be perfectly honest, I thought it was too dark. I was close to doing it and then *Buffy* came along, which I much preferred because it had a lighthearted side to it. It just seemed to come from a lighter place.

"Although, Joss also told us from the beginning that we were going to be serious about the dark, scary stuff. That it would be

Tony, with Alyson Hannigan, feels right at home with his young costars. © Sue Schneider/Flower Children Ltd.

real, with no gags. Which I thought was important because I do believe there is a dark side, a black side."

When asked specifically what scares him, Tony has a quick answer. "The unknown, I guess. When I was six, my uncle and aunt did a puppet show for me for my birthday—I think it was *Jack and the Beanstalk.* I spent the entire time behind the sofa because it scared me solid. That's about the size of it, really—the unknown."

Tony believes the secret of the series' success is its ability to incorporate several different genres into one. "Joss has proven that you can have real horror, real suspense, real situations and yet have real humor. I think it's amazing that Americans have this unique ability to switch abruptly between emotions.

"I used to marvel at the fact that one moment you can have a complete farce and then the next moment it turns into a real weeper and American audiences are right there. It's something the English have never been very good at doing. Joss has just taken that a step further by adding suspense."

Ironically, in both *VR.5* and *Buffy*, Head's character is responsible for watching over a young woman, but Tony says that's where the similarity ends. "The difference is that in *VR.5*, Oliver worked for an organization and he basically knew what he was doing. In *Buffy*, I'm on my own and occasionally don't have the faintest idea what I'm doing. I just know it is my duty and my life's mission to find this girl and teach her how to deal with vampires.

"And the fact that she is this young American high school girl and I'm very English creates a lot of fun to be had. So it's very different from *VR.5*. Very different."

Although the fortysomething Head is the senior member of the cast by a significant number of years, he says there is no generation gap off-camera.

"You always hear actors saying, *Oh, we're like family*. But in this case, it really is true. We all hang out together. We tend to gravitate to each other's trailers and hang out."

After the quick demise of *VR.5*, Tony is pleased at the reception *Buffy* has received, particularly from the critics. "We've had some extremely good press but one of the things that's been most flattering is we're regularly referred to as an ensemble show and the supporting characters are singled out. I think the show is doing very well for all of us, particularly Sarah, who is great.

"This bunch are really, really talented and dedicated and nice people but then again, I've been very lucky because in the twenty-one years I've been working, I've rarely come across egos that have gotten in the way of stuff. I've been really lucky with the people I've worked with and this is no exception."

For the *Buffy*-obsessed, there's probably very little anybody could say about the episodes that would be a revelation after having watched each one countless times until every frame is seared into memory. But there is more to a series companion than mere production facts and continuity bloopers. Hopefully, this episode guide will offer even the most knowledgeable *Buffy the Vampire Slayer* fan not only a complete reference source, but food for thought as well by examining the series from several different points of view.

Each episode listing includes a brief plot summary, anecdotal and production information including names of the recurring cast and guest stars, the most obvious bloopers, some noteworthy facts about the episode, and commentary and observation on the characters' development. One aspect of the series' overall theme—that life in high school is a real-life horror film—will be discussed in detail.

First, an acknowledgment to the executives and craftsmen responsible for helping bring Buffy into your home every week.

* Executive Producers: Joss Whedon, Sandy Gallin, Gail Berman, Fran Rubel Kuzui, Kaz Kuzui
* Co-Executive Producer: David Greenwalt
* Created by: Joss Whedon
* Producer: Gareth Davies
* Co-Producer: David Solomon
* Special Make-up Effects: Todd McIntosh
* Production Designer: Carey Meyer
* Costume Designer: Cynthia Berrgstrom
* Director of Photography: Michael Gershman
* Theme Music: Performed by Nerf Herder

The Episodes

Produced by Mutant Enemy, Inc. and Kuzui/Sandollar in association with 20th Century Fox Television

*These credits will not be repeated in the listings, unless to denote any changes.

First Season Regular Cast
Sarah Michelle Gellar (Buffy Summers)
Nicholas Brendon (Xander Harris)
Alyson Hannigan (Willow Rosenberg)
Charisma Carpenter (Cordelia Chase)

Anthony Stewart Head (Rupert Giles)

Season One

1. "Welcome to the Hellmouth"
(March 10, 1997) 120 min.

[Originally filmed as two separate episodes, "Welcome to the Hellmouth" and "The Harvest."]

Director: Charles Martin Smith ("Welcome to the Hellmouth"); John Kretchmer ("The Harvest")

Teleplay: Joss Whedon

Recurring Cast: Julie Benz (Darla); David Boreanaz (Angel); Ken Lerner (Principal Flutie); Mark Metcalf (The Master); Kristine Sutherland (Joyce Summers)

Guest Cast: Eric Balfour (Jesse); J. Patrick Lawlor (DeBarge, who is also called Thomas); Mercedes McNab (Harmony); Jeffrey Steven Smith (Student); Natalie Strauss (Teacher); Brian Thompson (Luke); Teddy Lane Jr. (Club Bouncer); Deborah Brown (Girl); Amy Chance (Girl); Tupelo Jereme (Girl); Persia White (Girl)

Plot: While trying to settle in to her new surroundings in Sunnydale, California, Buffy must come to grips with the realization that it is her destiny to be the Slayer—whether she wants to be or not.

This Week's Prophecy: On the night of the Harvest, the Master Vampire can draw power from one of his minions while it feeds. Once he's gathered enough strength, the Master Vampire will be able to break through the mystical barrier and come above ground. If he succeeds, his plan is to begin the annihilation of humans so "the old ones" can regain control of the earth.

Introducing . . . : The first episode introduces the main cast of characters—Buffy Summers, Willow Rosenberg, Xander Harris, Rupert Giles, Cordelia Chase, and the mysterious Angel.

Also introduced is the Master, the oldest, most powerful vampire, who has been trapped beneath Sunnydale for sixty years after getting stuck in a mystic portal while attempting to open the Hellmouth. The Master's attempts to gain his freedom comprise the overriding story arc of the first season. Among his many minions is Darla, who uses her schoolgirl look to lead unsuspecting young men to a grisly end.

As it happens, a lot of the Master's plans eventually involve the Bronze, Sunnydale's only nightspot for the high school set. When not beset by vampires looking for sacrifices to bring the Master, the Bronze offers the town's teens soft drinks, bands, and overfed cockroaches.

Analysis: The first episode picks up where the feature film version of *Buffy the Vampire Slayer* left off. In the movie, Buffy wipes out a horde of vampires by trapping them inside her school gymnasium and then setting it on fire. Los Angeles school authorities were not amused and Buffy was expelled. So she and her mom are hoping to make a fresh start in postcard perfect Sunnydale, California.

While the film version was more campy than creepy, it is established early on that the television series won't be afraid to evoke palpable unease in its viewers. When Buffy, on her way to rendezvous with her new friends, hears footsteps behind her, the tension is tangible. Her stalker turns out to be the enigmatic Angel, who both repels and intrigues Buffy. As many women can attest, there's something dreadfully attractive when a handsome face is combined with a whiff of danger.

The pilot episode effectively establishes the relationships between Buffy, her Watcher Giles, and her new friends Xander and Willow—who will become the Slayer inner circle. Xander represents the "every man" non-believer who is forced to believe—

Demons

During her brief time in Sunnydale, Buffy has come up against her share of demons. But there are plenty more who've yet to make an appearance at the Hellmouth hootenanny. In fact, demons are almost a dime a dozen, with thousands appearing in writings around the world. Below are a just a few of the more notorious.

Ashtaroth was usually depicted as an ugly demon riding a dragon and carrying a viper in his left hand. In addition to being the Treasurer of Hell, he was also the Grand Duke of its western regions. He encouraged sloth and idleness.

Asmodeus kept very busy because he was the demon of lust. He had three heads—a bull's, a ram's, and a man's. Not coincidentally, these three creatures were considered to be the most sexually lecherous creatures in the animal kingdom. Using the same line of thinking, he had the feet of a rooster.

Beelzebub was one of the powerful seraphim—the highest order of angels—first recruited by Satan. Once he switched sides, his specialty was tempting people with pride. He became associated with flies because he sent a plague of them to Canaan.

Belial was the demon of lies and was immortalized in Milton's *Paradise Lost*.

Mephistopheles is famous for being the demon summoned by Faust, who wanted to be granted immense power. Mephistopheles fulfilled all of Faust's desires on the condition that at some point, Faust would owe him one. When payback time came, all that was left of Faust was his torn and bloodied corpse, his soul having gone to Mephistopheles in Hell.

against any logic or reason—in all sorts of creatures that do a lot more than just go bump in the night. Complementing Xander is Willow, the whiz kid who faces the unbelievable with more amazement than doubt. Giles, whose British countenance should not be mistaken for meekness, assumes the role of mentor/father figure to the sometimes rebellious but always well-intentioned Buffy.

One of Buffy's primary character traits is her unwillingness to leave people behind, even if it means putting herself in jeopardy. She may be fighting an unending internal struggle over her role as the Slayer, but when someone is threatened, she has no choice but to try to save them. This is one of her great human strengths, but it is also an Achilles' heel the Master and others will use against her.

The pilot episode also establishes the fact that although Buffy is one tough chick, she's not invincible. She feels every punch and kick doled out by her undead adversaries. This vulnerability is an intriguing aspect of the series—she may possess superhuman strength and abilities, but Buffy's no Superman. The high mortality rate of previous Slayers propels Giles to push Buffy so hard, and the secret of her longevity will ultimately prove to be her loyal, if not exactly fearless, support group. Buffy does more than just get by with a little help from her friends, she lives to slay another day.

The Real Horror: Enrolling at a school after everybody else has already formed well-defined cliques. Anybody who's ever been "the new kid" can empathize with Buffy's nervousness at walking into unfamiliar surroundings, whether it be a new job, a new neighborhood, or especially a new school. Nothing is so nausea-inducing as having to decipher a high school's pre-ordained popularity pecking order and going through the agony of finding where you fit in—which is not necessarily where you'd like to fit in.

Although she'd like to be as popular as Cordelia, the queen of the "in" or "A-list" crowd, Buffy is drawn to Willow and Xander, who represent the vast majority of students who pass through high school just *this much* on the outside—they're close enough to see in but seldom get invited to join the party.

The situation with Xander's buddy Jesse reflects another common adolescent occurrence; a friend you've known all your life suddenly turns into a stranger, in this case an absolute monster. It's "hanging out with the wrong crowd" taken to a horrific extreme. But even though Jesse has become a vampire, he still looks like the same person he used to be, so Xander has difficulty accepting the change. He's hoping against hope that something will restore Jesse to the guy he was before. Fortunately for Xander, while his intellect and emotions are battling it out, Jesse is pushed onto the wooden stake Xander's clutching, causing Jesse to disintegrate in a puff of ash-like debris.

Bloopers: In the scene where Giles is piling ancient tomes in Buffy's arms, the bindings are first facing Buffy, then in the next shot, facing Giles, then finally, facing Buffy again.

Of Special Note: "Welcome to the Hellmouth" was combined with what was originally intended to be the second episode, "The Harvest," and presented as a two-hour pilot. Sunnydale High is actually Torrance High School, which was also used in *Beverly Hills, 90210.*

Nerf Herder, the band that performs the theme song, took their name from a bit of *The Empire Strikes Back* dialogue, when Princess Leia referred to Han Solo as a "nerf herder." And no, she was not being complimentary at the time.

Although most *Buffy* fans may be too young to remember, Charles Martin Smith, who directed the first hour of the pilot, was once best known as an actor, having gotten his big break— along with Richard Dreyfus, Harrison Ford, and Suzanne Somers—in *American Graffiti.*

Music: "Saturated" (during the scene where Buffy is debating outfits), "Believe" (being played on stage when Buffy arrives at the Bronze), "Things Are Changing" (as Buffy leaves the Bronze to look for Willow), and "Right My Wrong" (Buffy's confrontation with Flutie at the school gate) by Sprung Monkey, on their *Swirl* CD; "Wearing Me Down" (the song Cordelia says she loves) and "Ballad for Dead Friends" (as vampires descend on the Bronze) by Dashboard Prophets, from their *Burning Out the Inside* CD.

2. "The Witch" (March 17, 1997) 60 min.

Director: Stephen Cragg

Teleplay: Dana Reston

Recurring Cast: Kristine Sutherland (Joyce Summers); William Monaghan (Dr. Gregory)

Guest Cast: Elizabeth Anne Allen (Amy); Jim Doughan (Mr. Pole); Nicole Prescott (Lishanne); Robin Riker (Catherine); Amanda Wilmshurst (Head Cheerleader)

Plot: A girl's obsession with becoming a cheerleader may be the evil force behind a series of spells spontaneously combusting, blinding, and otherwise maiming other members of the squad. When the student witch realizes that Buffy knows her secret, she puts Buffy under a spell that will kill her, unless Giles can locate her book of Magic and reverse the spell.

This Week's Evil Creature: A very powerful witch trying to hold onto her youth.

Introducing . . . : Science teacher Dr. Gregory is introduced, as is Cordelia's frightening lack of driving skills. Also, "The Witch" represents the first non-vampire story line.

Analysis: Buffy's desire to try out for the cheerleading squad reflects the dichotomy within Buffy. She doesn't conform to the will of the Cordelias of the world in order to gain acceptance, and yet she wants to be accepted enough that being a cheerleader really matters to her—even though she'd never admit just how much. For as much as high school life has changed over the last half century in America, there remain a few constants—the jocks and the cheerleaders still rank near the top of the high school food chain hierarchy, golden children secretly envied and openly resented.

If anyone doubts the lengths some girls—and mothers on their behalf—will go to win a spot on the sidelines, consider the real-life incident that occurred in Texas a few years ago when an overzealous mother plotted to murder one of her daughter's competitors for a spot on the cheerleading squad. The surreal situation was the basis for the 1993 Emmy-winning HBO movie, *The Positively True Adventures of the Alleged Texas Cheerleader-Murdering Mom.* By comparison, using witchcraft to make the squad doesn't seem all that unbelievable.

The major revelation of this episode—that Amy's mother has literally stolen her daughter's youth by switching their bodies—provides a shocking plot twist that is indicative of *Buffy*'s storytelling conventions—just when viewers think they have things figured out, the story often takes a creative and surprising turn.

It's a Mystery: How and when did Amy steal Buffy's bracelet? We see Buffy make off with a lock of Amy/Catherine's hair, but the scene that showed Amy lifting the bracelet must have been left on the cutting room floor.

The Real Horror: Trying to live up to your parents' sometimes unreasonable expectations.

In this episode, both Buffy and Amy are confronted with the reality that they haven't always lived up to what their parents had hoped, either in achievement or character. In Buffy's case, her secret exploits have resulted in a complete family upheaval, but she's unable to explain to her mother why life with Buffy is so difficult. It's not that she wants it to be a problem but she can't help it—what teenager can?

When Joyce suggests that Buffy work on the yearbook committee—an activity on the low end of the 1990s school social scene—she's projecting her own past glories onto Buffy without taking into account that her daughter is a very different person

A cast that slays together stays together. The *Buffy* stars are honored by the Museum of Television & Radio. © Albert Ortega/Flower Children Ltd.

than she was. Projecting interests onto a child usually just sets the stage for hurt feelings. The child's belief that the parent doesn't have a clue is reinforced and the parent is injured that something that was once so important to them is summarily blown off, which is often interpreted as personal rejection.

In Amy's case, her mother so desperately wants to relive her youth through her daughter that she casts a spell enabling them to switch bodies. What Catherine "the Great" does isn't all that much more horrific than parents who drive their children into careers or activities in an effort to live vicariously through them. Catherine is *Gypsy*'s Mama Rose with a spell book. The biggest irony of the episode is that when Catherine is finally poised for her moment of triumph, she discovers that no matter how much she practices, no matter how strong her desire, Catherine as Amy simply doesn't have the innate skills to be great again. She failed to learn one of the most important lessons of parenting—your child's destiny is their own, and trying to recreate your youth through them can only lead to tragedy . . . or being trapped in a trophy case for eternity.

Bloopers: In the gymnasium, a sign reads: *1996 Cheerleading Tryouts*. It didn't read 1997 because the series was originally supposed to debut at the beginning of the 1996 season, but was pushed back because of production problems.

Of Special Note: Dr. Gregory is the first recurring character introduced on the series who will later wind up being killed off. Breaking the long-standing tradition of only killing off guest stars, having recurring characters regularly die will become a hallmark of the show.

Robin Riker, who played Catherine the Great, is no stranger to witches, having guest-starred in 1996 on *Sabrina, the Teenage Witch*.

Music: "Twilight Zone" by 2 Unlimited

3. "Teacher's Pet" (March 25, 1997) 60 min.

Director: Bruce Seth Green

Teleplay: David Greenwalt

Recurring Cast: David Boreanaz (Angel); Ken Lerner (Principal Flutie); William Monaghan (Dr. Gregory)

Guest Cast: Jean Speegle Howard (Natalie French); Jackson Price (Blayne); Musetta Vander (She-Mantis)

Plot: After the gruesome death of science teacher Dr. Gregory, Xander falls for the flirtatious charms of the new substitute, who brings new meaning to the term "man eater."

This Week's Phenomenon: Metamorphosis, an ancient belief that certain people are empowered with the magical ability to change themselves and others at will into other life forms. In this episode, the animal of choice is a She-Mantis, who can only maintain her human form by mating with, and then devouring, virginal young men.

Introducing . . . : The first death of a recurring character. In this case, science teacher Dr. Gregory, who is dragged off by some creature just minutes after giving Buffy a supportive pep talk.

Also new to the scene is the mutual sexual attraction sparking between Angel and Buffy. Up until this episode, Buffy has been wary towards, and annoyed with, her mysterious shadow. But her initial distrust is being replaced by flirtatious banter and seductive glances.

Analysis: Poor Xander. Not only is his sexual prowess repeatedly challenged by self-proclaimed womanizer Blayne, now he discovers that Buffy's mystery man, Angel, looks like he stepped straight out of a *GQ* ad. Meeting Angel for the first time, Xander obviously feels threatened on an "attractability" scale.

This episode is a showcase for Xander, as his creepy crawly encounters with the She-Mantis take center stage. But while the story allowed Nicholas Brendon to display his range of talents, his alter ego would have wished some things had been left unrevealed—like the fact that the creature only goes after virgins—and that the others are all too aware of the fact. Xander takes out his frustration over the revelation of his virginity on a sac of mantis eggs, which he chops apart with a machete.

#ET: The Real Horror: Learning how to cope with adult feelings of sexual desire while still an emotionally immature teenager. Among high school boys, it expresses itself as verbal sexual competition. It really is a guy thing, the need to boast and brag about "conquests" as a quantifier of manhood and virility—which for

Lesser Known Evil Creatures

When you live on a Hellmouth, all sorts of uninvited guests tend to pop into town. Below are some of the less commonly known monsters that may show up someday in Sunnydale.

The Baobhan Sith is an evil Scottish fairy who appears as a beautiful woman and dances with men until they are totally exhausted, and then eats them.

Rakshasa is an Indian vampire that appears human with animal features, usually those of a tiger. In addition to drinking the blood of its victims, Rakshasa also eats the flesh.

Strigoiuls are a type of vampires that like to hunt in groups. (Think velociraptors.)

Succubi are interesting vampire-like creatures. Female, they usually feed by having sex with the victim until he's exhausted, then feeding on the energy released during the erotic encounter. They can enter homes uninvited and can take on the appearance of other persons. And they will often visit the same victim repeatedly, like alien abduction, with the victim experiencing the visits as dreams.

Incubus is the male version of a Succubus.

many apparently continues until old age and death.

Xander represents the average teenage boy who feels compelled to play along with the game rather than admit sexual innocence and risk eternal ridicule from his peers. But even worse than being ridiculed by the guys is having the object of your fantasies find out that you're about as sexually experienced as Tickle Me Elmo. There's a reason why so many high school girls date older guys.

The Moral of the Story: Although hormones will be hormones, in this age of deadly, sexually transmitted diseases—and evil creatures who are drawn to Sunnydale like ants to blood—uninformed sex with a stranger can kill.

Bloopers: When the substitute teacher is first seen sitting at her desk preparing her sandwich, her sleeves are pushed up to her elbows. But during the close-up of her hands dumping the crickets on the bread, the sleeves of her sweater are clearly visible. Then in the very next shot of her taking a bite of the sandwich, the sleeves are pushed back up.

Of Special Note: The director of this episode, Bruce Seth Green, has some experience with television action heroes, having also directed episodes of *Hercules: The Legendary Journeys* and *Xena: Warrior Princess*. And his horror credentials include a stint on *Airwolf*, the onetime Jan-Michael Vincent vehicle.

Jean Speegle Howard, the actress who plays the real Natalie French, is the mother of actor-turned-director Ron "Opie" Howard.

Music: "Already Met You" (music in Xander's dream) and "Stoner Love" (at the end when Xander chops up the eggs) by Superfine, on the *Stoner Love 7* vinyl release.

4. "Never Kill a Boy on the First Date"
(March 31, 1997) 60 min.

Director: David Semel

Teleplay: Rob Des Hotel and Dean Batali

Recurring Cast: David Boreanaz (Angel); Andrew J. Ferchland (Collin); Mark Metcalf (The Master)

Guest Cast: Geoff Meed (Bus Passenger); Robert Mont (Bus Driver); Christopher Wiehl (Owen)

Plot: Buffy develops a crush on sensitive, poetry-loving Owen, who asks her out on her first date since moving to Sunnydale. But her night of hoped-for romance is interrupted by a new prophecy the Master is bent on seeing fulfilled in order to gain his freedom.

This Week's Prophecy: A great warrior vampire will be "born" and become the Master's secret weapon against the Slayer, ultimately leading her to doom—although exactly how he's supposed to do that remains a mystery at this point.

Introducing . . . : The Anointed One. Through this vampire, the Master plans on both killing Buffy and gaining his freedom so the "old ones" can once again rule the Earth. The twist here is that instead of being one of the more violent, nastier looking adult vampires, the Anointed One is a little boy—someone Buffy would never suspect of being an evil creature intent on seeing her dead— until it's too late. The Anointed One's role in this episode is limited to a surprise introduction at the end, but the character becomes the focal point of the season-ending story line in the finale, "Prophecy Girl."

Analysis: Buffy is going through some typical adolescent growing pains in this episode, complicated by her secret life as the Slayer. Still hoping to resume a fairly normal social life, Buffy is thrilled when Sunnydale's resident brooding, poetry-loving hunk takes an interest in her. So what if some apocalyptic prophecy is about to be set into motion? She'd rather go on a date.

Giles's feelings of guilt over Buffy's destiny are more evident here than in past episodes. Rather than pull Watcher rank and insist she do her Slayerly duties, he relents because he empathizes with her longing to be free, at least for a night, from the weight of being the world's savior—just as he once longed to live the life of a grocer, blissfully ignorant of the evil lurking in the shadows of the Watcher's world.

Buffy's sense of duty finally kicks in, but her lapse in responsibility may have disastrous consequences. Although she saved Giles and the others by incinerating the vampire believed to be the Anointed One, she is too distracted to consider the possibility that he wasn't the Anointed One after all—a fact that will come back to haunt her in the "Prophecy Girl" episode.

The Real Horror: Responsibility and sacrifice. One of the more sobering passages into maturity—except for those suffering from permanent arrested development—is the realization that we won't always be able to follow our heart's fondest desire. Sometimes, we either have to choose responsibility over selfish indulgence or sacrifice our personal needs and wants for the greater good. It can be a really depressing revelation, especially when it involves a potential love interest.

In Buffy's case, it's not so much that Owen might be Mr. Right, it's that she's Ms. Wrong for him. If she yields to her own desire for romance and a facade of normalcy with Owen, she stands the risk of literally killing him. For his own good, and hers, she has to break off the budding relationship. While on a surface level they may be the perfect couple, on a deeper, more profound plane they are incompatible.

Just as some of the world's greatest romances are ultimately unable to overcome fundamental obstacles such as religious differences, political beliefs, or even jobs that cause long separations, Buffy is forced to acknowledge that being the Slayer puts a serious, but necessary, damper on her social and love life. While most teens simply curry heartbreak or angry parents when they make irresponsible choices, Buffy's margin of error is much less and brings greater consequences. It would not only be irresponsible on Buffy's part to knowingly put Owen at risk, but pursuing a relationship of any kind with someone outside the inner Slayer circle could put Xander, Willow, and Giles at risk, as well.

Just like the overextended parent who fleetingly wonders what it would be like to have absolutely nobody to care for but themselves, or the executive who daydreams about leaving behind the stress and pressure of corporate America for a simpler, downsized way of life, Buffy learns that at the end of the day, being an adult—or being a Slayer—means having to take into consideration how our actions affect the people around us. We might be only answerable to ourselves but we are responsible to everyone we make a part of our lives.

Bloopers: When the shuttle bus is first seen from far away, all of the lights inside the bus are brightly lit. But when the camera cuts to an interior shot of the bus and its passengers, all the lights are off.

Of Special Note: Because he's unrecognizable under his vampire make-up, viewers may not recognize Mark Metcalf, who appeared on *Seinfeld* in the recurring part of the Maestro. But Metcalf's signature role is still as Douglas C. Neidermeyer in the 1978 film *National Lampoon's Animal House*.

The group performing during Owen and Buffy's date at the Bronze is Velvet Chain.

Music: "Strong" (the first song Buffy and Owen dance to) and "Treason" (the next song they dance to) by Velvet Chain, from the *Groovy Side* CD; "Let the Sun Fall Down" (when Buffy tells Owen they should just be friends) by Kim Richey, from *Kim Richey*.

5. "The Pack" (April 7, 1997) 60 min.

Director: Bruce Seth Green

Teleplay: Matt Kiene and Joe Reinkmeyer

Recurring Cast: Ken Lerner (Principal Flutie)

Guest Cast: David Brisbin (Mr. Anderson); Jeff Maynard (Lance); Justin Jon Ross (Joey); Jeffrey Steven Smith (Adam); James Stephens (Zookeeper); Barbara Whinnery (Mrs. Anderson); Gregory White (Coach Herrold); Eion Bailey (Kyle), Brian Gross (Tor), Jennifer Sky (Heidi)

Plot: During a field trip to the zoo, Xander and a gang of four school bullies become possessed by the spirit of a vicious hyena. With Xander as pack leader, they start a reign of terror at Sunnydale High. Buffy and Giles need to figure out how to exorcise the evil spirit before it permanently takes over Xander's soul.

This Week's Evil: Transpossession, which is when a person becomes possessed by the spirit of an animal, most often a predator of some kind. Certain tribes, including the Masai in Africa, believe an animal spirit can inhabit the body of a human, thereby elevating the person to a higher spiritual plane.

Introducing . . . : The primal side of Xander. After he is taken over by the hyena spirit, Xander's more "Basic Instinct" side emerges, where hedonistic desires flourish without any tempering codes of social conduct. Normally, his love for Buffy, combined with common courtesy and manners, would prevent him from going after her like an animal in heat, but as hyena-boy, he just follows his urges.

Analysis: If there was any doubt left about Willow's feelings for Xander, or his attraction to Buffy, it's completely dispelled in this episode. It's also clear that the thing that Willow finds most attractive about him in a romantic sense, and Buffy on a friendship level, is Xander's good-natured, macho-less personality. When he behaves in an animalistic fashion, both Willow and Buffy are instinctively put off by him.

When Xander nearly rapes Buffy, his claim that he's only being what Buffy finds attractive—dark and dangerous á la Angel—strikes at the heart of the *Men Are from Mars, Women Are from Venus* misunderstanding between the sexes. While Buffy finds Angel's sexiness heightened by his mysterious aura, in her fantasies about him she's not in any kind of real jeopardy because *she's* the one controlling the situation. But as soon as Xander pins her against the wall, their encounter becomes about power, not attraction. Which is why she then hits him with a desk.

This episode takes a sharp turn to the dark side, first with Xander and company eating Herbert the pig, Sunnydale's mascot, then with the cannibalistic murder of Principal Flutie by the pack, minus Xander. Whether intended or not, Flutie's death at the hands of his students can be seen as a symbolic morality play about the alarming escalation of juvenile crime that is just as much of a problem in the suburbs as in the inner city.

While the events of this episode threatened to destroy their friendship forever, in the end—after the hyena spirit is released from Xander—the bond between Buffy, Willow, and Xander is strengthened by the girls' ability to forgive and Xander's pretense of forgetting what happened.

The Real Horror: Predators, whether it be sexual or social. The modern extreme are gangs but less dramatic examples can be found in every school where packs of students, both male and female, are on the prowl. In this episode, Xander and his hyena-possessed crew represent the primal behavior that teenagers can fall into when in groups. Case in point—Spring Break in Fort Lauderdale or Palm Springs, or any place where hordes of hor-monally charged teenagers and young adults gather. Xander's overt sexual aggression towards Buffy reflects the kind of intense dis-parity that can exist between male and female sexuality during the teen years and serves as a powerful analogy for the intense drive young men experience as their hormones go into overdrive. In fact, the pack members' behavior is so typical of many teenagers, especially boys, that Giles initially dismisses Buffy's concern.

In some parts of the country, it's almost commonplace for high school students to have one of their own killed by street violence, and guns have become so prevalent that certain school districts have been forced to install metal detectors. Perhaps it's this perva-sive aura of violence, which is becoming as much a part of school life as Friday night football games, that gives "The Pack" such an edgy feel of realism.

Bloopers: When Willow is in the library supposedly watching a clip about hyenas that is playing on the computer, the animals shown with the white fluffy tails are not hyenas, but a type of wild dog.

Of Special Note: The actor who plays Dr. Anderson, the father of the family in the van, played Mr. Ernst on Nickelodeon's *Hey*

Slayer Music

One of the most distinctive aspects of the series is the music. In addition to supplying soundtrack cuts, the groups that contribute music to *Buffy* often appear on stage during scenes at the Bronze.

Joss Whedon says he likes to have some of the lesser-known bands provide music for the episodes in order to give them a little exposure. "And, I like hiring the unsigned bands because they're cheap," he laughs. "No, not really. A lot of great bands just don't get enough exposure. And for some reason, all these bands sent in tapes of music for us to use."

From these submissions, Whedon picked a song by Nerf Herder to play over the opening credits. It's appropriately titled, *Buffy's Theme.*

One group, Nickel, found out about *Buffy* through writer Marti Noxon. "She knows one of the guys in the band and suggested they send in some demos," says the group's manager, Rob Robinson. "To be honest, it's hard to tell if it's made any difference to us as far as record sales because the band's CD is only available over the Internet [http://www.notlame.com]. But I think it'll help as far as signing with a label, which we expect to do soon."

The bands are selected on an episode-by-episode basis. Whedon says he'll sometimes write a scene around a particular song he's just heard. "I'll hear the music then get a picture in my mind of what the characters will be doing."

As far as scoring *Buffy*, Fernand Bos, the series' music editor, says they alternate composers. "One week it's Chris Beck and the next week the team of Shawn Clement and Sean Murray."

Because of the surprising fan response to the music, Whedon says there are plans in the works to release a *Buffy* CD.

Dude. Eion Bailey was one of the stars of *Significant Others*, the short-lived Fox series by the creators of *Party of Five*.

Music: "All You Want" (when Xander joins Buffy and Willow at the Bronze) by Dashboard Prophets, from the *Burning Out the Inside* CD; "Reluctant Man" (as the Pack enters the Bronze) by

Sprung Monkey, on the *Swirl* CD; "Job's Eyes" (as the Pack prowls among the students in slow-mo) by Far, from the *Tin Cans and Strings for You* CD.

6. "Angel" (April 14, 1997) 60 min.

Director: Scott Brazil

Teleplay: David Greenwalt

Recurring Cast: Julie Benz (Darla); David Boreanaz (Angel); Andrew J. Ferchland (Collin/The Anointed One); Mark Metcalf (The Master); Kristine Sutherland (Joyce Summers)

Guest Cast: Charles Wesley (Lead Vampire of the Three)

Plot: It's the best of times and the worst of times for Buffy. The good news is, Angel loves her. The bad news is, he's a 240-year-old vampire.

This Week's Killer Vampires: Tired of Buffy killing off his family, the Master calls upon warrior vampires, the Three, to kill her. When they fail, Darla, the vampire who dresses like a schoolgirl, takes it upon herself to get rid of Buffy.

Introducing . . . : Angel's history and Xander's dancing. In the opening scene, Willow looks on lovingly as Xander jerks and gyrates his way across the dance floor. Due to the response of adoring fans, more of Xander's inimitable dancing style will be seen in future episodes.

More seriously, both the dark and sensitive sides of Angel are revealed as the truth about his past is uncovered.

Analysis: Buffy is both surprised and thrilled to discover that Angel returns her feelings. But this is a horror series and nothing will be easy, especially love. Just as it seems Buffy's deepest desire may come true, Angel shows his true face and it's not a pretty sight.

Trust is a major theme of this episode, with Buffy ultimately trusting her instinct that Angel is not a monster—even though she makes a halfhearted attempt to kill him when she is under the mistaken belief that he attacked Joyce.

Joyce Summers' character is fleshed out more in this episode. Whatever traumas caused them to leave Los Angeles, mother and daughter are shown to have a close, respectful relationship. Despite all the problems her daughter has experienced, Joyce is surprisingly trusting of Buffy—especially when finding Buffy home alone with an obviously older man.

Angel offers proof of his love for Buffy by killing Darla—the vampire who "made" him—fully knowing that her death will forever brand him an outcast among his people. This sacrifice helped cement Angel as one of contemporary television's most romantic characters, and his portrayer, David Boreanaz, as the object of millions of viewers' fantasies.

The Real Horror: The realization that love isn't always enough to overcome every obstacle facing a relationship; that there are circumstances beyond the couple's control that will ultimately determine its success or failure. This never seems as true as it is for teenagers. Their lives are still controlled, to varying degrees, by parents.

The impact of unrequited, unrealized passion is magnified in youth. First loves are so intense and the emotions behind them so exposed and raw because teens haven't yet learned to protect themselves; they haven't formed the emotional calluses that come with age, experience, and previous loss. Buffy and Angel's apparently hopeless, Romeo-and-Juliet situation represents any relationship conspired against by culture, family disapproval, age, or other circumstances.

It's a Mystery: When did Buffy call Giles and tell him about being attacked by three vampires? All we see is Buffy taking Angel home, encountering her surprised mom, then going upstairs to go to sleep.

Bloopers: When Buffy is walking home early in the episode, she walks past a store window lit in a greenish hue. After walking several steps, she hears a sound, stops a moment then keeps walking—right past the exact same green-lit window.

When Buffy is training with Giles in the library, she is wearing pants and a blue T-shirt. In the very next scene, she walks into her bedroom, says hi to Angel, and offers him some food—dressed in a white dress.

During Buffy's confrontation with Angel in the Bronze, she puts down her crossbow and walks three or four steps toward him. But when Darla appears, Buffy—who is still next to Angel—is able to just flip the crossbow up into her hand because it is suddenly right next to her foot. Also, how come Darla never has to reload her guns?

Of Special Note: The director of this week's episode was one of the producers of the ABC series, *Cracker*.

So popular is Xander's unique dancing style among *Buffy the Vampire Slayer* fans that it has spawned a Xander Dance Club Web site on the Internet.

Kristine Sutherland, who plays Buffy's mom, is married to *Mad About You* costar John Pankow. They have a nine-year-old daughter.

Music: The song playing over the final scene between Buffy and Angel in the Bronze is "I'll Remember You," by Sophie Zelmani.

7. "**J, Robot—You, Jane**" (April 28, 1997) 60 min.

Director: Stephen Posey

Teleplay: Ashley Gable and Thomas A. Swyden

Recurring Cast: Robia La Morte (Jenny Calendar)

The Episodes

Guest Cast: Mark Deakins (Voice of Moloch); Edith Fields (Nurse); Chad Lindberg (Fritz); Pierrino Mascarino (Thelonius); Jamison Ryan (Dave)

Plot: Willow accidentally scans a demon trapped in an ancient book into the school computer. Once free to roam through the world's computers via telecommunication lines, Moloch has some cyber followers build him a robot body. His plan is to first kill Willow, Buffy, and Xander, and then wreak havoc and destruction on the world—unless Giles and Ms. Calendar, the computer science teacher, can find a way to stop him.

This Week's Demon: Moloch the Corruptor, a particularly ruthless demon whose specialty was seducing the young and innocent into doing his evil bidding. He was only stopped after his soul was imprisoned by medieval monks in an ancient tome, where he was destined to remain until the words of the book were read aloud. Apparently, scanning served the same purpose.

Introducing . . . : Ms. Jenny Calendar, computer science teacher and self-described techno-pagan. A child of the Information Age, Ms. Calendar butts heads with, taunts, and openly flirts with computer-phobic, bibliophilic Giles. When Giles needs help to rid the Internet of Moloch, it's Jenny who arranges for an online circle to exorcise the demon from cyberspace. She teaches Giles that the mystical world isn't limited to ancient texts and relics— the divine also exists in cyberspace. Jenny's knowledge of and belief in prophecies and other mystical events and creatures foreshadows her future inclusion in the Slayer's inner circle.

Analysis: This time it is Willow's turn to try her hand at Hellmouth romance. It's in keeping with Willow's computer savvy that she is the only one of the group who would be amenable to an online relationship with the highly seductive "Malcolm."

But even though Willow is smitten with her suitor, she's not one to completely lose her senses. When Malcolm slips up and reveals that he's been checking up on Buffy, Willow grows leery.

She is obviously more loyal to proven friend Buffy than to an unknown would-be boyfriend. Willow might be lonely and desperate for some romantic attention, but she's not going to lose her head. Well, actually, she does almost lose her head when Malcolm/Moloch is released from the Internet and tries to kill Willow, Xander, and Buffy.

In an evocative scene, Willow goes after Moloch, venting her hurt and frustration at being lied to and manipulated, revealing just how much of an Achilles' heel her loneliness is. After Buffy tricks Moloch into short-circuiting himself, Buffy, Willow, and Xander compare their unlucky-in-love track records and, like many teenagers who remain out of the dating-scene loop, and wistfully conclude that they will never find a relationship the way other people do.

The Real Horror: The dangers of Internet intimacy. This episode is almost of the ripped-from-the-headlines variety, with Willow establishing a "relationship" with an unknown, unseen stranger by chatting on the computer. With the recent flurry of reported crimes being committed by people who find their victims online, the presence of a demon inside the modem telephone wires is already a perceived reality to some techno-phobes.

It's a Mystery: How did Buffy, on foot, manage to follow Dave, who was driving a car, to the computer research facility?

Bloopers: When Moloch is hacking into the school computer to see Buffy's school record, her birthdate changes from 10/24/80 the first time we see the computer screen to 5/6/79; and her grade changes from sophomore to senior.

Of Special Note: The director of this episode, Stephen Posey, who also works as a cinematographer, began his directing career working on a number of horror films, including *Slumber Party Massacre*, which had the distinction of being banned from movie theaters in Germany.

Moloch

There really is a record of a demon named Moloch. He was a Canaanite deity associated with human sacrifices, primarily sacrifices of children. In areas where he was worshipped, a bronze statue with the head of an ox and body of a man would be erected and infants would be placed in it to burn. He's usually shown as an old man with ram's horns, holding a scythe.

For the literary minded, Moloch is mentioned in Milton's *Paradise Lost* in Book 6, line 365.

> *Touch of Evil*
> Touch of evil
> On the faithful bestowed
> Burn for Moloch
> Sacrificial inferno
> Submitting the offspring
> Swallowed in flames
> Baptismal immolation
> Another soul claimed
> Hell on earth
> The pagan returns
> To please the deity
> Children shall burn
> Your children are mine
> Placate me with them
> You worshipped before
> You will kneel again.
> As the young are scorched
> We welcome the end
> The lord of the altar of incense unleashed
> Apocalypse begins

The voice of Moloch/Malcolm is supplied by Mark Deakins, who is better known to daytime fans as *The City*'s Kevin Larkin. For the uninitiated, *The City* was a short-lived, revamped version of the daytime soap *Loving*.

Runes

When Giles finds out Ms. Calendar is a techno-pagan, he mentions runes.

The term "rune" means mystery or secret. Initially, runes were ancient Norse and Teutonic alphabets and symbols ascribed with various magical powers, such as the ability to predict the future. These alphabetical signs have been passed down through the centuries.

In Western Europe during the Dark Ages, runes were believed to possess potent magical powers. They were the tools of magicians passed onto initiates by word of mouth, but belief and interest in the runes was diminished by the Inquisition and the resulting tortures.

Beginning in the 1980s runes regained popularity for divination purposes, and some modern witches inscribe their magical tools and personal jewelry with runic characters.

The voice heard while Giles is listening to the radio belongs to series creator Joss Whedon.

8. "The Puppet Show"
(May 5, 1997) 60 min.

Director: Ellen Pressman

Teleplay: Dean Batali and Rob Des Hotel

Recurring Cast: Armin Shimerman (Principal Snyder); Kristine Sutherland (Joyce Summers)

Guest Cast: Krissy Carlson (Emily); Chasen Hampton (Elliot); Lenora May (Mrs. Jackson); Natasha Pearce (Lisa); Burke Roberts (Marc); Richard Werner (Morgan); Tom Wyner (Voice of Sid)

Plot: The Sunnydale High School talent show turns sinister when one of the featured students, a ventriloquist with an eerily real dummy, is suspected in the gruesome murder of another student, whose heart was cut out.

This Week's Evil Creature: A demon which, in order to retain its human form, must eat a human heart and brain every seven years. This demon is the last of a group of seven demons, the others having been killed by Sid, the demon hunter. Unfortunately for Sid, he's the victim of a curse that left him a wooden dummy (think Pinocchio with hormones and an attitude). In order to be freed from the curse, Sid must kill the last of the demons, hopefully before he finds a suitable brain to eat.

Introducing . . . : Principal Snyder, who is determined to restore order to Sunnydale High. He feels his predecessor Mr. Flutie, who was eaten by a pack of hyena-possessed students in episode #5, was too soft on the students. The new principal's hard line motto is that children should be disciplined and controlled. Trying to understand them will only lead to a chaotic school and a limited mortality.

Snyder seems to have focused his attention on Buffy and her cohorts because, he says, they seem to be the school's number one bad element. He keeps appearing out of nowhere and his too-close-for-comfort interest in Buffy begins to take on a skin-crawling quality. Is he just an overzealous authoritarian or something more sinister, or possibly even demonic?

Also introduced is Willow's stage fright, which will play a major role in episode #9, "Nightmares."

Analysis: As the reluctant director of the talent show, Giles's anti-social personality is fleshed out. His discomfort at having to deal with hordes of students is palpable and is reflected by how disheveled he looks whenever interacting with the participants. He isn't kidding when he tells the new principal that the reason he became a librarian in the first place was to minimize his contact with the students.

Through Sid, there is more sexual innuendo than in previous episodes. When everyone still thinks it's Morgan providing the voice of the dummy and Sid says, "Once you've had wood, nothing else is as good," Buffy deals with the sexual connotation in a mature, calm manner. Considering that creator Whedon has stated that Buffy is definitely a virgin, at least at this point, she's an aware virgin at ease with sexuality.

At the end when Giles is locked in a guillotine, it's the first time the Watcher has been in real, immediate peril where he needs to be saved from imminent death. Yes, he's run from vampires before but this is the closest he's come to being the late Watcher. Although Buffy readily puts herself at risk to save anyone, she seems particularly panicked when she realizes that the demon will go after Giles. Although she might not yet realize it, Buffy has started to see Giles as a surrogate father figure.

The Real Horror: Mandatory participation in a high school talent show and the ensuing public humiliation for the artistically impaired. Nothing is quite so sadistic as forcing students, or anyone else for that matter, to get up in front of a roomful of people and perform. While some people, like the Cordelias of the world, have no shame or sense of embarrassment about themselves and are happy to get up on a stage and sing off-key, just to be in the limelight, others—like Buffy, Xander, and Willow—find the experience degrading. Ironically, the people with the worst self-image problems are the ones most damaged by this barbaric school ritual. Buffy sums up the prevailing attitude of most students when she tells her mother, "If you really want to support me, you'll stay far, far away."

A second, and more serious, issue is raised by Morgan's illness. The monster of this episode, a demon who coldly robs people of their lives for its own insidious gain, could be seen as the fictional embodiment of his terminal brain cancer, a disease that literally eats away at bodies to keep itself going. There are few horrors so great as the thought of dying a slow, painful death from disease, especially for a young person. Debilitating illnesses are not supposed to afflict children, but do, and anyone who has ever had a classmate die from disease knows how affecting the surreal and frightfully jolting realization is that there are no guarantees we will all live to enjoy a long, aged life.

Bloopers: Sid kills the demon by stabbing it through the heart with a jumbo-sized kitchen knife. But in the next shot, when Buffy is carrying the lifeless dummy away, there is no knife in the demon's chest.

Of Special Note: Principal Snyder is played by Armin Shimerman, who is known to *Star Trek: Deep Space Nine* fans as Quark. According to Whedon, the casting was simply lucky. "Armin came in to read because I guess he had some free time and he was hilarious. He was just great. We have to work around his *Deep Space Nine* schedule but we work him in when we can."

Lenora May, who plays Mrs. Jackson, appeared in the classic 1979 horror film, *When a Stranger Calls*.

The voice of Sid is supplied by Tom Wyner, who produced, directed, story edited, and narrated the animated series *Techman*.

Nicholas Brendon and Alyson Hannigan play best buds Xander and Willow. © Albert Ortega/Flower Children Ltd.

The scene that Buffy, Willow, and Xander perform for the talent show at the end of the episode is from *Oedipus Rex*.

9. "𝕹ightmares" (May 12, 1997) 60 min.

Director: Bruce Seth Green

Teleplay: David Greenwalt

Story by: Joss Whedon

Recurring Cast: Dean Butler (Hank Summers); Andrew J. Ferchland (Collin/The Anointed One); Mark Metcalf (The Master); Kristine Sutherland (Joyce Summers)

Guest Cast: Jeremy Foley (Billy Palmer); Scott Harlan (Aldo Gianfranco); Tom Magwili (Billy's Doctor); J. Robin Miler (Laura); Sean Moran (Stage Manager); Brian Pietro (Billy's Coach); Justine Urich (Wendell)

Plot: An attack on a young boy leaves him comatose and his wandering spirit unleashes everyone's worst nightmares, making them come true. While battling her own REM demons, Buffy races the clock to uncover the identity of the boy's attacker before reality folds completely.

This Week's Mystical Phenomenon: Astral projection, the belief that while the physical body is unconscious, the astral body is able to navigate freely through dimensions of time and space.

Introducing . . . : Dean Butler, who plays Buffy's dad, Hank Summers. Hank still lives in Los Angeles and only comes to visit Buffy on occasional weekends. This is also the first time that the depth of Buffy's emotional reaction to her parents' divorce is explored. She worries that she may have in some way contributed to their growing apart because of the havoc wreaked by her secret life as the Slayer.

Analysis: The opening dream sequence, in which Buffy confronts the Master and is paralyzed with fear as he leans in for the kill, is a clear indication that Buffy's unspoken fear of the Master's power is growing and a nice little foreshadowing of the season finale.

Life at Sunnydale High takes on a surreal, dreamlike quality when nightmarish events become daytime realities. In one of the most upsetting scenes in a series filled with disturbing images, Buffy's father tells her he left because he couldn't stand living in the same house with her. She's too much trouble and an overall disappointment and he really has no interest in maintaining a facade of a relationship. The girl who has faced down death on a weekly basis crumbles under the emotional barrage.

The bizarre happenings are related to Billy Palmer, a boy who lies comatose in the hospital after a brutal attack. The nightmares Billy's astral body has brought with him from his comatose state are enveloping reality. Buffy's worst nightmare—that she'll become one of the soulless creatures she's been chosen to destroy—comes true, but in a dramatic denouement, Giles figures out how to reverse the nightmares and restore reality.

The Real Horror: This prickly episode touches on our secret fears of public humiliation. Nightmares of standing naked in front of class, being on stage and not knowing your lines, getting lost in a familiar place, being chased by malevolent clowns, and becoming physically disabled or mentally incapacitated are common dream manifestations of universal anxieties. But concerns of ostracism are probably never as intense as during the unforgiving high school years when the smallest social misstep can become a permanent red-letter identity—as anyone nicknamed Stinky can attest.

Series creator Joss Whedon, who came up with the story idea for the "Nightmares" teleplay, accentuates the power of these fears by resurrecting them out of sleep and giving them flesh. To Whedon, true terror is found in the mundane, not the fantastic. While a vampire may give us the creeps, having a family member we thought we knew turn monstrous is far more frightening.

When Hank Summers tells Buffy that the family fell apart because she wasn't worth loving, Whedon tapped into the overriding fear harbored by most children of divorce. Having her nightmare of unworthiness and abandonment confirmed was more emotionally crippling to Buffy than climbing out of the grave as a vampire.

As Xander showed by cold-cocking the clown, the best way to keep our nightmares from dictating who we are and what we do is to recognize and confront them. But as the Master knew, fear is the strongest emotion and the one we're least able to control.

Bloopers: In the opening scene, when Buffy is talking about her parents' divorce, Willow turns her back to the camera and slides her backpack off her shoulder. Quick cut to Willow's face and the backpack is still on her shoulder.

It's a Mystery: At the hospital, after Buffy turns into a vampire, how is she able to stand in direct sunlight on not one but two occasions, and not so much as flinch, much less smolder?

Of Special Note: Take a close look when Willow opens her locker and you'll see a Nerf Herder bumper sticker on the inside of the door, an homage to the band that plays the show's theme song over the opening credits.

Dean Butler, who plays Buffy's dad, starred in *Little House on the Prairie* for five years as Almanzo Wilder, who marries Melissa Gilbert's character, Laura. Says Butler, "I am still regularly recognized anywhere I go."

10. "Invisible Girl" (May 19, 1997) 60 min.

Director: Reza Badiyi

Teleplay: Ashley Gable and Thomas A. Swyden

Story By: Joss Whedon

Recurring Cast: David Boreanaz (Angel); Armin Shimerman (Principal

Snyder)

Guest Cast: Ryan Bittle (Mitch); Denise Dowse (Ms. Miller); Clea DuVall (Marcie Ross); Julie Fulton (FBI Teacher); Mercedes McNab (Harmony); Mark Phelan (Agent Doyle); Skip Stellrecht (Agent Manetti)

Plot: After her boyfriend, best friend, and teacher are all attacked by an unseen assailant, Cordelia—who has just been voted May Queen—pleads with Buffy for help. The problem is, the assailant is a former classmate who is now invisible and bent on exacting revenge, with Cordelia her primary target.

This Week's Phenomenon: Invisibility. According to a basic tenet of quantum physics, reality can be shaped and created by our perceptions of the world and people around us. In the case of Marcie, the invisible girl, she literally faded away because she didn't exist in the eyes of others.

Introducing . . . : A kinder, gentler Cordelia. Sort of. When Cordelia realizes that she's the one who Marcie is after, she lets personal aesthetics go by the wayside and comes begging for Buffy's help, making it clear she does not have the ability or wherewithal to fight an invisible opponent. It's a new vulnerability for Cordelia, albeit laced with the same old self-serving pragmatism.

The first season's story arc involving the Master is pushed along by the appearance of the Codex, courtesy of Angel. The Codex is a book of prophecies concerning the Slayer that Giles had believed was lost. Its appearance sets the stage for the season finale, "Prophecy Girl."

Analysis: Once again, Buffy's good heart is emphasized by her inability to refuse Cordelia's plea for help. Even though she would really love to see Cordelia squirm, she can't. She is, after all, the Slayer.

It's also interesting to note that while Buffy often seems harried and at loose ends whenever she runs into Cordelia and her entourage in the hallways, Buffy is in her element in the library and all it represents. Her body language—languidly sitting back in the chair while listening to Cordelia—speaks volumes about Buffy's double life. Out in the scary, sociopolitical world of high school, she's just as insecure as anyone but in her Slayer's lair, she's confident and in command.

This episode marks the beginning of a change in Cordelia's relationship with Buffy and company. Cordelia's admission to Buffy that being the school's most popular girl isn't all it's cracked up to be is a surprising show of vulnerability. She also seems more willing to accept what she perceives as their social faux pas, as long as no one else in the school knows about it. Appearances are still everything to Cordelia, but she's beginning to show that there's something underneath her haughty exterior. Cordelia is not a bad person, nor is she stupid. She is simply a prisoner of her own inverted social standards.

Angel is also slowly becoming a more accepted presence. When he appears in the library to share his concern with Giles that something big is brewing with the Master, the Watcher immediately picks up on the fact that Angel is in love with the Slayer. Giles's response that the situation is poetic, "in a maudlin sort of way," shows both his sensitivity as well as his concern that such a pairing will probably only bring Buffy heartbreak.

Angel's role as guardian angel is further cemented when he turns up in the nick of time to save Giles, Xander, and Willow from being gassed by Marcie. Up until now, his interaction has largely been confined to Buffy; this episode shows that his concern extends to her friends as well.

The Real Horror: Unpopularity and exclusion. At some point or another in high school, nearly everyone feels left out of the loop, but for some students, it's a full-time position.

Some people cope by being sidekicks. These are the kids who gain acceptance and popularity by attaching themselves to a popular student—the way Harmony is joined at the hip to Cordelia—and the arrangement works for both parties. The otherwise out-of-the-loop student gets to bask in the reflected glory of Ms. or Mr. Popularity and takes on an almost subservient, we-aim-to-please personality. This is true especially among girls. For their part, the popular students like having a loyal coterie of "friends," none of whom are particularly threatening. Cordelia never has to worry about her boyfriend Mitch taking a shine to Harmony.

Other teens cope by mostly rejecting the social hierarchy as not worthy of their emotional time. This is the category that Willow and Xander fall into. They are aware they're not the most popular kids on campus and that they'll never be May Queen or captain of the football team, respectively. But they're pretty much at peace with their status—partly because they have each other and partly because they really don't take most of the kids on the A-list seriously.

In this episode, Marcie represents all the kids who somehow manage to pass through school nearly totally anonymous. Not only do their classmates exclude them, but teachers tend to overlook them as well. These kids aren't the nerds, who tend to hang with each other and thereby have their own clique. The Marcies of the world are teenagers who don't seem to fit in anywhere and spend most of their time completely alone. They are also the "quiet" ones who end up as snipers in clock towers, a fact Whedon has taken to another level with his apocryphal ending, which has Marcie, with other invisible kids, enrolled in a top-secret government assassins program.

Bloopers: Near the end of the episode, there's a quick shot of the front of the Bronze. The chalkboard on the right side of the screen clearly reads "Closed for Fumigation," meaning the shot is stock footage from the "Angel" episode, which made a major point of the club being exterminated for cockroaches.

In the scene where Buffy and Cordelia are being held captive, Buffy gets loose and manages to untie Cordelia's left hand before getting punched by Marcie. In the very next shot, the hand is still tightly tied to the chair.

Of Special Note: This episode was originally titled "Out of Mind, Out of Sight."

Denise Dowse, who plays the teacher, Ms. Miller, appeared for two years on *Beverly Hills, 90210* as Mrs. Teasley, the headmaster.

Clea DuVall, who plays Marcie, has had practice playing the supernatural. She costarred in *Little Witches*, a 1996 film about four girls at a Catholic boarding school who delve into the occult.

11. "Prophecy Girl" (June 2, 1997) 60 min.

Director: Joss Whedon

Teleplay: Joss Whedon

Recurring Cast: David Boreanaz (Angel); Andrew J. Ferchland (Collin/The Anointed One); Mark Metcalf (The Master); Robia La Morte (Jenny Calendar); Kristine Sutherland (Joyce Summers)

Guest Cast: Scott Gurney (Kevin)

Plot: The Codex, the book of Slayer prophecy given to Giles by Angel, foretells of a great battle between Buffy and the Master, which will result in her death and the opening of the Hellmouth. When Buffy finds out about her foretold death, she initially bolts, but eventually returns to face the Master and her destiny.

This Week's Prophecy: According to the Codex, the Slayer will face the Master and be defeated by him. Once freed, he will open the mouth of Hell and release an apocalypse of demons onto the Earth that will result in the annihilation of humankind.

Introducing . . . : Cordelia and Ms. Calendar's full initiation into the Slayer's inner circle, when they help fight the Master's minions and witness the opening of the Hellmouth.

Analysis: All the primary players go through a transition or a coming to terms with emotions as the first season's story arc ends. Xander has to come to grips with the reality that Buffy will never love him the way she loves Angel. After Buffy rejects Xander's romantic overtures, Willow provides a double whammy by refusing his suggestion the two of them go to the dance as buddies—making it clear that her feelings about him prevent her from being his platonic date.

Buffy's impending battle with the Master brings out Xander's mettle as a friend and once again emphasizes his dogged loyalty. Despite being romantically rejected by Buffy, Xander is still willing to risk his life to save her. So much so that he swallows his pride and enlists Angel's help. But it ends up being Xander, not Angel, who brings Buffy back from the dead by resuscitating her after she is drowned at the hands of the Master.

Cordelia and Jenny Calendar's presence when the Hellmouth opens after the Master is released, and Angel's decision to help Xander, are precursors to the increased involvement they will have with Buffy in the second season.

The Real Horror: Premature death. In fact, the concept is so unnatural that most people, much less teenagers, have a mental block when it comes to mortality. But dying in the prime of life just doesn't compute so it is rejected out of hand by most teens.

When Buffy is confronted with the knowledge that her life will end sooner rather than later, her reaction is to basically go through the famous steps laid out by "deathologist" Elisabeth Kübler-Ross. First, she denies her destiny. If she simply walks away from her role as the Chosen One, she can beat death. Then, she gets angry that she should have to sacrifice so much—she didn't ask to be the Slayer. Then she is overcome with sadness at all that she'll never experience, which is represented by the dress her mom surprises her with—the same dress she wears to go face the Master and her fate when she finally accepts her situation.

Buffy's stalwart march to possible Armageddon poignantly represents the overwhelming tragedy of someone facing death at a young age. Again, Whedon has taken a real life terror and disguised and remolded it as part of the series' mythology and within the context of entertainment—and very effective entertainment, at that.

It's a Mystery: How does Xander know where Angel lives, since it's never been revealed to the audience? When did Giles get his phone number and what last name does Angel give to the phone company?

Bloopers: When the Master pushes Buffy into the pool of water after biting her, she lands face down with her arms under her body. But when Xander and Angel show up, her arms are floating straight out from her body.

Of Special Note: This was the first episode of the series to be rated TV-14.

Joss Whedon says that even though he was confident the series would be picked up for a second season, he opted against a season-ending cliffhanger. "And I'll continue to do that every season because I hate loose ends. Like when *My So-Called Life* left me hanging just when Brian revealed he had written Jordan's letters for him."

What the Critics Say: "The clever season finale takes place on prom night, giving new meaning to the phrase 'high-school hell.' Buffy and company don't make it to the dance; they're too busy keeping the mouth of hell from spilling its contents into Sunnydale High. Bloodsucking brutes aside, the series' real delight is watching these appealing teens balance school, home, and the saving-the-world thing." —*TV Guide*

Nicholas Brendon plays it cool. © Albert Ortega/Flower Children Ltd.

Music: "I Fall to Pieces" (Xander lying on bed depressed) by Patsy Cline; "Inconsolable" (Buffy morbidly looking at the photo album) by Jonatha Brooke from the CD *Plumb.*

Season Two

Second Season Regular Cast
Sarah Michelle Gellar (Buffy Summers)
David Boreanaz (Angel)
Nicholas Brendon (Xander Harris)
Alyson Hannigan (Willow Rosenberg)
Charisma Carpenter (Cordelia Chase)
Anthony Stewart Head (Rupert Giles)

Female Empowerment

Buffy is the latest, and most striking, example of empowered young females that have begun to appear with greater frequency on television. Contemporary characters such as Agent Scully, Xena, Alex Mack, and Sabrina, the Teenage Witch represent a new trend; instead of being role models who are mostly bitches or doormats, these women are self-sufficient, self-aware, and intelligent protagonists who capably handle whatever life hands them.

This is not to say these are Super Woman caricatures. Empowerment doesn't mean perfection. It means being able to handle the situations fate and others throw their way, to rise to the occasion and to be a hero, whether by saving the world from annihilation or just getting through the day.

"I see Buffy as an empowered young woman handling an immense responsibility," says show creator Joss Whedon. "She's a hero in the strict sense, a leader. She may be as confused as anyone else, but she instinctively manages to do the right thing anyway."

Although the empowered young women of today owe a debt to the groundbreakers of the past, such as *The Avengers*' Emma Peel and *The Bionic Woman*'s Jaime Sommers, women in television—and society too, for that matter—have traditionally been defined by their relationships, not by their personal accomplishments.

"This is not to knock these shows, but when I was growing up I watched Mallory on *Family Ties* and Blair on *Facts of Life* worry about their dates and their boyfriends," comments Sarah Michelle Gellar. "There were no strong female characters and role models. Even Tracey Gold on *Growing Pains* always complained because she was a nerd—she wanted to be beautiful and popular.

"What we've done with Buffy is show strong female characters who are not the most popular in school—that's Cordelia. I'm not the most beautiful; that's Cordelia. I'm not the smartest; that's Willow. I'm not the funniest; that's Xander. I'm just me *and I like who I am.* And even though I make mistakes, I always come through."

For some characters, like Sabrina and Alex Mack, supernatural powers serve as an empowerment metaphor. But it's not just having otherworldly powers that empower them. Think back to *Bewitched*—although Samantha was capable of changing the world with a twitch of her nose, she was still superficially subservient to both Darrins, pretending to be the obedient wife while surreptitiously using her powers to get her husband out of scrapes. Forget that. What gives these current TV females their real power isn't magic but their unwillingness to defer—they know they are anybody's equal.

For others, such as Buffy and Xena, their strength comes primarily from their inner character and integrity, not the fact that they can handily kick most people's butts. They accept who they are and are comfortable with the knowledge that being feminine and being an empowered female are no longer mutually exclusive. They know that women can be smart and successful and capable—and secure enough to admit that, yes, they also still care about shoes and dates and looking pretty, too.

12. "When She Was Bad" (September 15, 1997) 60 min.

Director: Joss Whedon

Teleplay: Joss Whedon

Recurring Cast: Dean Butler (Hank Summers); Andrew J. Ferchland (Collin/The Anointed One); Robia La Morte (Jenny Calendar); Armin Shimerman (Principal Snyder); Kristine Sutherland (Joyce Summers)

Guest Cast: Tamara Braun (Tara); Brent Jennings (Absalom)

Plot: Buffy is back after spending the summer with her father in Los Angeles, but something is not quite right. She's bitchy and cruel and seems bent on driving everyone away. She almost succeeds when her behavior ultimately puts her friends' lives in danger.

This Week's Evil Plan: Resurrection. If the Anointed One can get back the bones and perform a ritual using the blood of the people who were present in the library at his death—Jenny, Giles, Willow, and Cordelia—then he will be able to revivify the Master.

Introducing . . . : A new season, new hairdos, and a new vampire population, including a preacher-type called Absalom. Gone are the Master's minions and in their place are the Anointed One's followers, who have come to Sunnydale to do his bidding. Also gone is the Anointed One's reverberating voice from season one.

Buffy returns to Sunnydale sporting a shorter, Jennifer Aniston-esque hairstyle and Xander has lost the bangs and gone for a shorter, more mature look.

A new school lounge. This season, Buffy and her friends relax in a bi-level campus lounge, complete with couches and a soda machine.

Analysis: Buffy may have physically survived her encounter with the Master but she hasn't gotten over it. Her uncharacteristically bitchy attitude is driving a wedge between her and the people she loves the most. It isn't until she's confronted with the cold reality that her actions have put her friends' lives in danger that she starts to snap out of her emotional straightjacket. She goes on a vampire-killing spree, which ends with her weeping on Angel's shoulder. The tears signal the return of the old Buffy, minus a big chunk of invincibility and Slayer innocence.

Buffy's not the only one who has changed over the summer. While her basic self-involvement remains the same, Cordelia's character has softened around the edges, making her more dimensional and less of a caricature. The question of whether Cordelia knows that Buffy is the Slayer is answered when she comes up to ask if she fought any demons over the summer.

Also for the first time, we see Buffy's parents together and hear their mutual concern for their daughter. It's revealing to see they both feel incapable of communicating with her, and powerless to help Buffy through whatever is troubling her.

The Real Horror: Realizing how much your best school friend has changed over summer vacation. Remember how on one hand it was great to see everyone again but on the other, there was that slightly awkward time of readjustment and reintroduction with the friend you hadn't seen all summer? In Buffy's case, there's more than just awkwardness at play—a major personality overhaul is apparent.

The distance between Buffy and her friends is an extreme example of classmates who grow apart over the course of a summer because they don't have the common denominator of school. But in her case, the time spent away from Sunnydale has exacerbated the unresolved issues brought about by her confrontation with the Master. For most teens, it's simply that without the forced bonding of school, many friendships drift apart.

Bloopers: When Buffy is in the car with her mother on the way to school, she is wearing a pink top. But in the next scene at school, she's wearing a white tank top. The pink top shows up again later, in what is supposed to be the next day.

Of Special Note: David Boreanaz is now a series regular. Brent Jennings, who plays the vampire preacher, has had some previous experience with creep kids, having costarred in the 1984 movie *Children of the Corn.*

Nicholas Brendon is more noticeably bulked up at the start of the second season. Part of the reason for so many new looks is that the original half season was filmed and completed toward the end of 1996 and the new episodes for the second season didn't begin shooting until the summer of 1997.

What the Critics Say: "This is a thoroughly entertaining season opener that has humor, wit, and style. The performances are stellar. Sarah Michelle Gellar is wonderful in the lead, displaying the full 12–to–20 range of adolescent angst. All of the regular players . . . are well-cast and believable in their roles." —*Hollywood Reporter*

Music: "It Doesn't Matter" (during the drive to school) by Alison Krauss and Union Station, from their *So Long So Wrong* CD; "Spoon" (as Buffy first enters the Bronze) by Cibo Matto from *Super Relax* CD, and "Super Relax" (the dance) by Cibo Matto from *Viva! La Woman* CD.

13. "Some Assembly Required"
(September 22, 1997) 60 min.

Director: Bruce Seth Green

Teleplay: Ty King

Recurring Cast: Robia La Morte (Jenny Calendar)

Guest Cast: Michael Bacall (Chris); Melanie MacQueen (Mrs. Epps); Ingo Neuhaus (Daryl); Angelo Spizzirri (Eric); Amanda Wilmshurst (Cheerleader)

Plot: The bodies of three high school girls are dug up from their graves by two would-be Dr. Frankensteins. But their creation is more than a science experiment, it's a literal labor of love.

This Week's Monster: A quite literally born-again high school jock and his ghoulish brother. After getting killed in a rock climbing accident, Daryl Epps is brought back to life by his genius brother, Chris, but after a couple of years, Daryl's libido has gone berserk for female companionship.

Introducing . . . : Giles and Jenny Calendar's budding romance. The flirtation finally graduates into a real date, take-out followed by a night out at the Sunnydale High football game.

Angel's jealousy over Buffy's friendship with Xander. Buffy admits to Angel that her erotic dance with Xander was simply a ploy to make him jealous. But Angel won't own up to his feelings.

Analysis: Although the story line about Daryl and his would-be Frankenstein bride had some unexplained gaps and requires a greater suspension of disbelief than usual, it serves as a conduit for the cementing of Buffy's relationship with Angel and Giles's attraction for Jenny Calendar. It also brings Cordelia one step closer into the inner Slayer sanctum.

After Buffy's emotional catharsis in the previous episode, things between her, Willow, and Xander appear to be back on an even keel, although they are still adjusting to the new dynamic brought about by Xander's revelation of his feelings for Buffy in the first season finale, "Prophecy Girl."

This season, Giles is seen outside the context of just being a Watcher and surrogate parent. His attraction to Ms. Calendar forces Giles out of the library and into the world, which he finds almost as frightening as the monsters Buffy fights—and a lot less familiar. Whatever his relationship with Jenny turns out to be, when living at the Hellmouth, it's a pretty safe bet that no romance will be without a certain element of horror. Not the least of which for Giles is attending a high school football game as a first date.

If Giles acts as a father figure for Buffy, then he's Willow and Xander's favorite uncle. Whether intentional or not, it's an interesting commentary on the rootlessness of teenagers today that neither Willow nor Xander ever seem to have any family commitments to attend. And they seem freer to come and go than Buffy, who often has to sneak out her window to go patrolling for vampires. Buffy's mom is a single parent trying to run a new business. But both Willow and Xander's parents are still married, and yet seem to have even less interaction with them than Buffy's mom does with her.

The Real Horror: Losing a family member to death. While in Sunnydale, death is sometimes just the beginning, in the real world, death is permanent. It leaves in its wake guilt, depression, fear, and loss. As supposedly the only animal aware of its mortality, man must somehow confront on a daily basis the knowledge that he and everyone he loves will someday die. Considering the powerful emotions caused by the death of a loved one, it's easy to see why the Frankenstein story has remained so compelling, pertinent, and timeless. Being able to overcome death, whether through magic, religion, or science, reflects a primal human desire.

It's a Mystery: If the surface of the main story line about human reanimation is scratched ever so slightly, it exposes more glaring plot loopholes in this episode than any other. First of all, when and how exactly did Chris manage to steal the body of his brother? If, as Willow points out, formaldehyde destroys the brain tissue, Chris would have had to steal the body before it was preserved. And nobody noticed the body was missing?

Chris is such a genius that he's figured out the secret of reanimating human tissue, but so humble that he's decided to keep it a secret, so his brother can go insane from loneliness and his mother emotionally wither over the believed death of her eldest son? And Daryl is so concerned with a few facial scars that he prefers to live in a basement? Has he never heard of plastic surgery and intensive therapy?

Bloopers: The pictures that Eric took of Buffy, Willow, and Cordelia could not have been the same photos he took earlier at school because none of the poses match what was seen on screen.

Of Special Note: Although Sarah Michelle Gellar does do quite a bit of her own fighting, she still has a stunt double, Sophia Crawford, who performs the more acrobatic moves. If you're curious to see what Sophia looks like minus the Buffy wig, check her out as Katya Steadman in the "Dragonswing II" episode of *Kung Fu: The Legend Continues.*

Anthony Stewart Head now provides the narration for the series prologue, which also has a new score.

14. "School Hard" (September 29, 1997) 60 min.

Director: John T. Kretchmer

Teleplay: David Greenwalt

Story by: Joss Whedon and David Greenwalt

Recurring Cast: Andrew J. Ferchland (Collin/The Anointed One); James Marsters (Spike); Robia La Morte (Jenny Calendar); Juliet Landau (Drusilla); Armin Shimerman (Principal Snyder); Kristine Sutherland (Joyce)

Guest Cast: Alan Abelew (Brian Kerch); Alexandra Johnes (Sheila)

Plot: Not only does Buffy have to organize Parent-Teacher night under the critical eye of Principal Snyder, she also has to contend with a new vampire in town, who is planning to make the Night of St. Vigius the Slayer's last.

This Week's Unholy Holiday: The Night of St. Vigius, in honor of a crusading vampire who slaughtered his way across Eastern Europe and into Asia. On that night, the vampires' strength will be at their greatest and they plan to flex their momentary muscle by killing the Slayer.

Introducing . . . : Vampires, a Love Story, starring Buffy's new nemeses Spike and Drusilla. He was known as William the Bloody but earned his current nickname because of his penchant for torturing victims with railroad spikes. She seems to be emotionally challenged and totally dependent on Spike. Relocating to Sunnydale from their previous home in Prague, Spike is hoping the mystical energy of the Hellmouth will act as a curative and restore Drusilla's fragile health. Together they bring a sort of Gothic punk quality to the show.

Analysis: This episode sets up a new series arc with the introduction of Spike and Drusilla. Although he may not be as powerful as the Master, in some ways Spike seems more dangerous because he's not as bound by tradition as the Master was. An unpredictable vampire offers a whole new set of potential risks for Buffy, which is ominously confirmed by Angel. Spike refers to Angel as his sire and mentor, obviously setting the stage for more revelations in later episodes.

When Spike and his horde of vampires crash Parent-Teacher night, the ensuing showdown between Buffy and Principal Snyder is powerful and revealing. Buffy is no longer the nervous student trying to appease the disapproving principal. She's his equal and then some. It's an eye-opener for Buffy's mom who, like most parents, tend to see their children in the context of the family dynamic, not as how they relate as individuals to others out in the world.

Finally, the question of just who Principal Snyder is becomes even more mysterious when it's revealed that he knows the attack was by vampires (and not PCP-addled gang members as he told the parents), but conspires with the police detective to cover up the truth. Again.

The Real Horror: Parent-teacher night. It was always just a little unnerving having your parents meet face to face with teachers who weren't terribly enamored with you. There's nothing like getting the parental wait-until-we-get-home glare, which is usually accompanied by immediate nausea and headache. Part of the uneasiness of parent-teacher conferences is that it's the collision of two worlds teenagers instinctively tend to keep separate, just as many adults tend not to completely share their life at work with their spouse at home.

Bloopers: When Buffy takes a break to go dance, she leaves her notebook open on the table where she and Willow were studying. But when Xander returns to get Buffy a stake, the books are gone and only her bag remains.

After a vampire announces to Spike that they've cut off the power, the trophy case behind him is still quite visibly lit.

Of Special Note: Mrs. Summers name, Joyce, is spoken for the first time. Principal Snyder's first name is also mentioned for the first time, when the detective at the end calls him Bob.

Joss Whedon said the decision to fry the "Annoying One" was made because a person is supposed to stop aging when they become a vampire and Andrew Ferchland was getting noticeably older and bigger.

Throughout the first season, Buffy burning down her previous school's gym was repeatedly mentioned. But in this episode, when talking to biker-girl Sheila, Buffy indicates she has actually burned down more than one building.

Music: "1000 Nights" (Willow and Buffy doing homework) and "Stupid Thing" (Spike watching Buffy at the Bronze) by Nickel, on the *Stupid Thing* CD.

David Boreanaz gives *Buffy* its bite. © Sue Schneider/Flower Children Ltd.

15. "Inca Mummy" (October 6, 1997) 60 min.

Director: Ellen Pressman

Teleplay: Matt Kiene and Joe Reinkmeyer

Recurring Cast: Seth Green (Oz); Jason Hall (Devon); Kristine Sutherland (Joyce)

Guest Cast: Gil Birmingham (Inca Guard); Ara Celi (Inca Princess); Joey Crawford (Rodney); Samuel Jacobs (the real Ampata); Henrik Rosvall

(Sven); Danny Strong (Jonathan); Kristen Winnicki (Gwen)

Plot: A mystical seal is broken enabling a five-hundred-year-old mummified Inca Princess to come to life as a beautiful sixteen-year-old. The only catch is that to stay alive she has to literally suck the life out of others. Xander falls for her, unaware of her deadly secret.

This Week's Threat: An Inca Princess bent on reliving her lost youth. Sacrificed to a mountain god when she was just sixteen, the princess has been entrapped in her mummified form by a holy seal. Once freed, she intends on making up for lost time, even if it means killing innocent people to keep herself from reverting to mummy form.

Introducing . . . : Oz, Sunnydale high school student by day, guitarist in a band at night. Unlike most of the boys in school, he seems singularly unimpressed with Cordelia but becomes instantly smitten with Willow when he sees her dressed as an Aleut at the Bronze's cultural diversity dance.

Analysis: Other than pouting because she has to try and find a murderous mummy instead of going to a dance, Buffy seems more like herself than she has in the previous second season episodes, although she's still prone to sudden ebbs of mortality-related brooding and self-pity.

As is readily obvious, more emphasis is being placed on the characters' romantic lives, or lack thereof, this season, meaning more teenage angst is on display than was in the first season. Not only is the group having to come to terms with the ramifications of Buffy's almost-death, they are also coping with changing interpersonal dynamics caused by the tangled romantic webs they're weaving.

Although Xander is clearly still in love with Buffy, he's also open to looking for love elsewhere. So when Ampata returns his interest, he's thrilled. She'll never be Buffy, but she could be his.

Unlike his lustful crush on Ms. French, the preying mantis of episode # 3, his feelings for Ampata are more romantic and soulful, which makes the revelation that she's really a murderous five-hundred-year-old Inca Princess, and his resulting loss, that much more tragic.

The Real Horror: Having chronically rotten taste in the opposite sex. Xander's recurring tendency to fall for the wrong girl continues with a flourish but his plight is nothing new. Like a lot of teenagers—and adults, for that matter—he can't have the girl he really wants and doesn't want the girl he could have, so he ends up with someone he shouldn't. He's so anxious to find *someone* that he rushes in without knowing who the person really is. Of course, in the world of the Slayer, this is not only a waste of time and emotionally frustrating, it could be fatal as well. Once again, Whedon is heightening reality to a horrific level.

Ironically, it was often the student in high school who seemed to have the most going for them that seemed to always be dating someone who—as was obvious to everybody but them—would eventually prove to be a disaster. Then after the inevitable break-up, the person with the rotten taste in romantic partners would feel foolish and depressed—until the next time. Unfortunately, teenagers who consistently pick the wrong love interest grow into adults who continue the legacy with more lasting, and destructive, results.

It's a Mystery: Other than the ones she stole off the real Ampata's body, where did the fake Ampata get her clothes? And how do they explain to Ampata's family in Peru and the local authorities that she's dead and laying in a trunk in Buffy's room?

Bloopers: When the mummy's guard attacks Xander and the fake Ampata on the bleachers, her bag is kicked away during the struggle. But when she stands up to run, it's back right in front of her.

Right before killing the mummy's guard, *faux* Ampata was standing at the mirror in the bathroom putting on lipstick but later that same night, she tells Buffy she has no lipstick.

The first time Buffy opens the trunk, the real Ampata's mummified head is laying on Buffy's right side. When she opens it the second time with Giles, it's on her left side.

Finally, Ampata sneaks up on Giles and grabs the seal before he's had a chance to glue the last piece of the seal back. But in the next shot, as she raises the seal and throws it to the ground, it's quite clearly in one whole piece.

Of Special Note: Seth Green, who plays the new recurring character Oz, has been acting since he was ten years old. His most recent television role was as Harry Byrd on the short-lived ABC series *Byrds of Paradise*, which just happened to costar Jennifer Love Hewitt, who just happened to costar with Sarah Michelle Gellar in *I Know What You Did Last Summer*. Talk about six degrees. By the way, Seth Green is not related to *Buffy* director Bruce Seth Green.

The band that Oz and Devon belong to, Dingoes Ate My Baby, is mercifully fictional. The music they play is actually from the group Four Star Mary.

Xander apparently got his license over the summer because for the first time, he offers to drive the gang to the Bronze.

16. "Reptile Boy" (October 13, 1997) 60 min.

Director: David Greenwalt

Teleplay: David Greenwalt

Guest Cast: Todd Babcock (Tom); Greg Vaughan (Richard); Jordana Spiro (Callie)

Plot: Angry that Giles has become a relentless task-master and hurt over Angel's reluctance to give into his feelings for her, Buffy rebels by going with Cordelia to a fraternity party. But her attempt at retaliation backfires when she and Cordelia are drugged so they can be sacrificed to a reptile-like demon.

This Week's Ritual: For fifty years, a demon-worshipping fraternity annually sacrifices three girls on the tenth day of the tenth month to a lizard-skinned creature in exchange for power, wealth, and professional success.

Introducing . . . : "Cordy." In the first season, Cordelia was only referred to as Cordelia, but in the second season she has picked up the diminutive Cordy, which serves two purposes. The first is to make her character more familiar and the other is to show her acceptance by and for Buffy and the gang. Although she is still fighting it, she now shares a bond with them and in her own way has come to recognize their value as people, and if not exactly friends, then at least partners in horror.

Analysis: In the past Buffy has pouted, she's been snappish and moody and whiny about having to go trolling for vampires instead of going out with her friends, but she has never pulled a bona fide teenage rebellion before. Her insubordination provides the catalyst for growth in her relationship with Giles. The scene in which Buffy admits her deception to Giles emphasizes how their relationship has taken on a parent-child aspect—her unhappiness at disappointing him and his admission that he pushes her because, in essence, she's so important to him and he dreads the thought of something happening to her.

In the moving conclusion, Giles protectively holds Buffy's arm as they walk up the stairs from the frat house dungeon/basement—one of the first times they've made any sustained physical contact that wasn't fight-related.

"Reptile Boy" also unveils some evolvement regarding Angel's character. When Angel joins forces with Giles, Willow, and Xander to save Buffy, his full acceptance by the others is confirmed. But he's still keeping his emotional distance from Buffy, much to her frustration. When she finally confronts him about it, he tells her he's afraid to lose control. Her line about wanting to die when he kisses her can be interpreted to mean 1) she wants to die from ecstasy; 2) she wants to die from sadness knowing they can't ever be together; 3) she wants to literally die and join him as his eternal mate; or 4) a combination of all of the above. Whatever the correct answer, the bottom line is, she's got it bad and that ain't good.

The Real Horror: Getting caught in a *really* big lie. There are few things more mortifying than having a carefully crafted lie blow up in your face. There is nowhere to hide and anything you say just makes matters worse because it is indefensible. Most teenagers lie to go somewhere, see someone, or do something they know they shouldn't because it's either dangerous or has been—or would be—forbidden. So when caught, the crime isn't just the lie but the irresponsibility of putting themselves in an unwarranted situation.

Naturally, when Buffy lies, the consequences are a little more horrific than being grounded or having driving privileges taken away—she ends up chained to a wall, about to become a human canapé for a scaly green demon. But the underlying truths are still the same—the greater the consequences of the lie, the greater the chance you'll get found out.

Of Special Note: Greg Vaughan, who played creepy frat boy Richard, was Charisma Carpenter's romantic interest on the series *Malibu Shores*.

Music: "Bring Me On" by Act of Faith; "She" by Louie Says.

17. "Halloween" (October 28, 1997) 60 min.

Director: Bruce Seth Green
Teleplay: Carl Ellsworth

Recurring Cast: Seth Green (Oz); Juliet Landau (Drusilla); James Marsters (Spike)

Guest Cast: Robin Sachs (Ethan Rayne)

Plot: Halloween takes a terrifying new twist when make-believe becomes reality. This is particularly bad news for Buffy, who is suddenly a defenseless eighteenth-century noblewoman—an opportunity not lost on Spike, who sets out to kill the powerless, not to mention clueless, Slayer.

This Week's Spell: A black magic incantation made to the spirit of Janus turns everyone into the real-life incarnation of their Halloween costume. Janus is the two-faced Roman deity that represents opposites such as good and evil.

Introducing . . . : Ethan Raynes, a shopkeeper who shares a mysterious connection to Giles that dates back to his pre-Sunnydale days.

Analysis: While many TV series' holiday-themed episodes are contrived and anomalous from the overall series, this episode inventively incorporates a holiday into a story line that actually maintains the character and context of the series. When Ethan casts a spell through the two-faced deity, Janus, he's releasing the inner fantasies of those who bought costumes in his shop. Xander, who feels emasculated after Buffy saves him from being punched out by a bully, dresses up as a commando. Buffy, on the other hand, dreams of being someone whose biggest worries are cosmetic and not supernatural, so she pretends to be a noblewoman from the 1700s.

Buffy's tendency to use brute force over diplomacy is highlighted when she smashes the brute bullying Xander into the soda machine. Unlike another empowered TV female, Xena, Buffy tends not to be conflicted about the use of force. In fact, it's become second nature to her, which is good when patrolling for vampires in the dead of night but not always appropriate for all daytime social situations.

The biggest surprise of the episode comes courtesy of the B-story line, when Giles confronts Ethan and it's revealed that they know each other from the past. The final shot of Giles in the now-empty costume shop, reading a note left by Ethan that indicates he'll be back, is the precursor for the future revelation about Giles's past.

The Real Horror: Getting what you wish for. It's better to play the hand you're dealt because granted wishes usually come with unexpected consequences. Beyond that, it's depressing to discover that living out a situation we've fantasized about for a long time seldom lives up to our expectations. For a pop cultural example of this phenomenon, rent the Bo Derek-Dudley Moore movie *10*.

For Buffy, the irony is that her wish—to be a seventeenth-century girl whose sole job was to be dainty and pretty—actually turns out to be a turn-off for Angel, because that's exactly the kind of girl he *isn't* attracted to. And an additional Hellmouth consequence is that it almost caused her to end up as Spike's treat.

Bloopers: I realize this is really picky but . . . when they are reading the Watcher's diary, Willow mentions that the excerpt is from when Angel is eighteen years old. Since we know he is now 241, that means he was born in 1756. So he would be eighteen in 1774. However, when she becomes the noblewoman, Buffy says the year is 1775. Since one must assume that in her fantasy she was the noblewoman from the diary, she's off by a year. But who's counting?

When Buffy smacks the soda machine, she hits the "Dr. Pepper" button. But a *diet* Dr. Pepper comes out.

When Spike is watching the videotape of Buffy fighting, he asks for the segment to be rewound. But the shot seen after the rewind is actually the end of the fight when Buffy stakes the vamp with a wooden sign, meaning the tape was actually fast forwarded.

If vampires can only enter a home when invited, why was the vampire able to sneak into Buffy's house through the kitchen door?

Of Special Note: Robin Sachs, who plays the up-to-no-good Ethan, is known to *Babylon 5* fans for two separate roles—Hedron and Na'Kal. And who can forget his performance in the movie *Vampire Circus*?

This episode sets the stage for a future romantic liaison between Cordelia and Xander. Creator Whedon admits that the idea of pairing Xander and Cordy as a Sunnydale odd couple had been originally intended for this episode, but since the potential plot twist was leaked in *TV Guide*, it was delayed.

Slayer Mythology

In 1845, Boston shipyards were plagued by a series of grisly murders. The attacks ended when a quiet young woman arrived in town...

In 1893, in the Oakland Territory, a series of savage attacks claimed the lives of seventeen homesteaders. The murders stopped when a young woman blacksmith passed through town...

The year is now 1997, and Sunnydale, California, is on the brink of ruin. Can another girl come to the rescue?

As developed by Joss Whedon, the television Slayer is a sort of an all-purpose demon hunter. Since there have always been demons throughout history, there has always been a Slayer, a girl born with the necessary strength and skills to find and kill vampires.

Although vampires are her primary focus, Buffy must also fight all the other evil elements that are continually drawn to Sunnydale because of the Hellmouth's mystical energy.

When one Slayer dies, she's replaced by the next Chosen One, who is trained for her duties by a mentor called the Watcher. There's even a Slayer's Handbook. However, in Buffy's case, Giles realized the manual would be of little use with someone as individualistic and strong-willed as she is.

A Watcher's main job is to help the Slayer identify the evil she's facing, keep her focused on the task at hand, and keep her alive as long as possible.

Music: "Shy" by Epperley; "How She Died" by Treble Charger.

18. "Lie to Me" (November 3, 1997) 60 min.

Director: Joss Whedon

Teleplay: Joss Whedon

Recurring Cast: Robia La Morte (Jenny Calendar); Juliet Landau (Drusilla); James Marsters (Spike)

Guest Cast: Jason Behr (Billy "Ford" Fordham); Julia Lee (Chantarella); Jarrad Paul (Marvin); Will Rothhaar (James)

Plot: A one-time classmate—and former object of Buffy's prepubescent fifth grade desire—shows up unexpectedly in Sunnydale. But it turns out his visit is neither social nor neighborly. Instead, he's in town to trade Buffy's life for vampire immortality.

This Week's Antagonist: The past. Buffy lets her affection for an old school crush blind her to his sinister motives. And one of Angel's cruelest deeds comes back to haunt him—and put Buffy at risk.

Introducing . . . : The darkest side of Angel's dark days as a vampire. It turns out that Angel isn't only personally acquainted with Spike, but he also has a history with the childlike Drusilla. Well, childlike if it's the child from *The Bad Seed*.

Analysis: Everybody seems to be having some trust issues in this episode. When Billy "Ford" Fordham shows up unexpectedly in Sunnydale, Xander finds someone else to be threatened by while Angel instinctively doesn't trust him. But Buffy is too busy catching up with her old friend Ford, and using him to make Angel jealous, to notice that something isn't quite right.

When Buffy discovers Ford's murderous motives, her moral indignation is briefly tempered by his reason for doing it—rather than die an excruciating death from brain cancer, he will sell his soul, and stay alive. Ford's admission brings her up short. Up until the moment he tells her he's dying, she had gone around killing vampires without a moment of internal conflict. They were bad and needed to die. Simple. But Ford was no demon, at least not yet. He was scared and angry and desperate. Not too dissimilar from Buffy when she thought she was going to die at the hands of the Master. Even though she's right that we always have a choice, sometimes both options suck.

The final scene between Buffy and Giles, where he tells her life only ever gets more complicated and less uncertain, establishes that the Watcher is now as much a confidant as he is Slayer coach. He's the one adult she can turn to for guidance, a role her parents simply can't fulfill. Giles and Buffy are now officially family, with all the plusses and minuses that entails.

The Real Horror: Discovery of the gray zone. To most young children, the world seems a very simple place. There are good guys and bad guy, and telling them apart is as obvious as the black or white hat they wear. Our parents will be around forever, we'll always be best friends with our best friends, and whatever lofty dreams we have for the future will somehow come true.

At some point, we are all introduced to the reality that most of life plays itself out in shades of gray and not definites, and that situations don't always have a happy ending. Children who grow up in poverty or deteriorating inner cities tend to lose their innocence at such a tender age that permanent hopelessness settles into the gaping void left by the premature disillusionment. But for the others, the jolting realization that life is a lot more complex and ambiguous than previously thought usually occurs during the teen years.

Teenagers tend to think that once they're adults, most of the troubles they face will automatically be solved. And for the most part, they are. The law says you can drive, drink, smoke, have sex, stay out all night, wear what you want, eat what you want—all without parental permission.

But what never seems to be explained, or perhaps understood, is that passing out of childhood into young adulthood then full-fledged adulthood simply means exchanging one set of problems and obstacles for another. And the adult version is a lot harder game to play. While there's nobody telling us what to do, there's also nobody to really fall back on. We're stuck with the consequences of our choices, which are made all the harder because the more life we experience, the more we realize that right and wrong, moral certitude and ambivalence, honesty and deceit, love and infidelity, good and evil, can coexist and often do—it all comes down to a matter of degree.

Charting our individual moral ground, and establishing our requirements of others, is part of life. But the disturbing part is knowing that no choice comes with a guarantee that what we're doing is the absolute right thing.

Bloopers: When Buffy is fighting the vampire in the alley, the length of her hair changes noticeably from one shot to the next. One assumes the stunt double was still wearing a wig that matched Sarah's first season hair length, not her shorter second season 'do.

Perhaps this isn't exactly a blooper, but it wasn't fine film-making, either. While it's a given that Buffy possesses supranatural physical agility and strength, she's never been able to defy gravity before so noticeably. In the Sunset Club, as the vampires are beginning their feast, Buffy jumps from the ground floor to the balcony like a chop-socky Michael Jordan. The feat is so implausible and the wire work so obvious that it detracts from the drama of the moment.

Of Special Note: Juliet Landau, who plays Drusilla, is the daughter of Oscar-winning actor Martin Landau, who's probably still best known for his work in *Mission: Impossible*.

The actor portraying Dracula in the movie playing at the Sunset Club is Jack Palance, who'd go on to win an Oscar for *City Slickers*—and Academy Award infamy for his acceptance speech, which included one-handed push-ups as a visual aid.

19. "The Dark Age" (November 10, 1997) 60 min.

Director: Bruce Seth Green

Teleplay: Dean Batali and Rob Des Hotel

Recurring Cast: Robia La Morte (Jenny Calendar)

Guest Cast: Carlease Burke (Detective Winslow); Stuart McLean (Philip Henry); Robin Sachs (Ethan Raynes); Wendy Way (Dierdre)

Plot: As a rebellious youth in London, Giles and a group of friends dabbled in black magic. Now their old demon playmate is in Sunnydale looking to kill the last two survivors of the group— and using Ms. Calendar's body to do it.

This Week's Demon: Eyghon. A demon of Etruscan origin, this walking evil is also called the sleepwalker because it can only exist on Earth by possessing someone who is unconscious or dead.

Introducing . . . : Giles's demons, both inner and outer.

Analysis: Up to now, the only inner demons Buffy has fought have been her own. But in order to defeat Eyghon, she also has to battle Giles's guilt and self-recrimination over bringing the demon into the Earth's realm through his experimentation with black magic twenty years earlier.

Their conversation at the end brings a momentary role reversal, with Buffy being Giles's confidant and offering understanding solace while Giles bares his soul and acknowledges his regret over not being able to live up to Buffy's expectations. Of all the consequences of his youthful stupidity—his friends' deaths, Ms. Calendar being possessed by a pointy-eared demon, and the com-

Alyson Hannigan gets gnarly at a *Buffy* convention. © Sue Schneider/Flower Children Ltd.

plete trashing of his apartment—the thing that seems to weigh on him most heavily is the sense of letting Buffy down, both in a Watcher sense and a parental sense.

Buffy, however, has learned a few lessons of her own. She hasn't always made the best choices or been the standard-bearer of model behavior, and in the process, has put those closest to her at mortal risk. But just as Xander and Willow forgave her at the end of "When She Was Bad," tacitly letting her know that real friends allow room for error, Buffy reassures Giles that the lowering of his pedestal a notch has actually strengthened their bond and made her feel that much closer to him.

The Real Horror: Realizing adults don't have a clue, either. When you're little, the adults you hold in the greatest esteem seem to have all the answers. And if there's something they don't know, like how a caterpillar turns into a butterfly, they go look the answer up in a book.

Then comes the inevitable moment when you find out that they've done some pretty stupid things in their life and that if they don't have the answers for themselves, they're certainly not going to have them for you. And these are the people running the world.

Buffy's momentary disillusionment with Giles, his shame over what he's done, and his remorse over the sense that he's been lessened in Buffy's eyes, is a scenario that plays out in real life on a daily basis. The ramifications of such a fall from grace can range from mild recrimination to permanent rifts. But usually, people accept such revelations first with disappointment, followed by a period of awkwardness then finally reluctant acceptance of the fact that even those we look up to the most can be just as unsure and imperfect as we are.

Bloopers: It's amazing that Cordelia was able to tell the others that the police were talking to Giles about a homicide since that fact was never mentioned in Cordelia's presence. She entered the library after Detective Winslow told Giles about the death.

When Giles answers the door of his apartment, his watch reads 11:55. But when he sends Buffy away, he immediately gets on the phone to London and comments that it's 5:00 A.M. there. When he gets off the phone and sits down to take a drink, his watch is visible again, and reads what looks to be 12:05. Apparently, they didn't think to change the real time on Anthony Head's watch.

Of Special Note: Carlease Burke, who appears as Detective Winslow, has made a career out of playing law enforcement characters, upholding the peace in *Ghost in the Machine*, *Betty Broderick: The Last Chapter*, *Death Warrant*, *Woman with the Past*, and *Freddy's Dead: The Final Nightmare*.

We now know that Giles is forty-one. He has said several times he's known Ethan for twenty years and he told the police he knew the dead guy twenty years ago. When confessing his past to Buffy, he told her he was twenty-one when he encountered Eyghon.

20. "What's My Line?" Part 1
(November 17, 1997) 60 min.

Director: David Solomon

Teleplay: Howard Gordon and Marti Noxon

Recurring Cast: Seth Green (Oz); Juliet Landau (Drusilla); James Marsters (Spike); Armin Shimerman (Principal Snyder)

Guest Cast: Kelly Connell (Norman Pfister); Saverio Guerra (Willy); Bianca Lawson (Kendra); Eric Saiet (Dalton)

Plot: Tired of Buffy's meddling, Spike commands a sect of bounty hunters to kill her once and for all. But in addition to the Slayer hitmen, there's also a new girl in town, who claims that she, too, is a Slayer.

This Week's Evil Clan: Three members of the Order of Taraka, a group of human and non-human bounty hunters who continue to send members until their quarry is dead. Apparently these killers are so fearsome, even vampires dread them.

Introducing . . . : Kendra, the *other* Vampire Slayer. Did the prophecy give birth to twin Slayers, or is Kendra not who she claims to be?

Oz finally gets introduced to his mystery girl in the waiting room of the world's leading software company, which is recruiting at Sunnydale High as part of Career Week.

Analysis: For the most part, Buffy's angst over her lot in life, and the occasional brooding or self-pitying anger it ignites, has fit in the given context in which it was displayed. However, in this episode, it seems as if the petulance is being forced, which results in Buffy coming across as if she is in the throes of a particularly bad case of PMS. Her sudden testiness at Giles in the library smacked of an Alanis Morisette-esque display of inappropriate surliness. Moody and broody is more in keeping with Buffy's character as developed than bitchiness is, which is exactly why her 'tude in "When She Was Bad" was so effective.

Using the plot point of the school's Career Week as the reason for her churlish behavior seems incongruous, especially because when we last saw Buffy and Giles together, she was comforting him over his Eyghon experience. The unevenness of the characterization seems more related to the direction than the actual written dialogue.

This episode features a Kodak *Beauty and the Beast* moment for star-crossed

Demonic Possession

Someone like Jenny Calendar, whose personality and body have been taken over by a demon, is said to be possessed. Although most people still associate possession with projectile pea-soup vomit and scary children with bad skin who can rotate their heads (thank you, Linda Blair), there are other, more accepted signs of demonic possession.

In the Middle Ages, anyone displaying unusual behavior or a strange personality was automatically suspected of being possessed by the Devil. This is why so many old, ugly, or poor people were accused of being possessed.

The Catholic Church still defines true signs of possession as someone displaying superhuman strength, often accompanied by fits and convulsions; changes in personality; having knowledge of the future or other secret information; and being able to converse in languages not previously known to them.

Included in the list of other signs or symptoms for declaring demonic possession are: sexual thoughts and changes in the voice to a deep, rasping, menacing, guttural croak—which made Ms. Calendar a textbook case—and, most importantly, a violent revulsion toward sacred objects and texts.

lovers Buffy and Angel. After he is injured helping stave off the first bounty hunter, Angel tells Buffy he's uncomfortable having her touch him when he's "that way." That is, with his demon face accessory, which she says she didn't even notice, leading to a passionate Slayer-Vampire kissfest.

Watching this intimate moment is a mystery girl, who later announces she's Kendra the Vampire Slayer, setting the stage for Buffy to have a full-blown identity crisis.

The Real Horror: Realizing you're not just being paranoid—everybody really *is* out to get you. In Slayerdom, that means bounty hunters and terminal consequences, but in the heightened reality that is high school, with its insular social community, the effect can sometimes feel just as deadly. Like that numbing moment when you realize a former friend is spreading vicious stories about you, or when you fall out of favor with a certain clique and become the object of their contempt.

Adults can also readily empathize with Buffy's feelings of isolation and persecution. Ex-spouses sometimes discover that once the marriage is over, people they thought were friends have taken sides in the break-up and turned against them. And in the backstabbing corporate world, employees who steal credit for others' work in hopes of leapfrogging past them on the promotion ladder are as plentiful as members of Sunnydale's vampire community.

While the problem sometimes resolves itself, more often than not it requires confrontation, which is an entirely different horror.

It's a Mystery: How did Kendra know where Angel lives? And how come Willow was able to stay out all night, if her parents are so strict that she's not even allowed to have male friends in her bedroom?

Bloopers: When the door of the bus carrying one of the bounty hunters opens, the camera zooms in on the steps, which are initially white but then suddenly turn maroon as the bounty hunter's foot comes into frame.

Of Special Note: Bianca Lawson, who plays Kendra, has costarred on two series, the Sherman Hemsley sitcom *Goode Behavior*, and *Saved by the Bell: The New Class*—in other words, the one after Elizabeth Berkeley graduated to Hollywood infamy in *Showgirls*.

Episode director David Solomon, a co-producer in the first season, was promoted to executive co-producer in the second season.

21. "What's My Line?" Part 2
(November 24, 1997) 60 min.

Director: David Semel

Teleplay: Marti Noxon

Recurring Cast: Seth Green (Oz); Juliet Landau (Drusilla); James Marsters (Spike)

Guest Cast: Kelly Connell (Norman Pfister) Saverio Guerra (Willy); Bianca Lawson (Kendra); Danny Strong (Student Hostage)

Plot: Buffy must save herself from the Order of Taraka assassins, and Angel from Spike, who is planning to kill him during a ceremony that will give Drusilla back her strength. Complicating matters is the second Slayer, who goes strictly by the rules, which includes killing vampires, not saving—or dating—them.

This Week's Evil Ceremony: An ailing vampire can be restored to health by performing the ritual the night of the first moon that requires killing the sick vamp's sire.

Introducing . . . : Xander and Cordelia's first kiss; Willow and Giles's first kills; Drusilla's first day back at full vampire strength; the Slayer's Handbook.

Analysis: This episode took a giant leap in character development, beginning with Buffy's new appreciation for her role as the Slayer. Ever since she arrived in Sunnydale, Buffy has moaned and groaned about the crimp being a Slayer put on her life. But when the prospect of not being the Slayer arises, Buffy suddenly realizes that it's not just a job she can walk away from. It's part of who she is, for better or worse.

Kendra, the Slayer-in-Waiting, makes Buffy realize that her calling is an honor, not a sentence of drudgery. Compared to Kendra—who was given up by her parents as a young child so she could train full-time to be a Slayer—Buffy lives the life of a jet-setter. Through Kendra's eyes, Buffy finally sees the glass as half full—she's got devoted friends who offer her companionship and support—and who have saved her life on many occasions.

While Kendra and Buffy are coming to terms, Xander and Cordelia go through some changes of their own. After a close encounter of the yuck kind with a gruesome grub monster, Cordy and Xander's customary bickering leads to an unexpected but very passionate kiss. Believing they were just carried away by the stress and terror of the moment, they sweep the incident aside. But the chemistry apparent between the two is an indication that this love connection will be continued in future installments.

During the gang's final confrontation with Spike and the assassins, the killing isn't left to only Buffy this time. Although Xander accidentally killed a vampire in the past (his friend Jesse in episode #1, "Welcome to the Hellmouth") most of the slaying has been at the hands of Buffy. But in the church, Xander, Cordelia, Giles, and Willow all participate in the slayage. The group is now truly blood brothers.

The Real Horror: Being replaced. Nobody likes to feel dispensable. For adults, the most glaring example is in the work place, where employees who suddenly lose their jobs often fall into deep depressions, spurred by feelings of worthlessness.

In high school, emotions are much more fragile and the smallest slight can result in a traumatic crisis. Kids who suddenly fall out of a group's favor slink around like social pariahs, their confidence and self-worth dramatically shaken. And nearly everybody has experienced the nauseating pain of being dumped by a boyfriend or girlfriend in favor of someone else. When we are replaced, whether in a job, as a friend, as a lover, or even as teacher's pet, the message is clear—we don't matter enough; we're not worth the care.

In Buffy's case, the prospect of being replaced as the Slayer goes to her fundamental being. It's not just what she does, it's an integral part of what makes her Buffy. Without that core, her purpose and direction in life would suddenly be uprooted.

The same is true for everyone—who we are in the eyes of others and what we do are just as much of who we are as our genetic code. When any of these foundations are undermined, it damages the whole structure—usually only temporarily but in the most severe cases, irreparably.

It's a Mystery: How did Kendra's parents know their daughter was a Slayer-in-waiting? And are there other Slayer schools elsewhere in the world? And why did Kendra's accent occasionally sound Irish when she's presumed to be from the Caribbean?

Bloopers: Early in the episode, Spike talks about how the ceremony has to take place the night of the full moon. But later, Giles says the ceremony takes place on the night of the new moon. A new moon and full moon are not the same thing and happen on different days of the month.

Of Special Note: Kelly Connell, the actor who guest stars as *faux* salesman Norman Pfister, is probably best known to TV fans as Rome, Wisconsin resident Carter Pike in *Picket Fences*.

Buffy's crack to Kendra about making sure not to watch the in-air movie if it stars Chevy Chase is amusing, considering Sarah made a brief appearance in Chase's dreadful 1988 film, *Funny Farm*, playing one of many students in a classroom.

22. "Ted" (December 8, 1997) 60 min.

Director: Bruce Seth Green

Teleplay: David Greenwalt and Joss Whedon

Recurring Cast: Robia La Morte (Jenny Calendar); Kristine Sutherland (Joyce Summers)

Guest Cast: Jeff Langton (Vampire #2); Jeff Pruitt (Vampire #1); James G. MacDonald (Detective Stein); John Ritter (Ted Buchanan); Ken Thorley (Neal)

Plot: Buffy's mother has a new beau, Ted. Although to everyone else, he's Mr. Wonderful, Buffy's Slayer sense tells her there's something very wrong about Ted—but nobody will believe her. So when an altercation with Ted leads to tragedy, Buffy becomes an outcast even among her family and friends.

This Week's Antagonist: The perfect man. He's a gourmet cook, he washes dishes, he's attentive, he's romantic, he's gainfully employed, he's committed—in other words, he's just *way* too good to be true. And because he's everything to everyone, he's a far more insidious adversary than any of the monsters or living-dead creatures Buffy has previously encountered.

Introducing . . . : Joyce Summers as sexual being. Up until now, Buffy's mom has been presented as a harried, mostly absent single parent whose chief function is to remind Buffy that if she screws up in Sunnydale, there won't be another chance. But with the introduction of a love interest, Joyce's character becomes more complex as she is torn between her desire for a relationship with Ted and her love and loyalty to her daughter.

Analysis: Although they don't realize it, Joyce and Buffy have a lot more in common than would at first be apparent. They are both lonely and yearn for romance in their life. Buffy doesn't think she'll ever get it because of her life as the Slayer and because the only guy she's interested in happens to be a vampire. Joyce worries that she may never experience love again because of age, work obligations, and being a single parent.

The final scene between Buffy and her mom reveals a new resonance between them, as if Joyce suddenly sees her daughter as an insightful person whose intuition shouldn't be so quickly dismissed. And Buffy appreciates the fact that her mother is also a woman who makes bad decisions out of a desire to have some romance in her life—something Buffy can relate to.

The rekindling of the romance between Giles and Jenny is a nice counterpoint to Joyce's bad choice in androids. Unlike the perfect Ted, Giles often falls short, but it's his genuineness that ultimately brings Ms. Calendar back around.

The Real Horror: The prospect of stepparents. Even in the most stable of households, family dynamics are a tricky and fragile thing. But when a single parent introduces a new person into the equation in the form of a lover or spouse, it can turn into an explosive situation as everybody tries to figure out the new parameters such an arrangement brings.

In Buffy's case, it's not just that the unspoken desire to see her parents back together is made less likely by the appearance of her mother's new boyfriend, it's that the whole hierarchy of her home life is being turned upside down. Instead of being answerable to just her mother and father, she is having to account for herself to a virtual stranger. It's an invasion and a threat. By usurping Joyce's parental authority, Ted is also creating a wedge between mother and daughter as part of a divide-and-conquer strategy.

While younger children may adjust more easily to a new authority figure in the house, teenagers, who are in the midst of striving for independence as it is, are more likely to resist a situation in which they suddenly have one more person telling them what to do. Their predicament is often made worse by the natural parent being reluctant to cause any tension in the new relationship, just as Joyce deferred to Ted when it came to Buffy.

The episode also touches very lightly on the reality of abuse by stepparents or live-in lovers. Again, out of a desire not to lose the relationship, some parents, especially women who need the financial support of their partner, may turn a blind eye to physical or emotional abuse against their children, rationalizing it as discipline. However, in Buffy's case, she was able to turn the tables on Ted and turn him into a pile of short-circuitry.

It's a Mystery: When did Sunnydale build a miniature golf course? During the second season's first episode, "When She Was Bad," Willow comments that there's not even a miniature golf course in town.

Bloopers: During the first confrontation in Buffy's bedroom with Ted, after she smacks him back, her diary is laying on the floor in the middle of the doorway in one shot but disappears in the next.

Of Special Note: John Ritter is best known for his role as Jack Tripper on *Three's Company*. The vampire Buffy assaults in the cemetery is played by Jeff Pruitt, the series' stunt coordinator, who reportedly suffered an injured hand after Sarah whacked him with the lid of the garbage can.

23. "Bad Eggs" (January 12, 1998) 60 min.

Director: David Greenwalt

Teleplay: Marti Noxon

Recurring Cast: Kristine Sutherland (Joyce Summers)

Guest Cast: Brie McCaddin (Girl at Mall); James Parks (Tector Gorch); Jeremy Ratchford (Lyle Gorch); Danny Strong (Jonathan); Eric Whitmore (School Security Guy); Rick Zieff (Mr. Whitmore)

Plot: As if it's not bad enough that there are two new cowboy vampires in town, Buffy has to play single mother to an egg as part of an class assignment on responsibility. But when the student's eggs turn out to be from a Hellmouth creature, Buffy finds herself facing an opponent even more frightening than vampires—and a lot grosser.

This Week's Adversaries: In addition to the Gorch Brothers, two low-rent cowboy vampires who were into massacring Mexican villages even before they were undead, the Hellmouth has belched up the bazor, a prehistoric demon parasite that uses its larva to possess human hosts.

Introducing . . . : The brighter side of Angel. Compared to his somber mood of the past, Angel is positively giddy in this episode. Ah, young love—relatively speaking. The only moment Angel turns somber is when the topic of Buffy wanting children one day is brought up. But other than that, he's like a 241-year-old teenager in love. However, you just know the fates won't allow Buffy and Angel to remain happy and untroubled for long, and the shot of the headstone that reads *In Loving Memory* seems to be an obvious foreshadowing of bad things to come.

Analysis: "Bad Eggs" is mostly a poor man's homage to the classic science fiction film, *Invasion of the Body Snatchers*. In that film, a man discovers that something inside what looks to be giant pea pods are taking over people's bodies and minds. The possessed person was devoid of emotion and followed the command of an unseen force.

This episode is merely a Hellmouth version of the same story and has a much happier ending than either the original *Invasion of the Body Snatchers* movie or its remake. In those films, it appears there's no way to reverse the loss of our humanity, whereas in this episode, Buffy manages to kill the bazor and restore everyone's personality and self.

In a way, this episode may have been much stronger had it concentrated on the loss-of-self aspect, with those closest to Buffy turning into deadly strangers, rather than diluting it with the rather weak story line involving the Gorches, who appeared to be there mostly for comic relief. For a series that has had horror at its core, neither element was developed enough to generate any real sense of threat or danger and all the characters seemed to be merely going through the motions.

The Real Horror: Responsibility and all it entails. The irony of Buffy being saddled with an egg baby is that she's already assuming the ultimate responsibility for keeping the world safe from evil. However, the eggs are used as a metaphor for all the kinds of responsibility that teenagers must assume as they make the transition into adulthood. For Buffy, it means juggling her mother's expectations with her secret life as the Slayer as well as not completely losing her head over Angel.

It's a Mystery: When Buffy and Angel are talking about children, he tells her he can't have kids. She responds by noting there are probably lots of things a vampire can't do. However, as noted elsewhere in this book, according to vampire mythology, vampires *can indeed* have children. The offspring of a vampire and a human is called a *dhampir*. Traditionally, the father is a vampire and the mother human and the child is usually male. So either the writer made a glaring vampire lore error or it was intended to mean Angel specifically can't have children. But why that would be is unclear.

Bloopers: When the girl is playing pinball in the closed arcade, her handbag moves up and down her arm from shot to shot.

Of Special Note: The mall where the opening sequence was shot appears to be the Sherman Oaks Galleria, which was made infamous by Moon Zappa in the song "Valley Girl."

24. "Surprise" (January 19, 1998) 60 min.

Director: Michael Lange

Teleplay: Marti Noxon

Recurring Cast: Seth Green (Oz); Robia La Morte (Jenny Calendar); Juliet Landau (Drusilla); James Marsters (Spike); Kristine Sutherland (Joyce Summers)

Guest Cast: Eric Saiet (Dalton); Vincent Schiavelli (Gypsy Uncle); Brian Thompson (The Judge)

Plot: It's Buffy's birthday and everyone seems to have a surprise for her. Angel professes his love, the gang throws her a surprise party, and Drusilla is back with a vengeance—and an itch to annihilate the world.

This Week's Horror: A revitalized Drusilla. In honor of her refound health, Dru is planning a coming-out party that will wreak horror and destruction on the world.

Introducing . . . : Jenny Calendar's true identity. She is Jana, a member of the gypsy tribe that put the curse on Angel that restored his soul, after he killed their most beloved daughter.

Analysis: The series takes a giant, dark turn beginning with this episode. Up until this point in the season, the overall tenor of *Buffy* had been relatively light, once Buffy was able to put her trauma over the Master to rest. Or as light as one can get living on a Hellmouth. But Buffy's suddenly disturbing dreams, in which she sees Drusilla killing Angel, are portents of an end to the relative calm that had been hovering over Sunnydale.

In a rather surprising revelation, Jenny Calendar turns out to be much more than she seems. Originally sent to Sunnydale to keep an eye on Angel, Jenny now finds herself torn between what her people expect of her and what she knows to be true in her heart. Her Gypsy uncle is unmoved by Jenny's pleas on Angel's behalf. To honor the girl he killed, even one minute of happiness for Angel is too much. As each scene between Buffy and Angel becomes more and more charged with sexual tension, it is clear to the audience that Angel's moment of happiness is inevitable, and will happen sooner rather than later.

That moment happens after Buffy and Angel narrowly escape being char-broiled. Their brush with death emboldens Buffy and she lets Angel know she is ready to take the next step and make love with him. The final scene, where Buffy is sleeping in pure contentment while Angel is suddenly propelled out into the street in searing agony, sets the stage for the next phase of their relationship.

The Real Horror: Juggling fear of loss with sexual responsibility. Now that Buffy has found what she believes to be true love, she lives in terror of losing Angel, because like any teenager experiencing romantic love for the first time, she can't imagine ever feeling this way about someone again. In Buffy's case, there's the added element that the future, and whether she'll even have one, is a huge unknown. Although she doesn't want to be careless or irresponsible, she also knows that as the Slayer, she truly might not live to see another day.

In her dreams, she sees Angel killed and so the fear uppermost in her mind is his loss of existence. It doesn't occur to her that Angel could be lost to her in another way; that the person she has fallen in love with—the *soul* she has fallen in love with—could change.

It's a Mystery: Since when is Sunnydale a port city with cargo ships sailing in and out?

Bloopers: In the dream sequence, the monkey switches directions as the scenes cut back and forth between Willow and Buffy.

Of Special Note: Although Mercedes McNab, who plays Cordelia's snotty friend Harmony, is listed in the opening credits, she doesn't appear in this episode because her scene was cut. According to Joss Whedon, "Mercedes was in a scene where

Cordy and Xander try to broach the idea of dating to their friends. Cordy mentions him to Harmony, who looks and sees him dancing like a fool for Willow." The scene was cut because the episode was running too long.

Joss Whedon's name is now "above the title" during on-air promotions—*Joss Whedon's Buffy the Vampire Slayer*.

Music: "Anything" by Cari Howe; "Transylvanian Concubine" by Resputina.

25. "Innocence" (January 20, 1998) 60 min.

Director: Joss Whedon

Teleplay: Joss Whedon

Recurring Cast: Seth Green (Oz); Robia La Morte (Jenny Calendar); Juliet Landau (Drusilla); James Marsters (Spike); Kristine Sutherland (Joyce Summers)

Guest Cast: Ryan Francis (Soldier); James Lurie (Teacher); Carla Madden (Woman); Vincent Schiavelli (Gypsy Uncle); Parry Shen (Student); Brian Thompson (The Judge)

Plot: Angel and Buffy consummate their relationship but the joy Angel experiences has disastrous consequences. Willow discovers the truth about Xander's relationship with Cordelia. Jenny and Giles become estranged after he learns her true identity.

This Week's Nemesis: The Judge, an ancient demon who had been conjured to rid the earth of the plague of humanity, as the vampires like to say. The Judge was so powerful, he could not be killed. An army eventually subdued and dismembered him, burying his parts in various far reaches of the world.

Introducing . . . : Angelus. You've read about him! You've heard about him! Now meet the vampire evil enough to have sat at the right hand of the Master—who makes even Spike look like a good-natured evil being.

Warding Off Vampires

Everybody knows that a stake through the heart kills a vampire and that a cross and holy water will repel one, but not many people know the different ways to keep a vampire dead and gone and preventing former loved ones from rising out of their graves sporting a new set of sharp teeth. Here are a few lesser-known methods that have been developed by people over the ages to protect themselves from the undead.

Put Coins on the Corpse's Eyelids—Many cultures believe a payment is necessary before a soul can travel to the world of the dead. So by placing coins on the dead body, the soul won't be trapped in the body and forced to become a vampire.

Put Stakes in the Ground Above the Corpse—That way the vampire will impale itself while trying to dig its way out of the ground.

Stuff the Corpse's Mouth with Garlic—Garlic has long been identified as having the power to ward off vampires. Plus, stuffing garlic in the body's mouth has the added advantage of preventing a vampire from chewing on itself.

Fill the Coffin with Seeds—According to certain folklore, a vampire will have to count every seed before it can leave the grave.

Bury the Corpse Face-down—That way when the vampire begins to dig its way to freedom, it will be digging in the wrong direction. And if they fall for that, we've got some lovely oceanside property in Transylvania to sell them.

Put a Headstone Over the Grave—According to some lore, headstones weren't originally meant to mark a grave as a memorial, but were used as a weight to prevent a vampire from escaping the grave.

Bury the Corpse at a Crossroads—For centuries, many cultures feared and avoided crossroads because they were thought to be the center of ghostly activities, especially at night. So a vampire buried at a crossroads would be trapped within the unhallowed ground.

Decapitate or Stake the Corpse— When in doubt, why wait until they rise?

Oz joins the inner circle.

Analysis: When things go bad in Sunnydale, they go *really* bad. Willow's discovery of Xander and Cordelia's clandestine relationship brings unexpressed feelings to the surface and marks an irrevocable sea change in their friendship.

Most of this episode deals with Buffy's confusion over Angel's sudden disappearance after their night of passion. As confident as she is about her Slayer skills, she wears her insecurities on her sleeve about her sexual inexperience. She needs to be reassured by Angel and when she can't find him, she becomes increasingly vulnerable emotionally. When she finally tracks him down, she finds him cool, aloof—and cruel. The encounter leaves Buffy the lowest she's ever been, more demoralized even than when targeted by the Master.

Buffy's realization that she is the one responsible for "killing" Angel, and her inability to kill him when she has the chance, provide some of the series' most heartwrenching and agonizing moments. When her mother brings out a cupcake with a birthday candle on it, all Buffy can do is watch it burn down, her wishes now gone the way of Angel's soul.

The Real Horror: Loss of your first true love. In real life, what was thought to be eternal love often turns out not to be either because the couple grows apart or one person loses interest and wants to move on. Few things are more demoralizing for teenage girls than having their first sexual experience only to find out that the boy she gave her heart and body to didn't really love her the way she thought he did. But in Buffy's world, Angel hasn't changed simply because he's looking for more wild oats to sow, but because he's lost his soul.

Now she has to deal with two painful truths—the man she loves has literally been extinguished and she's partly responsible for the transformation.

It's a Mystery: Does Oz have his van painted regularly or does he own a fleet of them? In the "Halloween" episode, his van was black-and-white striped but now it's a solid color.

Just how big *is* Sunnydale? Not only is it a port city, as revealed the previous episode, but it's also the home of a fully equipped Army base.

Bloopers: The final shot of the previous episode had Angel kneeling in the pouring rain calling for Buffy (reminiscent of Marlon Brando's impassioned screams for "Stella!" in *A Streetcar Named Desire*). However, at the beginning of this episode, which picks right up where "Surprise" left off, there's no rain to be seen. Angel even looks dry.

Possibly the most notable blooper of the entire series takes place in this episode, the result of a major continuity gaffe. The sequence occurs this way:

After Buffy runs out of the library in despair, Xander tells the group he has a plan that requires Cordelia's help. They agree to meet at Willow's house in a half hour, where they will hook up with Oz and his van.

Cut to Buffy's bedroom where she lays on her bed and cries herself to sleep. She dreams about seeing Angel and Jenny at a funeral and Angel saying, *You can't see what you don't know.*

The next scene shows Buffy confronting Ms. Calendar and learning about the curse. Then immediately after this comes the scene where Xander and Cordelia are at the Army base stealing a missile launcher—an event that was supposed to have occurred the night before.

When asked about the error, Whedon owned up. "I was watching the final mix before air when I caught that *huge mistake*. No one else caught it but since I *caused* it I get only tiny shriveled kudos. So my theory now is that he was having her come over to [Willow's house] to *practice* being a trashy army girlfriend. We'll just run with that, okay?"

Of Special Note: Brian Thompson, who plays the Judge, appeared in the series pilot, "Welcome to the Hellmouth" as Luke, the Master's right-hand vamp whom Buffy reduced to dust during the final fight scene in the Bronze.

In a bit of synergy and advance promotion, one of the movie theaters at the mall is playing *Quest for Camelot*, an animated feature film Warner Bros. released in May 1998.

The movie Buffy is watching at the end of the episode is *Stowaway*, which starred Shirley Temple.

26. "Phases" (January 27, 1998) 60 min.

> Director: Bruce Seth Green
>
> Teleplay: Rob Des Hotel and Dean Batali
>
> Recurring Cast: Seth Green (Oz)
>
> Guest Cast: Larry Bagby III (Larry); Keith Campbell (Werewolf); Jack Conley (Cain); Camilla Griggs (Gym Teacher); Megahn Perry (Theresa Klusmeyer)

Plot: A werewolf is prowling Sunnydale, and Buffy needs to capture the creature and find out who it is before the bounty hunter who is gunning for it beats her to it. Xander unwittingly learns a fellow student's secret. Willow is growing impatient with Oz, who's being a bit too gentlemanly for her tastes.

This Week's Nemesis: A werewolf or lycanthrope, as Giles would say. According to Giles's research, a person inflicted with the curse transforms three nights a month—the night before the full moon, the night of the full moon, and the night after the full moon.

Introducing . . . : Willow and Cordelia's acceptance of each other. After weeks of tension caused by Willow's discovery of Cordelia and Xander's romance, Willow has accepted the relationship enough to feel comfortable talking to Cordelia about her frustration at Oz's apparent reluctance to get physical.

Analysis: This episode has several story line threads running through it. In a nice change of pace, the primary focus is on Willow and Oz instead of Angel's transformation back into Angelus, alleviating some of the intensity of the two previous episodes.

This installment makes it clear how much Willow's character has grown since the series' inception. She takes the initiative to confront Oz about why he's hesitating with her. A year earlier, Willow would have never dreamed to be so bold, but her association with the Slayer has given her self-confidence. Ironically, though Oz turns out to be a werewolf, it appears that Willow is going to be the more assertive partner in their relationship.

While *Buffy*'s scripts always combine horror with comedy, the writers up the humor quotient with this episode. Giles's barely disguised glee over getting the chance to deal with a werewolf, Willow's biting comments about the man in her life, and Xander's confrontation with Larry in which neither knows what the other is talking about—make this episode more giggle-inspiring than most.

The Real Horror: Teenage mood swings. It's not too far a stretch to see Oz's transformation into a werewolf as being symbolic of the emotional ups and downs experienced by practically all teenagers as their bodies and psyches go through the metamorphosis into adulthood. Oz, in fact, has no more control over the change in his appearance and character than does the teenager who one moment is a silly school kid and the next an angst-filled pre-adult.

Just as Oz can do nothing about his transformation except recognize the problem and learn to cope with it, teenagers can only ride the wave of hormones until they settle back into more manageable levels.

It's a Mystery: Why Oz waited until after his second transformation to call his aunt to see if Jordy was a werewolf. Didn't he realize something was up the morning before when he woke up somewhere outside naked?

Bloopers: When trapped in Cain's net, Buffy's flashlight goes on and off throughout the scene. After Willow falls in the woods, her clothes have visible dirt stains. But when she comes into the library in the very next scene, her clothes are completely clean. Giles's glasses appear then disappear through the scene when he's preparing the tranquilizer gun.

Of Special Note: According to Alyson Hannigan, a scene was shot for this episode—which was later cut—in which Cordelia and Willow get into a verbal cat fight before turning their mutual aggression onto Xander, at which point they both hit him and knock him down. By the scene's end, Cordelia and Willow have become more bonded, which explains why Willow and Cordelia were seen commiserating in the Bronze about their respective men.

Music: "Blind for Now" by Lotion.

27. "Bewitched, Bothered, and Bewildered"
(February 10, 1998) 60 min.

Director: James A. Contner

Teleplay: Marti Noxon

Recurring Cast: Elizabeth Anne Allen (Amy); Seth Green (Oz); Robia La Morte (Jenny Calendar); Juliet Landau (Drusilla); James Marsters (Spike); Mercedes McNab (Harmony); Kristine Sutherland (Joyce Summers)

Guest Cast: Tamara Braun (Student); Jennie Chester (Kate); Jason Hall (Devon); Scott Hamm (Student); Kristen Winnicki (Cordette)

Plot: After being rejected by Cordelia on Valentine's Day, Xander plots revenge. He turns to witchcraft but his plan to make

Cordelia pine after him backfires with potentially deadly consequences.

This Week's Predicament: Love potions. As explained by Giles, they are the most unpredictable of spells because when someone under the spell is rejected, their hurt can turn violent.

Introducing . . . : Cordelia and Xander as an official couple and Amy (first seen in episode #2, "The Witch") as a practicing witch.

Analysis: In this episode, Xander and Cordelia finally come to grips with their feelings for each other. After dumping him to remain cool in her friends' estimation, Cordelia realizes that she's become a follower, a sheep. And being a sheep is not cool. Even though Cordelia retains her innate sense of superficiality, she has grown enough to where she is more comfortable being her own person regardless of what others think. And Xander's willingness to follow his heart and take on Cordelia's image-conscious baggage shows his growth as well. These changes are indicative of the meticulous character development on *Buffy*. While some series' characters fit neatly into cookie-cutter patterns that don't bend over the years, Buffy and her pals learn from their encounters, grow, and evolve.

While the Buffy-Angel story line doesn't occupy the front burner in this episode, a few scenes foreshadow events to come and provide enough tension to heighten the sense of impending doom.

The Real Horror: Being the unwanted object of someone's desire. Although : t as poignant as unrequited love, unwanted crushes can be just as difficult to deal with. How does one make it clear in a nice way that someone's romantic desire is not returned? Especially, as in the case of Xander and Willow, when the person happens to be a friend?

The case of Buffy and Angel is a darker example of unrequited obsession, with Angel in essence stalking Buffy, determined to kill her so he can have her with him forever, in the same way a jilted lover turns violent when rejected. It's hard enough for adults to deal rationally with rejected desire, but it's especially difficult for teenagers whose emotions are heightened to begin with. Recent real-life events in which spurned students have gone on shooting rampages at their schools reflects the depth and intensity youthful obsession can reach. The love potion Xander has Amy cast is symbolic of this occasionally out-of-control hormonal state that afflicts nearly all high schoolers.

Bloopers: The board Xander nails onto the basement door jam appears to move from one shot to the next.

Of Special Note: Four Star Mary is the ghost group for Dingoes Ate My Baby.

Music: "Pain" by Four Star Mary; "Drift Away" by Naked; "Got the Love" by the Average White Band.

28. "Passion" (February 24, 1998) 60 min.

Director: Michael E. Gershman

Teleplay: Ty King

Recurring Cast: Juliet Landau (Drusilla); Robia La Morte (Ms. Calendar); James Marsters (Spike); Kristine Sutherland (Joyce Summers)

Guest Cast: Richard Assad (Shop owner); Richard Hoyt Miller (Policeman); Danny Strong (Student)

Plot: Angel's obsession with Buffy takes a dark and deadly turn, putting everyone around her at risk.

This Week's Anguish: Regret.

Introducing . . . : The darkest side of Angel.

Analysis: Of all the episodes, "Passion" is probably the most viscerally disturbing because of the unexpected death of Jenny Calendar. Even though by now everyone knows that creator Joss

Whedon has no qualms about killing off recurring characters, never before has such a *regular* recurring character died. And seldom has a death been as upsetting, because of the prolonged chase, with Jenny running for her life from Angel.

Viewers have gotten used to seeing Buffy, Willow, Giles, Xander, and Cordelia in life-threatening situations only to be saved at the last minute. But there would be no last-second reprieve for Jenny. And what made her demise all the more poignant was that she had just begun to mend bridges with Buffy and Giles. The scene in which Giles comes home in anticipation of a romantic evening with Jenny and finds her dead body in his bed is particularly wrenching.

The shot of Angel peeking through the window at a grief-stricken Buffy and Willow, smiling at the pain he's caused, reinforces his title as television's most evil villain. With each despicable act, it becomes increasingly difficult for viewers to think of his character—or his soul—as redeemable.

The Real Horror: Realization of mortality. Even though Buffy and her friends have seen more death than any big-city homicide detective, for the most part they were all able to maintain enough emotional distance to keep it from paralyzing them. But Jenny's death was extremely personal, especially for Buffy, who must live with the knowledge that Jenny would be alive if she had followed her duty and killed Angel when she had the chance.

The permanence of death and the void left by it is reinforced for the gang daily because suddenly Jenny isn't at her computer and can't be found walking the halls anymore. Where Jenny once *was*, now she *isn't*. And there's no bringing her back. It's similar to what happens when a class suffers the lost of a student. The empty desk serves as a reminder that the absence is forever, a concept almost innately alien to the teenage mind. However, once it does sink in, the effect can be profound because it comes with the realization that we are all subject to the whimsy of fate.

It's a Mystery: Why didn't Jenny have a cross handy to ward off Angel, knowing he could come into the school any time he wanted?

Of Special Note: The voice heard during the graveyard scene belongs to Anthony Stewart Head.

When Giles comes home and finds Jenny, Puccini is playing on the stereo.

Music: "Never an Easy Way" by Morcheeba.

29. "Killed by Death" (March 3, 1998) 60 min.

Director: Deran Sarafian

Teleplay: Rob Des Hotel and Dean Batali

Recurring Cast: Kristine Sutherland (Joyce Summers)

Guest Cast: James Jude Courtney (Kindestod); Andrew Ducote (Ryan); Willie Garson (Security guard); Richard Herd (Dr. Backer); Juanita Jennings (Dr. Wilkinson); Denise Johnson (Celia); Robert Munic (Intern); Mimi Paley (Little Buffy)

Plot: While in the hospital battling a debilitating flu and high fever, Buffy suspects a demon is killing children.

This Week's Evil Creature: *Der Kindestod*, a demon usually invisible to adults, who kills children by straddling them and literally sucking the life breath out of the child.

Introducing . . . : The budding friendship between Giles and Joyce Summers.

Analysis: This episode reinforces Xander's new role as Buffy's primary protector. Previously, it was Angel who would stay behind and watch her back but now that Angel is the enemy, Xander has filled the void. This change first became evident in episode #26, "Phases," when Xander killed Theresa the vampire, thereby saving Buffy, who had been momentarily stunned into inaction.

Xander's devotion to Buffy creates conflicting emotions in Cordelia, who on one hand does care for Buffy but on the other doesn't like playing second fiddle to anyone. Her growth as a character, without losing her I-should-be-the-center-of-the-universe uniqueness, is particularly evident in this episode. Even though she still shows flashes of her self-centered superficiality, it's now balanced by a sweet, caring side that enables viewers to understand why Xander is attracted to her.

The Real Horror: Childhood illness. While unexpected, youthful death is a horror unto itself, prolonged illness is a special kind of horror because it robs a youth of the very vigor and vitality that marks childhood and the teen years. While part of Buffy's fear of the hospital was the repressed memory of seeing Celia killed, she was also reacting to the idea of being ill and not having all of her faculties to rely on. Although losing one's physical strength and capabilities would be particularly wrenching for a Slayer, it is just as frightening a thought for any flesh-and-blood teenager who inherently believes themself to be healthy and not subject to the ravages of illness.

It's a Mystery: Why is the access door to the basement located in the middle of a children's ward? Also, if Buffy is so terrified of hospitals, why was no mention of that made in episode #9, "Nightmares," in which significant action takes place inside a hospital?

Bloopers: On the door to the basement, a sign reading "Basement Access" suddenly appears from one scene to the next.

In the scene in Buffy's hospital room when she sees the Kindestod, the clock first reads 2:27, but later in the same scene, it reads 2:15.

Of Special Note: This episode had many familiar TV faces in guest-starring roles. Richard Herd, who played Dr. Backer, costarred on *T. J. Hooker* for three years as Captain Sheridan, and Andrew Ducote most recently starred as Willie on *Dave's World.*

James Jude Courtney, the evil Kindestod, is also a professional stuntman.

Roughly translated, *Der Kindestod* means *kid killer.*

30. "J Only Have Eyes for You" (April 28, 1998) 60 min.

Director: James Whitmore Jr.

Teleplay: Marti Noxon

Recurring Cast: Juliet Landau (Drusilla); James Marsters (Spike); Armin Shimerman (Principal Snyder)

Guest Cast: Meredith Salinger (Grace Newman); Christopher Gorham (James Stanley); John Hawkes (George); Miriam Flynn (Ms. Frank); Brian Reddy (Police Chief Bob); Brian Poth (Fighting Boy); Sarah Bibb (Fighting Girl); James Lurie (Mr. Miller); Ryan Taszreak (Ben); Anna Coman-Hidy (Girl #1); Vanessa Bednar (Girl #2)

Plot: The spirit of a young man who killed his lover in a fit of passion years ago forces Buffy to confront her guilt over the loss of Angel's soul.

This Week's Spirit: A poltergeist. These spirits are frequently considered harmless ghosts who cause mischief but no real harm because they are generally believed to be the spirits of young people. However, there have also been reports of malevolent poltergeists. According to Giles, a poltergeist is someone who died with unresolved issues, and the only way to make the ghost go away is to resolve those issues.

Introducing . . . : The official cover-up of the Hellmouth when it's revealed that Principal Snyder and the police chief are aware of its existence. It was intimated in episode #14, "School Hard," that Snyder knew more than he was letting on, and it's now clear that he is fully aware of Sunnydale's evil underbelly.

Witches

Witches are women who use supernatural powers, in the form of black magic, for evil purposes. Male witches are called warlocks. Witches are either possessed by evil spirits or under the guidance of some mystical power or deity. Because of their association with magic, the term sorcery has long been synonymous with witchcraft in the English-speaking world. (However, Neo-pagan witches hold a deep and abiding respect for the free will of all living creatures and abide by the motto, *Do what you will, but harm no one.*)

Records reveal that belief in witchcraft dates back to prehistoric times. There are several references to sorcerers in the Old Testament and the Greek writer Homer makes references to witchcraft. Among the Germanic peoples, belief in and fear of witches was widespread.

Witch mythology varies from country to country. For example, while in many cultures witches have been historically depicted as ugly, old women, a more modern view of witches tends to cast them as ordinary or beautiful women who just happen to have the power to cast spells.

In Europe, witches are often portrayed as thin and gaunt, much like the Wicked Witch of the West as she appears in *The Wizard of Oz*, but in Central Africa witches are thought of as fat from eating human flesh. The notion of witches buzzing around on brooms actually came from a long-standing European tradition, which has become part of American pop

---

Also, new digs for Dru, Spike, and Angel, since their old warehouse burned down after Giles firebombed it at the end of "Passion."

Analysis: Although at first it seems that this episode will simply be a ghost story, it uses the story of the student who killed his teacher-lover as a treatise on forgiveness. It also offers some intriguing parallels between Buffy and Angel and the former ill-fated lovers.

culture thanks to Halloween.

Sometimes witches use animals as protectors or to help them carry out their evil deeds. In Europe they use cats, dogs, or weasels; in Japan, hyenas or owls; in Africa, baboons. Some witches even turn into animal forms.

From the mid-fifteenth to the mid-eighteenth century—during what's been referred to as Europe's "witchcraft craze"—witches were accused of having special links to the devil. Thousands of people were convicted of witchcraft and executed, the most notable American example being the Salem witch trials of 1692, during which nineteen persons were hanged.

In the early years of the witch hunts, the accused were mostly women. One interesting study concluded that women who were economically independent made up 89 percent of the women executed for witchcraft in New England. Scholars believe that was no coincidence. In *Mystic Cats*, author Roni Jay explains, "In the thirteenth century, people were becoming disillusioned with the Church and the whole structure of society. The Church needed a scapegoat, and it picked on witchcraft—after all, old women were less likely than anyone to put up a serious defense. Over the next few centuries, thousands of women throughout Europe were executed for witchcraft—and many cats were condemned along with them."

Poor kitties.

In an interesting twist, the ghost of the student takes over Buffy and the ghost of the teacher briefly possesses Angel. Their reenactment of the tragedy of James (in Buffy's body) and Grace (Angel) has a happier outcome, enabling James and Grace's spirits to leave in peace. In a particularly touching scene, Grace/Angel tells James/Buffy that they are forgiven and that they loved them with their dying breath. For the first time since Angel's transformation, we sense that Buffy might be ready to start forgiving herself for what happened.

The other brief story line in the episode has Dru, Angel, and Spike moving to a new residence. The tension between Angel and Spike is palpable. After Dru and Angel go off to feed, Spike gets up out of his wheelchair, signifying that a showdown with Angel is now inevitable.

The Real Horror: Guilt. While guilt is an emotion that never dulls with age, like all passions, it seems to be felt more keenly among the uncallused hearts of teenagers.

Through the story of James, Buffy finally confronts her guilt over having destroyed the person she loved the most. Initially, she is resistant to the idea that James deserves forgiveness, because Buffy doesn't feel she does.

It's a Mystery: How is it possible that Willow has been browsing Ms. Calendar's computer when Angel smashed and burned it in "Passion"?

Bloopers: In the scene (set in 1955) showing James prior to killing himself, he's listening to a version of "I Only Have Eyes for You" by the Flamingos which wasn't released until 1959.

Of Special Note: Miriam Flynn, who plays Ms. Frank, is also a well-known cartoon voice-over artist whose characters include Jean Tazmanian Devil in *Taz-Mania*.

Music: "Charge" by Splendid; "I Only Have Eyes for You" by the Flamingos.

31. "Go Fish" (May 5, 1998) 60 min.

Director: David Semel

Teleplay: David Fury and Elin Hampton

Recurring Cast: Armin Shimerman (Principal Snyder)

Guest Cast: Charles Cyphers (Coach Marin); Jeremy Garrett (Cameron Walker); Wentworth Miller (Gage Petronzi); Conchata Ferrell (Nurse Greenleigh); Danny Strong (Jonathan); Shane West (Sean); Jake

Patellis (Dodd McAlvy)

Plot: Buffy suspects the Sunnydale swim team is being filleted by a mysterious sea creature.

This Week's Danger: Better living through chemicals. An overzealous coach exposes his athletes to an experimental inhalant in hopes of improving their performance—and succeeds *too* well.

Introducing . . . : Xander as jock. In order to keep an eye on the school's quickly disappearing swimmers, Xander tries out for and makes the team.

Analysis: One of the more lighthearted episodes, comparatively speaking, "Go Fish" doesn't do much to advance the characters or the second season story arc, but it reestablishes Buffy and her gang as some of the more quick-witted high school students around. And after spending most of the second season in a state of perpetual angst, it's nice to see Buffy back in the guise of frustrated high school teenager.

Buffy and the gang believe that a fish-like monster is killing off members of the swim team. But in an inventive plot twist, it turns out that the boys haven't been killed by a monster, they are turning *into* monsters—a fact Buffy comes to understand after watching one swimmer rip open his skin to reveal a fish-man, actually, a fish-boy, underneath. She manages to escape the fish-men with the help of Coach Marin, who later claims ignorance when questioned by Giles.

This particular scene was quite out of character for the series. Even though *Buffy* deals with vampires and monsters, the characters have always come across as real and their reactions to their situations have always rung true. The fact that the coach would be so unrattled by discovering his swimmers were turning into fish-boys seemed incongruous. Although Giles and Buffy dwell in a world of monsters, presumably the majority of people at the school live in blissful ignorance. So the coach should have been in a state of shock or severe disbelief. On the other hand, his blasé reaction to the turn of events should then have immediately caused Giles to suspect that Marin was in some way involved in whatever was going on.

The Real Horror: A winning-at-all-costs attitude. Anybody who has ever so much as attended a high school sporting event knows how much pressure is placed on winning. For coaches, it may mean whether or not they keep their jobs. For the athletes, it's either an ego-booster or a ticket to college, or both. And for the school, winning means prestige and, through boosters and game attendance, money. Although the pressure is often greatest at the collegiate level, high school athletes also feel the heat.

Stories of performance-enhancing drugs are commonplace, so this episode merely heightens a prevalent reality of modern-day athletics.

It's a Mystery: How exactly did the coach use steam to transfuse fish DNA into the athletes? And how did he have the knowledge to do so?

Since when does Sunnydale High have such direct access to the city's sewer tunnels, which apparently run directly under the school?

32. "𝔅𝔢𝔠𝔬𝔪𝔦𝔫𝔤" 𝔓𝔞𝔯𝔱 𝔍 (May 12, 1998) 60 min.

Director: Joss Whedon

Teleplay: Joss Whedon

Recurring Cast: Seth Green (Oz); Juliet Landau (Drusilla); Bianca Lawson (Kendra); James Marsters (Spike); Armin Shimerman (Principal Snyder)

Guest Cast: Julie Benz (Darla); Nina Gervitz (Teacher); Zitto Kazann (Gypsy Man); Jack McGee (Doug Perren); Max Perlich (Whistler); Richard Riehle (L.A. Watcher); Shannon Welles (Gypsy Woman); Ginger Williams (Girl)

Plot: The story of Angel "becoming" a vampire at the hands of Darla—how as Angelus he waged a reign of evil and terror and how the vengeful gypsy reinstated his soul so Angel would suffer eternal torment for his deeds—is interwoven with Buffy's determination to kill Angel once and for all.

This Week's Demon: Acathla, an ancient demon capable of opening up a whirlpool that will draw everything in this world into the demonic reality beyond, where all non-demon life would suffer eternal torment.

Introducing . . . : Angel's biography.

Analysis: By presenting Angel's full 200-plus year story, series creator Joss Whedon is able to simultaneously show Angel as both victim and criminal. Just as Buffy is conflicted in her emotions, loving the Angel that was while despising what he has now become, counterpositioning the two faces of Angel makes for some serious dramatic conflict.

The fact that Angel eventually loses his soul because of the love he and Buffy share makes his transformation back to Angelus a tragedy of Greek proportions. It also makes their final confrontation inevitable. There is no way Angelus can let Buffy go. They both cannot live—one must die.

Since the time of Angel's transformation, Buffy has often been portrayed as more preoccupied and less quick-witted than she was previously. She has put herself and others in danger over the course of the second half of the season. But in this episode, her preoccupation and obsession with Angel finally proves fatal. Using Angel as a decoy to keep Buffy away, Drusilla stages an ambush on the library. Xander and Willow are injured, Giles is kidnapped, and Kendra is killed, leaving Buffy—now a fugitive from the law—to wallow in a sea of regret and guilt. This suspense-filled installment left viewers fervently anticipating part two, the season finale.

The Real Horror: Not being able to turn back the hands of time. Everyone has regrets but the errors in judgment made as a teenager seem to resonate more and take on greater importance. In the world of the Slayer, errors in judgment can prove fatal as proved by Buffy's relationship with Angel.

If Buffy had it to do all over again, she wouldn't. But she doesn't have that choice, so now she's left to deal with the fallout of her misbegotten passion for Angel, the guy from the ultimate wrong side of the Hellmouth tracks.

It's a Mystery: All right, just how old is Angel? In the 1997 episode "Some Assembly Required," Angel stated that he was 241 years old. According to the Watcher diary in "Halloween," Angel was eighteen years old in 1775—prior to becoming a vampire—which means he was born around 1756. However, in this episode, Angel was bitten by Darla in 1753, years before his previously established birth.

Beyond that, in the "Angel" episode, it was mentioned that Angel's soul had been restored sometime in the twentieth century, circa the 1920s. However, in this episode it's revealed to have taken place in 1898.

Bloopers: During the scene where he's killed by Drusilla, Doug's hand moves on and off the statue from one shot to the next.

Of Special Note: Julie Benz reprises her role as Darla for the first time since Angel killed her.

The building used for Hemery High in the flashback to 1996 is the same building used for the Hill Valley Clock Tower in the first two *Back to the Future* films.

33. "Becoming" Part II (May 19, 1998) 60 min.

Director: Joss Whedon
Teleplay: Joss Whedon

Recurring Cast: Seth Green (Oz); James Marsters (Spike); Robia La Morte (Ms. Calendar); Juliet Landau (Drusilla); Armin Shimerman (Principal Snyder); Kristine Sutherland (Joyce Summers)

Guest Cast: Max Perlich (Whistler)

Plot: As Angel feverishly tries to unleash Acathla on the world, Spike reveals a few plans of his own as he teams up with Buffy to stop world annihilation. Meanwhile, Willow tries again to restore Angel's soul using the spell left behind by Jenny Calendar.

This Week's Threat to Humanity: Angel as the instrument for Acathla.

Introducing . . . : Joyce Summers to the world of the Slayer. When attacked by one of Drusilla's vamp-goons in front of her mother, Buffy is forced to spike the vampire and finally reveals to Joyce her real identity as the Slayer.

Re-Introducing . . . : Angel with soul. Briefly.

Analysis: One of the biggest dramatic questions of the second season was how to restore Angel's soul and maintain the integrity of the series. Considering all he had done since losing it, not the least of which was killing Jenny Calendar, it seemed as if the series had backed itself into an escape-proof corner.

If Angel had anguished over what he had done to strangers the first time his soul was restored, how could he ever face Buffy and the others, especially Giles, now? And even if they could get over that hurdle, how could Angel and Buffy ever pick up where they left off, knowing that it was their love that unleashed the demon inside him in the first place? Talk about no-win situations. There would be no easy answers to end this season's story arc.

With the final episode, the series took some major turns and some major risks. The first was the revelation to Joyce that her daughter was the Slayer. In many regards, this opens the series up and creates many new story possibilities for the seasons ahead.

It also gives the Joyce Summers character a chance to grow and not be stuck in the she-must-be-dumb-as-a-post category not to notice something strange is going on with her daughter. Now she can be the voice of informed concern. It also opens up the possibility of a relationship between Joyce and Giles, who has become Buffy's well-defined father figure anyway.

Although we've learned that in Sunnydale few things are as they seem, the decision to cast Angel into hell with Acathla was, in the end, the only logical way out of the Angel-as-evil story line.

With the season finale ending with Buffy on a bus heading out of town, Whedon sets up the third season to be a different kind of journey for Buffy. In the first, she had to face her own mortality and come to terms with her destiny. In the second, she had to learn sacrifice and what it's like to love. In the third season, Buffy will have to deal with issues closer to home, such as her mother—and a hostile principal who obviously knows her identity. In other words, the third season will see Buffy graduate not only from high school, but from adolescent to full-fledged adult.

The Real Horror: The greater good. In life there are occasions when it's necessary to do what's right, as opposed to what would serve our own best interests. It's never easy and many people simply cannot do it. But in Sunnydale, those occurrences take on cataclysmic importance, so Buffy had no choice but to sacrifice Angel and her own happiness for the sake of others.

Obviously, a sword wound cannot kill a vampire, so she didn't kill Angel. She banished him to an existence of eternal torment because if she didn't, the world would have come to an end. Instead, her world did. Sending Angel to the agonies of hell just as his soul is returned to him is something that Buffy may never overcome.

The biggest irony is that many of the people she is suffering for have no appreciation of her sacrifice. Her mother wants her daughter to have a different fate and to ignore her calling. The school principal is looking to keep a lid on the local troubles. Even Xander is too interested in seeing Angel suffer to fully realize what it will cost Buffy emotionally.

It's a Mystery: Was the spell Willow used to restore Angel's soul the exact same one the gypsies first used, including the caveat that Angel would lose his soul if he experienced one moment of true happiness—or did it restore his soul with no strings attached?

Also, does Kendra's death mean that another Slayer will be called?

How did Buffy know it was Drusilla who killed Kendra?

Bloopers: During the final fight scene with Angel, Buffy's hair goes back and forth from loose to pulled back from shot to shot.

Of Special Note: The week this episode aired, the WB announced that they were spinning off a series to star David Boreanaz as Angel for the 1999–2000 season.

Music: "Full of Grace" by Sarah McLachlan.

Bibliography

The primary source materials utilized in the preparation of this book were interviews with the cast and executives of the series at Television Critics Association conventions, comic conventions, and other events at which the author was present. The author also consulted production information supplied by the WB network, television and radio transcripts, and a number of newspaper and magazine articles.

The following is a selection of articles that may be of interest to *Buffy* enthusiasts.

Abramowitz, Rachel. "Sideburn, Baby, Burn!" (Luke Perry) *Premiere*, August 1992.

Baldwin, Kristen. "A Couple of Suckers." (Spike and Drusilla) *Entertainment Weekly*, October 31, 1997, p. 84.

—. "Touched by Hell's Angel." *Entertainment Weekly*, May 22, 1998, p. 52.

Brady, James. "In Step with Sarah Michelle Gellar." *Parade*, July 6, 1997, p. 18.

Cohen, David S. "Buffy the Vampire Slayer." *Script*, November/December 1997, p. 48–52.

Dunn, Jancee. "Sarah Michelle Gellar and the Power of Buffy-Hood." *Rolling Stone*, April 2, 1998, p. 42–45.

Hensley, Dennis. "Miracle Worker." *Movieline*, December/January 1998, p. 20.

Hine, Thomas. "TV's Teenagers: An Insecure, World-Weary Lot." *New York Times*, October 26, 1997, p. A1.

Howard, Megan. "Slayer-Speak." *Entertainment Weekly*, October 31, 1997, p. 84.

Jacobs, A. J. "Interview with a Vampire Chronicler." (Joss Whedon) *Entertainment Weekly*, April 25, 1997, p. 23.

Koltnow, Barry. "*Buffy* Star Isn't Just Another Buff Blonde." (Kristy Swanson) *Los Angeles Daily News*, August 1, 1992, p. 22.

Kutzera, Dale. "Buffy, Vampire Slayer." *Femme Fatales*, July 1997.

Lippert, Barbara. "Hey There, Warrior Grrrl." *New York*, December 15, 1997, p. 24.

Martinez, Jose. "Buffy's *Scream*ing Good *Summer* Vacation." *Venice*, October 1997, p. 59–60.

Pope, Kyle. "Limping 'Buffy' Gets a Lift from WB." *Wall Street Journal*, May 14, 1997, p. B1.

Rebello, Stephen. "Vampire Pop." *Movieline*, August 1992, p. 35–38+.

Rice, Lynette. "*Buffy*'s Green Sinks His Teeth Into Regular Role." (Seth Green) *Hollywood Reporter*, March 17, 1998, p. 6.

Rochlin, Margy. "Slay Belle." *TV Guide*, August 2, 1997, p. 16–21.

Rogers, Adam. "Hey, Ally, Ever Slain a Vampire?" *Newsweek*, March 2, 1998, p. 60.

Strauss, Bob. "Busy *Buffy* Star Leaps into Two Feature Film Roles." *Los Angeles Daily News*, October 14, 1997

Walstad, David. "Kristy Swanson the 'Vampire Slayer' in the Campy Summer Comedy.' *Los Angeles Times*, August 1, 1992, p. F2.

Index

Index

Index

Index